BURIED BY EARTH
A Dystopian Shifter Romance
Jemma Weir

JEMMA WEIR

ALSO BY

HIGHLAND RIFT PACK

Buried by Earth

Bitten by Frost

Battered by Storms

ERNIE SMITH

Finding Death's Scythe

In the Cards

The Life and Chaos of a Retired Old God – Short Story
Collection

STANDALONE

Wishing For Truths – Short Story

CONTENTS

CHAPTER ONE

At the top of the hill, Hale wiped the sweat from his forehead and scanned the desolate wasteland for any signs of danger. The Rift Scar spread out as far as the eye could see. Grey craggy summits faded into the clear blue sky. Flurries of dust gusted about him as the wind caught the dry dirt. There were no trees, no grass, no sign of life at all.

He just hoped it stayed that way for the rest of the patrol.

So far, it had been uneventful except for the oppressive heat. He tugged at the neckline of his body armour to create some airflow. It was too hot to help much. He would've taken the Kevlar off, except it had saved his life more than once.

Hale sighed and let go of his body armour. Even if he'd gotten some cool air, it wouldn't have helped. The moon would be full tonight, and it already called to him, pulling at his wolf.

Hunt. Run, Fang, Hale's wolf, whispered in his mind, more images than words. It showed them running with the pack, leading the hunt.

Soon, Hale said, pushing the image away, trying not to let his wolf distract him, which wasn't easy. The full moon was the only time they had a space where they were allowed to shift forms unless they took a turn patrolling as a wolf in the Rift Scar. Or they wanted to risk getting locked up.

Even though Shifters had been around for over a hundred years, humans didn't trust that they had control over their other halves. Any Shifter caught in their animal form outside approved locations would serve years in jail, or worse, depending on the judge.

His wolf huffed but pulled back at the idea of shifting here. Even in his human form, the place stank like meat left out too long in the sun. With his wolf's sense of smell, it was a dozen times worse.

Hale rolled his shoulders and did another once-over of the horizon. The Highland Rift Scar was the smallest of the four in the UK. The Scars had been left behind after humans had won the Fae War in the early nineteen hundreds. But while the fae had retreated and poorly sealed their Rifts, they'd left a multitude of dangerous and violent creatures behind. It was Hale's responsibility to keep their population under control so they didn't venture into the local towns.

'Any sign of activity?' Shane asked as he stepped up beside Hale.

Shane had a thick trunk neck, square jaw, and stocky build. He'd been with the Highland Rift Pack for almost six months and had bulked up enough to pass for a pro wrestler. Hale suspected it had more to do with boredom than anything else.

The population of the closest town, Huntly, barely hit 5,000 people. There was little else to do but patrol the Rift Scar, exercise, or find someone willing to have a good time. Huntly had attracted plenty of the latter, with Shifters stationed close by. Especially near the full moon when energy ran high––and sometimes running just wasn't enough of a release.

'Nothing so far,' Hale said as he moved his rifle to a more comfortable position. Just because it was boring now didn't mean it would stay that way. Hale had split the team in half since they were on the border. That meant it was just him and Shane while the other three of his team worked parallel to their route.

'Good,' Shane said, looking over the grey landscape but didn't add anything else. He'd been quiet most of the day, which was unusual for him.

Shane should've been in charge of this patrol, but after the way Hale's day had gone, he'd needed a distraction. Being both the alpha and rift warden meant he was in charge whenever he joined a patrol. Unfortunately, it seemed to have annoyed Shane, though that hadn't been Hale's intent.

Shane looked like he was going to say more, but he shook his head and started down the hill but stumbled, foot catching on something. Hale reached out, just managing to grab the back of Shane's Kevlar vest to pull him backwards. Shane grunted, falling into Hale, nearly sending them both to the ground.

'You good?' Hale asked as they stabilised.

'Fucking Rift Scar,' Shane muttered, pulling away. He reached down to yank out a skull that had been long since been picked clean and bleached white. It was the size of a ten-year-old, but it had a muzzle and savagely long teeth.

'Imp,' Hale said. The creatures were one of the most common in the Rift Scar. The two-legged predators were small in stature, but their claws and teeth were sharp enough to cause serious harm.

Shane grunted and threw the skull down the hill hard enough that it broke. The sound echoed over the dusty ground, making Hale's trigger finger twitch where it lay safely along the frame of the gun. The patrol might have been quiet so far, but there was no need to push their luck.

It was almost like Shane was hoping for a fight, which was possible. He'd been restless for the last few weeks, volunteering for extra shifts in the Rift Scar. Hale had been happy to let him. They were always short-staffed, and it wasn't like they had a lot of options. Humans couldn't go into the Scar. The Rift venom—something that most Rift creatures carried—was nearly always deadly to them. That only left those from the Rift Bloodlines. Shifters and Elementals. With the Highland Rift Scar being so far north, few of those wanted a job here.

Shane started moving down the hill again. He kept shifting his grip on his gun. Whatever was going on with Shane, he wasn't in a good place. But how the hell did Hale get Shane to open up to him?

'Spit it out, Shane,' Hale said at last, stopping at the bottom of the hill. In front of them was flat and open. If there were dangers, they'd see and hear them coming.

'Are you going to tell me what happened with the prime alphas?' Shane said, not looking at him.

'They were just reviewing how the year had gone,' Hale said, wishing he'd kept silent. The meeting had been less of an update and more of a lecture.

The prime alphas made up the governing force for Shifters in the UK. Six wolves who each managed their own little sliver of the country. They didn't appreciate someone like Hale making suggestions or criticising how they ran things.

'Did they talk about making any changes?' Shane asked, turning back to Hale with hope in his eyes.

Which meant Hale hadn't been half as discreet as he should have been.

'They've decided everything should remain the same for at least the next year,' Hale said. If the prime alphas had their way, it would remain the same this year and every year after that. To hell with how this pack suffered.

'The land?' Shane asked, but his eyes had already gone dark, no longer showing hope.

'There will be no change on the land rental,' Hale said, words tasting sour in his mouth, though he didn't show how he felt to Shane. 'They don't believe changing the contract this year is cost-effective.'

Cost efficiency had nothing to do with their decision. But Hale couldn't tell Shane that.

Shane scowled at him. 'We can't continue with only being allowed to shift once a month. It's not enough, Hale. Our wolves need more than that.'

Wanted more. Not needed. But that didn't make it any easier or more comfortable.

More. Need, Fang said, disagreeing with him.

Hale ignored his wolf. Fang had already made his opinion well-known over the last seven years. Theoretically, a Shifter never needed to turn into their wolf form except over the full moon. That pull was nearly impossible to stop, which was the main reason they had the one day they did. That part was more efficient than sending the wolves home or to Glasgow every month.

'We've made do for this long,' Hale said, trying not to show any of his own frustration. As the alpha, he had less luxury than most to show those feelings. 'We'll make do for another year.'

'That's bullshit. Nowhere else in the UK are Shifters forced to drive over four hours to another pack's territory so they can shift outside a full moon. Not to mention the need to ask permission every single time,' Shane said, looking back at Hale, eyes flashing to the yellow of his wolf, but he turned away, hiding them. 'It's not right.'

'The decision has been made,' Hale said, voice firmer as a trickle of his power slipped out at the challenge.

Shane stiffened. 'You should have fought harder,' he said, not turning around this time.

'You weren't there for the conversation, so don't assume I didn't fight for us,' Hale said. Because he had, and the prime alphas hadn't been interested in listening. But he couldn't say that. That truth wouldn't help the pack because suffering was the point.

The prime alphas wanted a place where they could send wolves who misbehaved, and because the Highland Rift Scar was in the middle of nowhere, it had become that place. Wolves would spend six months to a year here, then they'd go home, back to their family pack, knowing that if they didn't behave, they'd be sent north again.

Because this pack was never anything more than a job and a punishment.

Hale couldn't tell Shane the real reason because the prime alphas didn't want to tell anyone they deliberately kept the Highland Pack in this state. That way, the wolves blamed Hale, and when they went home, the prime alphas looked like the better option. It would be another reason for them never to risk getting sent north again.

Hale had been fighting for years for a better option.

'We can't keep this up forever,' Shane said, but he turned away and headed in the direction they'd been going.

Hale wanted to keep arguing, but there wasn't anything he could tell Shane that he hadn't already said.

Stop, Fang said, focus sharpening on the skull fragments as they reached the bottom of the hill. His wolf had seen something Hale had missed.

Hale looked at the ground. There were tiny marks in the dust around the fragments. He drew in a breath, searching for the scent of anything out of place, but there was only the overall rot of the Rift Scar. It was hard to follow trails in his human form here. Everything smelled similar until you were on top of it.

'Hale?' When Hale didn't respond, Shane's hands tightened on his gun as he scanned the area.

'Scorpion,' Hale said, following the line in the dirt. Although they were the most common creature in the Rift Scar, they were only the size of a Yorkie and had a stinger containing Rift venom. Unfortunately, they usually made up for their size by running in groups of twenty or more.

So much for a quiet patrol.

SAM TURNED HER OLD Jeep onto a little used dirt track off the main road. The ground was rough and deeply rutted, but it would take her to the Highland Rift Scar's northeast border and her last stop of the day.

Trees climbed up either side of her, mostly old pines with thick and expansive roots that poked out the track, making the conditions worse. But at least she was finally under some shade, and maybe her poor car's air-con might be able to compete with the heatwave. She was doubtful. It was already mid-afternoon, and the heat was only rising.

Sam hit a rut so deep that the steering wheel nearly jerked out of her grip. There was no sound of crunching metal, thankfully. The Jeep had fared well over the last six months, and so far, nothing had broken. With the way the Rift Scar's dust ate away at machines, there was always a chance the next thump would crack something major.

She'd been asking the local council to lay a proper road or improve this one for years. Unfortunately, since she was pretty much the only one who used it, the council didn't want to cough up the hazard pay for the repair crew or a rift ranger to protect them. Not that either was really needed. Sam hadn't seen a Rift creature, or anything remotely dangerous, in the five years she'd been working as a rift surveyor.

In the council's defence, having a rift ranger as an escort was law, and they weren't exactly cheap. They were already paying for Sam to have one every time she went to take soil samples and environmental readings at the Scar's edge. It was a bill she was glad she wasn't paying.

'You need to get better seats,' Lacey, today's personal ranger escort, said, grunting as they hit another rut. She was a lean Shifter with a runner's build, light brown hair, and a heart-shaped face. She wore her Kevlar vest over a thin, short-sleeved T-shirt and Kevlar-lined jeans tucked into heavy combat boots. Both were pale grey, designed to blend into the Rift Scar.

Lacey hadn't turned away from the trees that lined either side of the road as she'd spoken. 'Or you need more driving lessons,' she added as they hit yet another rut. She kept one hand on her rifle to stop it from bouncing around.

Sam gave Lacey a quick smile, hiding her own wince. That last one had hurt Sam as well, but she wouldn't admit that. Upgrading the Jeep wasn't an option, and she doubted it would help. The road was just that bad.

'Sorry. Maybe you or Hale would have better luck convincing the mayor to fix the road than me?' Sam said, scraping the side of the Jeep on the undergrowth as she avoided a pothole big enough to lose a wheel. The dry weather had cracked it wide open, and the next time it rained, it was going to be a problem. Maybe she should just fill them in herself?

'More chance of convincing the mayor to fix the weather,' Lacey said, patting her head. Her normally well-controlled, short brown hair had frizzed out like a bush in the dry heat.

'No chance of that before the weather warden returns from the hospital with her mum,' Sam said. The local Storm Elemental had been out of town for almost a week, and the weather had gone to pot without her. Again, the council was too cheap to do anything about it.

Before the Rifts had opened, Scotland had been a rainy, windy, and cold place to live, with summer temperatures rarely exceeding twenty-five degrees. After the Rifts had opened, they had destroyed weather patterns worldwide, causing hurricanes, droughts, and floods. Scotland had gone from cold and wet to a scorching hot forty degrees, then to below zero and back with no way for anyone to predict it.

The Storm Elementals quickly became the only way to stabilise the weather. They moved the rain clouds to where they were needed and calmed the storms before hurricanes ripped apart whole towns. The country had hoped that time would fix the damage, but it never got better. Eventually, the government had no choice but to create a permanent job for a weather warden within the various councils. Not that everyone had been happy about it, mainly because they blamed the Elementals for the weather problems in the first place.

'I don't think it's likely to be soon. Her mum's diagnosis isn't good,' Lacey said, wiping the sweat from her forehead. 'If the council doesn't do something, we could be in for an interesting summer.'

'Maybe the mayor will finally succumb to pressure and advertise a second weather warden position?' Sam said.

'Why not just wish for the Rift Scars to heal themselves?' Lacey said, snorting as Sam pulled into the small clearing at the end of the road and parked under the shade of some trees.

Sam forced a smile. It was a new saying people had started using in the last year or so, but she wasn't a fan. In her opinion, wishing for something that wasn't possible but everyone desperately wanted was no longer funny.

'This is the last one, right?' Lacey asked as she unhooked her seat belt and looked around the area intently, pulling her rifle closer.

Sam followed her gaze, though she doubted she'd spot anything. They were still another half mile away from the Rift Scar border, but the trees thinned after this section, and the dust got thicker. Unless she particularly needed to drive closer, keeping the car at a distance would help minimise the damage. As it was, she was going through about a car a year.

'Yep,' Sam said. She'd already double-checked her phone at the last stop. The new company app worked offline, which was just as well since the signal near the Rift Scar was spotty at best. Though with the local tower down, it was non-existent right now.

'Nice! An early finish for us then,' Lacey said, smiling at Sam.

'Unless some bright spark loses the data again,' Sam said. That had happened last month. Some intern had incinerated the wrong samples and overwritten a bunch of reports. No one was quite sure how. Sam had needed to spend a week doing double the work to catch up.

'If they do, they will have to wait until Monday. There's no way you're getting another guard until Monday with over half the rangers out for the full moon,' Lacey said, giving Sam a quick once-over. 'You all set?'

Sam nodded and tugged at the armour to show she still had it on. Even though this was their fifth stop today, Lacey always checked. The armour was too big and uncomfortable, especially in this heat. But in the unlikely event that one of the Rift creatures attacked, she'd have some protection.

For maybe thirty seconds. If she was lucky.

But it was protocol to wear it, regardless. One that the rift warden insisted she followed before she was allowed near the Rift Scar. Sam had also suggested she'd be safer if she could carry her own gun, but since they classed her as a civilian, she'd lost that argument.

Lacey huffed a breath as she shoved the door open and got out. All the cool air the air-con had created was lost as the heat rushed in. 'I'll be right back. Cross your fingers for nothing but dust and trees.' Lacey would do a quick circuit of the area before they'd move to where Sam would collect the samples.

Sam shivered despite the heat as the door slammed shut. Lacey's words were light-hearted, but they were a visceral reminder that there was real danger in being out here.

Lacey disappeared into the trees, striding fast, her rifle ready. Sam more than appreciated it. The last thing she wanted was to find herself face to face with a Rift scorpion or worse.

Even if she wasn't as vulnerable as Lacey thought.

HALE WALKED AROUND THE track marks, trying to find the direction they were headed. It wasn't easy; the trail was faint, and with the ground so dusty, one strong breeze could erase it altogether.

'It's just bounce marks from the skull fragments,' Shane said, looking at the ground. Tracking wasn't a skill he'd picked up.

Hale shook his head. 'No. It's definitely tracks.'

'I've seen scorpion tracks before; they are usually several feet wide,' Shane said, frowning like he still didn't believe Hale.

We alpha, should trust us, Fang said with a little snarl.

He's frustrated; give him some space, Hale said, though he agreed with Fang, especially considering they were out in the field. Shane doubting Hale was only going to make working together harder.

Hale took a breath, not letting his frustration show; there was no point in starting another argument. 'It's just one set of tracks. One scorpion.'

'Are you sure it's a scorpion, then?' Shane said, looking at the ground again. 'They don't generally travel on their own?'

'Yes,' Hale said, standing. Shane was right, but nothing else in the Rift left tracks like that.

'Which way is it headed?'

'East, towards the border,' Hale said, wishing he'd kept a ranger in wolf form with him to track it properly. He'd learned a lot in seven years, but visually tracking in these conditions wasn't easy.

'One lone scorpion near the border seems unlikely,' Shane sneered.

Hale shook his head, ignoring Shane's tone. Likely or not, that was what he was seeing. 'Unlikely doesn't mean it's not headed towards the rest of its group or out of the Scar.'

The creatures may not have been able to leave the Rift Scar for long without getting sick and dying, but it was long enough to kill people and do damage.

'You're—'

'Enough,' Hale snapped, his wolf energy slipping out at the word.

Shane's jaw tightened, and his grip on his gun shifted, but he stopped arguing. Hale wanted to curse. This was exactly what he'd been trying to avoid. His wolf was strong, and he hated using the weight of it to stop an argument. It wouldn't help deal with Shane's issues either; no one liked it when their alpha threw their weight around.

Shane need put in place. Should not challenge us, Fang said.

Hale didn't bother answering his wolf this time. It was another argument he wouldn't win.

'Whether you believe in my tracking ability or not, something left these tracks. This close to the border, we need to deal with whatever it is before it sets up a nest,' Hale said, struggling to pull back his anger.

Shane gave a sharp nod, not looking at Hale. But the stink of his anger made it over the rot of the Rift Scar.

Hale focused on the scorpion's trail. It was still travelling solo, heading northeast. They followed it for half a mile in silence, but there was still no sign of any other scorpions. He didn't like not knowing what it was doing or why.

The need to reach out to the other half of his patrol grew the longer they followed the trail. Unfortunately, there were few ways to communicate in the Rift Scar. Something about the place interfered with short-wave frequencies, so they usually relied on the mobile network, at least when it worked.

The mobile towers near the Highland Rift Scar were currently down, and the company that had put them in was fighting with the local council about who should pay for the repair. The Rift Scar dust tended to eat away at electronics and damage them far more quickly than normal. Hale wasn't expecting them to find a solution for a few more months if past experience was anything to go on. They carried flares for emergencies. But something that didn't make sense didn't exactly warrant a flare to gather everyone together.

Check safe? Fang said, pushing him to check on their pack. *Use pack bonds.*

Opening himself up to the pack bonds would only show the emotions of the wolves within his pack. He'd be able to feel if they were afraid, but not why. There also weren't any specific thoughts exchanged, so it was impossible to use the link to communicate or for Hale to send specific warnings. But his wolf was right. At least he'd know his people were safe.

Letting the connection to his pack open was always the easy part. Almost as soon as he made the decision, the links rose around him like he was at the centre of a spider's web, with dozens of threads spinning away from him. Most of his pack had a second, much stronger, connection back to their family packs, and it made Hale's threads hazy.

No other alpha had to endure this halfway house connection, but since the rest of the UK's packs often sent their wolves north for a limited time, Hale's link to them was always temporary. None of the alphas wanted to let go of their hold when their wolves would be back in a year or less. It was the other reason he rarely opened up the pack bonds. It was always frustrating.

Our pack, Fang said. *Keep.*

You know we can't, Hale said, though only one Shifter was due to leave soon. It was a fight that happened every time one of them left at the end of their year term. His wolf huffed and chose to ignore Hale. Some instincts went deeper than others, and this one had always been a problem for his wolf.

Taking a breath, Hale focused on the closest threads, trying to sense their emotions. Shane pulsed loud and clear, his residual frustration a bright spark. There was a tinge of surprise when Shane sensed the connection open, but Hale ignored it and pushed past him, searching for the others.

Three of his pack were out on patrol further north. A mix of boredom and focus came at him from their direction, which was a good sign that everything was well. He carefully closed down the connection once he was sure his wolves were fine. If it had been Elementals on patrol, he wouldn't have been able to check on them, but everyone in this group was a Shifter.

'Is the pack okay?' Shane asked, voice tight.

Hale glanced back at Shane. His eyes were the yellow of his wolf, but he wasn't looking at Hale. Shane would have sensed the link open, but he'd only have been able to sense Hale, not the rest of the pack.

'Everything is fine,' Hale said. 'I just wanted to be sure nothing had gone wrong with the other patrol.'

If kept link open, would always know, Fang said, letting out a huff of air again.

Except leaving the connection open like that was harder to manage. But it wasn't worth arguing with his wolf about it, so he didn't bother replying.

They barely made it more than a few feet when the wind shifted, bringing a familiar stink of death to his nose.

Shane stiffened, finally giving Hale a direct look as he caught the scent. First scorpions, and now this. At least there was no longer any doubt from Shane that they'd been following a trail.

Without a word, Hale started forward, raising his rifle to his shoulder. Shane did the same, falling in behind and slightly to his left.

CHAPTER TWO

SAM TAPPED THE STEERING wheel as she waited for Lacey. There was no sound outside, no birds or bugs, nothing at all. It was normal this close to the Rift Scar, but it still never felt right, no matter how many times she was near the border, which was nearly every damned day.

The trees here were over a hundred years old, mostly pines, with an occasional birch spotted through them. They'd come up in the wake of the Rifts closing and now towered over the clearing. Heather and ferns grew around their roots, providing plenty of space for animals to live and thrive, but none would go near it. It was like the wildlife sensed the rot, even though it was still a half mile away.

Sam fanned herself uselessly, looking around for Lacey, though it would be at least another ten minutes before she'd finished her checks. Technically, Sam was supposed to stay inside the Jeep, but it was stuffy, and she'd spent enough time trapped in it today. Lacey would have said if she'd sensed anything in the clearing, so getting out should be safe enough.

Sam opened the door after one last check of the area and slipped out. The peace from the land seeped into her even as new sweat beaded down her spine, and the faint rancid taint of the Rift Scar filled her nose. But it was good to be outside on her own land, even if it was miles from her house.

A flash of darkness caught her eye. It stood out oddly against the bark of a tree, too dark to be just a shadow. Sam frowned, moving towards it. The tree was younger than the rest, smaller and narrower, its bark rough and mottled with lichen. But that wasn't all that was growing on it.

Black sludge oozed from several sections where the bark had fallen off. It almost looked like claw marks, but Sam knew better. In the sections around the missing bark, there would be a scarlet fungus, eating away at the tree, trying to kill it from the inside.

Once it got past a certain point, nothing could stop it. Nothing in science could kill the fungus. Sam and other scientists had tried and failed to find a cure. Once it got a hold, it attacked like a cancer and spread too fast to stop. The solution was almost always to cut the corrupted wood out and burn it. But if the infection went too deep, then the tree would die because of the damage.

But Sam knew a better way. Something that normal scientists couldn't do. Except she couldn't let anyone know about it. Being an Earth Elemental wasn't something that she could share.

Not all Elementals had been accepted––though accepted might have been stretching it, tolerated might have been closer. There was one element that had remained separate and feared. Earth.

The government believed the connection that was formed between the Earth Elemental and the land would put lives at risk. It wasn't true, but it hadn't stopped them from creating laws that still held ninety years later.

Earth Elementals were forbidden from owning land and living in one place longer than a year. That way, they couldn't create the connection the government feared.

Sam's mum had managed to stay under the radar. Hiding what they were from the government so they could live in peace. Her mother had hated it, ranting more than once to Sam about how their magic wasn't dangerous. All they could do was heal plants and sense what was on the land.

Sam did another quick check around her, considering her options. It would be at least another five minutes before Lacey finished a full circuit around the clearing. Sam would have just enough time to give the tree an energy boost, though it would only be a temporary fix. To save the tree long term, the fungus would need to be removed, but there wasn't enough time to do that now with Lacey so close.

Letting out a slow breath, Sam made her decision. Saving the tree was worth a little risk. She lowered the walls in her mind a fraction.

The Land around her exploded with life, expanding the connection wider than she'd planned. The tendrils that had settled into her when she'd stepped into the clearing jumped into focus, trying to tug her in every direction.

A rabbit bolted between the trees a mile away. Sunlight soaked into the old pines around her, warming them, giving them life. Bugs chewed at a fallen branch. A shallow stream ran for miles through her forest before falling over a small cliff into a pool below.

None of the descriptions did the sensations justice as her mind struggled to keep up with the images the Land was sending her. It flowed through her, taking a part of her with it as it showed her everything it could reach. Like a child following a group of fireflies, unfocused and wanting Sam to see all of it at once. Except Sam couldn't do that. No matter how far she stretched her mind, there were limits.

Sam tried to pull back, box off the sensations so she could focus on one thing. Just the tree in front of her.

The fungus itself wasn't visible to her through the connection. Everything that came from the Rift was like that––like the corruption was just an illusion. But it wasn't. It was just so different that the Land couldn't understand it.

The tree slowly came into focus. It was in a worse state than she'd thought, life already leaching away as the fungus stole everything it had. She just needed to gather up some energy from the healthier trees to feed into it.

And fast. She was limited in time before Lacey came back.

The view of the tree changed with the thought.

Footsteps crushed the sparse grass. Lacey as she continued her patrol around the area. *Nearby, something metal lay on the ground, unnatural against the pine needles.*

Sam cut off the connection, fear tightening her chest. Had Lacey sensed Sam? She'd always been worried that by using her magic around others, she'd give herself away somehow, but this wasn't how she ever wanted to test that theory.

There was no shout from Lacey of worry or fear, no sign she was returning to investigate what had happened. In theory, she shouldn't. Lacey was a wolf. She shouldn't be able to sense Sam. No one except another Earth Elemental should be able to feel the magic, and even then, there was no guarantee.

But Sam understood so little about her magic that part of her worried. She needed to try this healing when she was somewhere safe. Somewhere there was no one about to sense her if she got distracted.

The decision to try again later made, she stepped back from the tree and drew in a slow breath, trying to let go of the fear.

'Sam?' Lacey said, making Sam jump. 'Why didn't you stay in the car?'

'I know, I'm sorry. I wasn't going anywhere, I promise,' Sam said, moving back to her Jeep so Lacey wouldn't see the fungus. If she did, she'd have to report it, and they'd cut the tree down.

Lacey sighed. 'You need to be more careful, Sam. You're only human. If even one scorpion got through and stung you, you'd be dead.'

'Or an Elemental,' Sam said, then wished she could take it back.

Most humans died after being stung by a Rift scorpion, but there was another possibility. Something a lot rarer. They became an Elemental, which was the exact opposite train of thought she wanted Lacey to follow.

'You'd have more chance of surviving if a Rift venom-infected wolf came along,' Lacey said, then her lips thinned. 'Actually, strike that. Too many people would think it was one of us.'

Sam winced. It was a sore point among Shifters. During the Fae War, wild wolves had been driven insane by the Rift venom and had attacked humans. Those who'd survived had become the first wolf Shifters.

But just because they'd been made that way, it didn't mean they could pass their abilities on with a bite any more than an Elemental could. But unfortunately, some people still believed Shifters were lying and claimed they were dangerous. Or keeping all their power to themselves, depending on who was making the accusation. But the truth was, the only way to safely become an Elemental or Shifter was to inherit it from a parent.

'Why don't we go get the samples and get out of here?' Sam said, deciding that changing the topic was best as she opened the back of the Jeep and dragged the sample kit towards her. 'I'm dying to get out of here and grab a shower.'

Despite the rather dark turn of the conversation, Lacey smiled.

'You and me both,' Lacey said as she grabbed the second box that held the scanner and passed it to Sam. That way,

Lacey would have both hands free for her gun. 'Right now, I think that even a human would smell us coming.'

Sam laughed, more tension easing out of her as they turned and headed towards the Rift Scar's eastern edge.

Hale expected a scorpion, but what he found was something else altogether. An imp.

It was sprawled out on its side, unmoving, and without a doubt, the source of the smell. The creature was a metre tall, with pale skin and no hair. It might have looked like a deformed child, except no child ever had arms almost as long as their body or a short muzzle. Its lips were curled back to show a row of sharp teeth, stained black from its own saliva.

Hale watched for signs of danger as Shane moved closer to the body. Neither scorpions nor imps liked to hunt without others of their own kind. They also didn't normally leave their kills. Food wasn't exactly easy to get in the Scar. But there was no sign there was anything but the one imp.

'Dead?' Hale asked despite the smell. Scorpion venom itself wouldn't kill a Rift imp, but it would paralyse it, allowing the scorpions to come in and take their time in dealing with its victim. It was a horrible way to die, even for a Rift imp.

Shane used the gun barrel to nudge the body. It moved more like a statue than a living thing, revealing a large gash on the side of its neck. It was no longer bleeding. Definitely dead. Shane stepped away, letting it fall back into place.

'Any signs of more?' Shane asked, looking at the ground. It was relatively undisturbed. The scorpion must have caught the imp unaware.

'No,' Hale said, backtracking a few paces, searching for the direction the imp had come. There only seemed to be two sets of prints, and they'd been headed towards the Rift Scar northeast border as well. 'Both of them looked to be alone.'

Even alone, there wasn't any reason for them to head towards the border. They couldn't survive outside the Rift Scar for long; even if they'd been cast out from their groups, they'd have gone deeper into the Scar.

'What the hell are they doing?' Hale said, not realising he'd spoken aloud until Shane snorted.

'You want to understand how these creatures work?' Shane said, tilting his chin towards the wasteland around them. 'Just look around. Chaos. Death. Destruction. What more do you need to know?'

Shane wasn't wrong exactly, but he also wasn't helpful. Some, like the imps, wanted to play with their food, but most were just like any other animals protecting their territory. But when that territory shouldn't have belonged to them in the first place, it was something that was hard to remember.

'Rift scorpions don't kill for sport. They kill for territory and food. It killed this imp, and didn't eat it, then it moved on,' Hale said, wiping sweat off his brow as it tried to drip into his eye. 'Something isn't right.'

Shift. Hunt with nose, Fang said, echoing Hale's unease as his wolf pushed at him to change into their wolf form.

Not here. Not enough time, Hale said, pushing back his wolf. Shifting took time, and having Shane carry Hale's gear just so he'd be able to track, or vice versa, was impractical.

Claws safer, Fang replied, but his wolf always thought that.

It didn't always have the greatest of forethought. Another reason it was better to patrol in human form. Though, there was always a place for scouts who could run faster and further in their wolf's form through the Scar. But as fighters? Guns often proved to be more effective.

Guns faster, Hale said, much to his wolf's annoyance. Fang stopped arguing, though he was far from convinced.

'Do you want to call the others?' Shane said, looking north towards where the other team would be patrolling. Again, his frustration was still there, but the concern for the pack curbed it.

'Not yet. I don't want to risk them crossing its path without knowing it's there,' Hale said. If he'd had any other way of sending a warning without bringing them towards him, he would have. 'Let's continue to follow the trail.'

He turned towards the border again, keeping his gun ready in case there was something ahead he couldn't see. The ground was growing slightly flatter, but there were still plenty of places a scorpion could hide from sight.

Two gunshots echoed over the wasteland.

Hale froze only long enough to determine that the gunshots had come from the direction of the northeast border before he started running. Shane moved to follow him, footsteps heavy as they abandoned the trail they'd been following.

The two shots hadn't been close, nor had they come from the other patrol's direction. He was still two miles out from where the Rift Scar ended, but there shouldn't have been any civilians with guns on the border, which meant there had to be more of Hale's people out there.

'I thought we were the only patrol out here today?' Hale asked, forcing himself to keep an even pace as worry tightened his chest. The last thing he needed was to stumble on top of the scorpion he'd been following and be unable to react in time.

There were no follow-up gunshots, which could have meant anything.

'Lacey's out playing bodyguard today,' Shane said, breath coming in heavy pants as he struggled to keep up. It was all well and good focusing on strength, but there was a balance, and he'd clearly sacrificed speed to bulk up.

'With Sam?' Hale asked, gut twisting as his wolf pushed at him to go faster. Sam wouldn't be able to protect herself from a scorpion.

'Yes,' Shane wheezed.

Hale cursed, pushing for more speed despite his earlier worry.

SAM WIPED THE SWEAT from her forehead as she followed behind Lacey. They'd done this trek enough times now that it was practically muscle memory as they slipped between the progressively thinning trees.

The pines dropped away first, then the ground changed, becoming brown dirt with patches of grey that looked like a malignancy, which was exactly what it was––the corruption of the Rift Scar leaking into the surrounding earth. Or at least it was trying to.

Records going back for the last hundred years had shown no signs that the border had shifted even once since the Rifts had been closed. They certainly hadn't in the past five years Sam had been doing this job. Nor had any of the other three UK Rifts. But if the government wanted to pay her to come down here to take samples and readings, then evaluate them, who was she to argue? It was easy money.

Sam stopped short of where the dirt changed from mottle grey and brown to entirely grey. Only things that came from the Scar grew after this point. Not that there was much of that. The few plants they had were all toxic or carnivorous. Thankfully, none of that grew near any of the borders.

She turned away from the grey wasteland, carefully laying down her two boxes. Then she opened up the larger one to grab a pair of gloves and a mask from the top compartment. She had to fight the thick latex over her sweaty fingers. The mask stuck to her face, making the hot air even hotter. But both had become regulation requirements.

'You know I wouldn't tell anyone if you didn't wear the mask,' Lacey said from where she'd moved to stand between Sam and the edge of the Scar. 'It's not like you've got sick in the past five years from not wearing them.'

'And here I was thinking I was starting a new fashion trend,' Sam said, spitting out the mask as she tried to take a deep breath. This batch was made of a flimsy material with a simple metal wire for the nose. All it did was make breathing harder. She'd have removed it like Lacey had suggested, but someone had got sick, and Sam didn't want to advertise she was different if she didn't have to.

She took the old Corruption Detection Scanner, or CDS, out of the smaller box first since it was temperamental. It was a heavy rectangular device about the size of a car battery, with a needle that would move to the right to show her how much Fae Magic was in this section. On the side of the box was a thick wand about a foot long, with a large cone on the end that she used to direct where the readings were coming from.

The CDS was almost as old as she was, which, at twenty-six, said a lot. It was long overdue for replacement. If she'd been working at any of the three southern Rift Scars, it would have been. But no one was all that worried about the swath of land that had once been Aberdeen. It was too far north, with too few people for them to do much more than make sure the Scar wasn't getting bigger.

Which was more than a little short-sighted. The north-east of Scotland was far from abandoned.

Sam turned the CDS on. It immediately started making a high-pitched whine, the needle twitching from left to right. The new version of the CDS had more functionality, but this one simply measured the levels of the magic. This close to the border, those levels were high. If she had taken the readings back near the car, the device would have been silent.

'So, what's the verdict? Did the Rift Scar suddenly decide, after over a hundred years of doing nothing, that it was going to get smaller in the last day?' Lacey said, using the shoulder of her T-shirt to wipe the sweat from her face.

Sam gave Lacey a justly deserved eye roll at the question. It was the same one she asked every time she was stuck on protective duty with Sam. 'I won't know until I get the data back to my computer. But how about I bet you it hasn't changed?'

Lacey snorted. 'Now you're just trying to steal my money.'

'Though maybe if the machine showed a change, they might finally send me the new model at long last,' Sam said, grunting as she walked with the machine in a two-metre-wide circle, watching the needle jump and dip as she passed closer to the border, then away again.

'They might even believe you if any of them saw how well these trees are surviving this close to the edge,' Lacey said, nodding at the treeline as Sam passed her. 'Down south, it's at least another mile back before anything can survive.'

Sam tried not to flinch at the comment. It had been casually said, and Lacey had never once looked at her, but it still made Sam nervous. She didn't like anyone noticing things were different. Though Lacey was far from the first person to comment on how well the trees did here.

Returning to where she'd left the rest of her kit, she turned the CDS machine off, then loaded it back into its case and sealed it up to minimise how much dust would get into it. She'd be able to pull the graph when she got back home and compare it to previous visits. Then she opened the second box, revealing half a dozen vials nestled in the foam padding.

Over half of them were already labelled and ready to run through the analyser when she got home. She took out one of the unused ones, along with its clean, matching scoop, and crouched next to one of the mottled sections of dirt.

The ground was dry and cracked after days of no rain. She scraped at the top layer to loosen it. The dust rose, tickling her nose despite the mask and making her gag on the stench of rot.

'Just when you think it can't get any worse,' Lacey said, the back of her hand raised to cover her mouth. 'Makes me wish for your human nose.'

Sam grunted noncommittally. The second use of the word human in less than an hour made Sam uncomfortable, so she changed the subject again.

'Are you looking forward to tonight's run?' Sam asked as she poured the sample of dirt into the vial and sealed it. She was careful to keep the dust away from her skin and tried her best not to breathe it in. Mostly because of the stench; the mask did nothing to help that.

'Always. I'm glad the council agreed to continue letting you rent us your land for the full moon. I couldn't even imagine what it had been like before you started that. Having to go south four hours to the Glasgow pack lands or home every month to our family pack,' Lacey said, shuddering. 'A lot of us had been worried by the delay.'

'I'm glad I could help, though it's not quite signed yet,' Sam said, putting the sample into the case and the scoop into the bag with the others she'd used. She'd been worried, too. The money she got from the pack for that one night paid most of her bills. 'But it isn't like the council has a lot of choice but to agree. Unless they want to change their policy.'

The government still banned wolves from shifting any-where except for specific locations. Most of the other packs owned their own land that their Shifters could use to change and hunt. But here in the Highlands, the local councils refused to allow the pack to have the same. As a result, the pack could shift in the Rift Scar, and for the full moon only, on Sam's land. Everywhere else was off-limits to protect the public, even if they were more likely to get hit by a car than bitten by a wolf.

'Heavens forbid they change the policy,' Lacey said, rolling her eyes. Then she hesitated and added, 'Why the delay?'

'The mayor has a new legal consultant, and he wanted to check that the agreement lined up with their local policies,' Sam said, shuffling over a few feet to another section of dirt where it was just brown to take another sample.

'Oh,' Lacey said, seeming to deflate, like she'd been hoping to hear something else.

'It's unofficially official,' Sam said, looking up at Lacey, not liking her worry. The mayor wasn't about to change the policy without a reason. 'They aren't going to change their minds.'

Lacey looked away, then back at Sam. 'You didn't consider changing the contract?

'You don't want me to rent you the land?' Sam asked, stomach dropping. The Shifters renting the land really was the difference between being able to pay all her bills and not. Being a rift surveyor wasn't exactly a well-paying job, despite the risks.

'No. Not that. The opposite,' Lacey said, eyes flaring faintly yellow as her wolf peeked out. 'I thought you might be considering renting us the land for more time?'

Sam froze, more from the question than the brief glimpse of Lacey's wolf. Renting the land for more than just the full moon would mean that the wolves would be on Sam's land all the time. If that happened, how would she be able to hide what she was? She was already nervous enough about being there on the full moon that she left and stayed in a hotel overnight.

Lacey looked away, blinking rapidly as she struggled with her wolf. Sam had seen enough wolves go through this that she knew when to keep her distance and give them space. But she'd never seen Lacey struggle like this before.

'It's not that I wouldn't consider it, Lacey,' Sam said as she sealed and stored the sample she'd been holding. 'But no one has asked, at least not that I've been told.'

Lacey started to turn back to Sam, inhaling sharply, then her face shut down and her gun came up. Fear settled into Sam's gut. The change could only mean one thing.

'Leave the case,' Lacey said, but Sam had already moved back to her feet, closing the distance between her and Lacey. Even if they'd never run into anything in the Rift Scar before, that didn't mean that Sam hadn't been made to run this same drill every few months like clockwork.

Stay close to the rift ranger. Don't run. Don't panic. Do as you're told.

Sam was doing her very best with the 'don't panic' part of the plan, but it was hard. Her heart pounded so loud in her ears that she wasn't sure she'd hear Lacey give a command.

Then the gunshot made it impossible to hear anything at all.

CHAPTER THREE

As Hale ran faster, Shane lagged. It was a struggle not to let the gap grow too large, but Hale couldn't risk leaving Shane alone without knowing what else might be out here.

Shane not in danger, Fang said, but he was hesitant as well, disliking the conflicting pull between pack and protecting Sam. *Shane can protect self.*

Which was true, but even so, they couldn't abandon Shane despite his recent attitude.

Hale risked opening the pack bonds just enough to see if Lacey was hurt. The web of connections sharpened in his mind. Lacey was ahead of them, an edge of worry and focus coming through the link.

That didn't mean Sam was okay. She wasn't pack, so he'd no way to check on her, but the lack of fear or other emotions from Lacey gave him hope.

If made mate, could do it, Fang said.

Sam isn't our mate, Hale said. *Even if she was, she's human.* There was no way for her to have a connection with him. Not that Hale believed in mates in the first place. It was a myth that persisted over the years. Hale thought it stemmed from a need to belong rather than any foundation in truth.

But regardless of what Sam was to them, the need to protect her was as strong as if she were pack. And not knowing if she was okay was killing him.

Hale's heart skipped a beat as he finally got close enough to see Sam. She was pressed tight to Lacey's back, staring down at a scorpion a bare few feet away from them. Lacey's gun was still pointed at the creature, ready to take another shot if needed.

The scorpion had two bullet holes in its thick shell, black blood oozing onto the ground as it twitched. It was at least two feet long, its dark grey colour almost blending in with the soil, so only the bright red stinger stood out.

He scanned the area, looking for more. The ground here was mostly flat, so he could see relatively far. There wasn't any sign of any more scorpions.

Shane caught up, wheezing heavily as Hale slowed his pace further so he could walk the last few metres toward Lacey and Sam. He inhaled deeply, pulling in the scents around him, searching for any sign the scorpion had hurt either of them. Nothing else but fresh gunpowder rose above the rancid scorpion scent. He released the breath, the knot in his stomach loosening, but not by much.

Lacey didn't turn fully away from the dead scorpion as she nodded at them. She was taller than him––but most people were––with more attitude than sense. She had her gun pointed towards the still-twitching scorpion, ready to react if needed. Not that there appeared to be any more danger.

'Are you alright?' Shane asked, his breath still coming in heavy pants as he looked Lacey up and down. A Shifter getting stung wasn't fatal, but it wasn't pleasant.

The venom would trap them in the form they were in. So, if they were a wolf, they'd be stuck that way for a day until the venom wore off. Not to mention it hurt like hell.

Lacey nodded and rolled her eyes at him, but her lips curled in a small smile, clearly pleased with the attention. The pair had been off and on since Shane had arrived.

'We're fine,' she said, nodding at the dead scorpion. 'It was just the one. It never had a chance. Right, Sam?'

Sam nodded and gave a strained smile. She was petite at five feet, with green eyes, high cheekbones, and a small, narrow nose. She looked pale but unhurt as she took a step away from Lacey. He wished he could pick up Sam's scent under the rot of the Scar, then he'd be sure she really was fine. Unlike with a Shifter, one scratch from the stinger was all it would have taken for her to be gone.

Is strong, Fang said. *Make good mate.*

But strength wouldn't have stopped her from dying if she'd been stung, and neither would whether or not she was his mate. Besides, he still didn't believe there was such a thing.

'You're sure you're alright?' Hale asked Sam as she tucked a strand of blond hair behind her ear. She'd tied it up in a messy bun on top of her head, but more than a few curls had escaped. He had to stop himself from reaching over to tuck another strand back in. That wasn't his place.

His wolf huffed a breath, unhappy with Hale's continued decision to hold back, but he didn't argue further. They needed to focus on other things. But later would be another matter.

'I'm fine,' Sam said, spreading her hands as if to show him. The Kevlar vest wasn't a great fit, and it moved awkwardly on her slim build, pulling up her pale T-shirt to show a flash of skin.

Desire trickled through him, and he had to force himself to remember all the reasons why getting involved with Sam was a bad idea. First and foremost was that Sam was human. Humans never made good partners to Shifters. At least, not that Hale had ever seen. They grew to resent the pack and wolf over time, and it never ended well, least of all for any kids involved.

He'd already seen what the pressure of being human in a pack had done to his mother. He wasn't going to wish that life on anyone else. Even if Sam wanted it, which wasn't a given.

Sam not mother, Fang said, giving him a mental nudge. Like he was tired of Hale being stupid. Then, despite having just given up the argument, he added, *Sam our mate.*

Sam isn't our mate, Hale said, sharper than he intended, making his wolf whine in displeasure at him. *I'm sorry. She's human. She can't be our mate. I've already told you.*

His wolf huffed another breath, still unhappy.

'Did you cull the rest of its group of scorpions?' Lacey asked. She kept her gun up and eyes constantly moving. She'd become very proficient working in the Rift Scar over the last year she'd been here, despite the attitude. Hale was going to miss her experience when she left next month.

Hale's wolf gave another loud huff at the idea of losing another of their pack, but Lacey's year was up. It was time for her to go home, even if his wolf didn't like it.

'There were no others,' Hale said, looking at the scorpion again. It looked healthy and whole except for the bullet wound. There didn't seem to be any reason it would be out here on its own.

When Hale looked back, Lacey and Shane were staring at each other, something unspoken passing between them before they turned away. Maybe the pair was back together again, though with Lacey leaving soon, she'd seemed even more distant than before.

'Did you see what way it was headed?' Hale asked Lacey. She frowned, considering.

'Does it matter?' Shane said, cutting in again with that short, frustrated tone he'd been using all day. 'Let's just get it moved back from the border.'

Hale swallowed his growl. He was going to have to deal with Shane's attitude soon. There was a time and place for him to vent his problems, but in front of Lacey and Sam was definitely not it.

'I don't like not knowing why this scorpion was out here on its own. It's probably best if you both continue this another day,' Hale said, turning back to Sam and Lacey.

'I can protect Sam,' Lacey said, lifting her chin. 'The scorpion didn't get anywhere near us.'

'And if one turns into five?' Hale said, snapping at her. It seemed everyone wanted to argue with him today.

She lowered her head a fraction, accepting the decision, but he suspected she'd have her complaint about it later. In depth. 'I'll help Sam get her stuff,' Lacey said.

Sam looked between them with narrowed eyes, and Hale was glad he couldn't get a hint of her scent right then. He suspected he might not like it. She understood pack politics well enough not to add to the tension by arguing as she followed Lacey.

Make good mate, Fang said again.

Hale ignored him.

'We'll walk you back to the car and then deal with the body,' Hale said, nodding at the scorpion.

Lacey's lips thinned, but she didn't argue this time as she handed Sam the second case so Lacey could have her hands free for the gun. It was probably overkill to have the three of them escort her out. But at the same time, Hale's stomach twisted at the idea of leaving any of his pack, or Sam, alone until he understood what was happening.

After they got Sam back to the car, he was going to bring the patrol together and decide how to deal with this. Unfortunately, it would probably mean they'd still have to split up to cover enough ground, but at least everyone would know what they were dealing with.

SAM FELT HALE'S EYES on her as they walked to the car in silence. They burned into her back, tugging at the residual adrenaline from the scorpion attack. Each step made her want to stop and turn to face him. To let him close the gap and ask her again if she was alright.

Which was bloody frustrating.

Letting anyone that close would risk them discovering she was an Earth Elemental, something she couldn't allow. Not when the cost of her father discovering the truth had led to the death of both of her parents.

So, no matter how good the attraction felt, or how easy it would be to reach out and brush off that tiny smudge of grey dust she'd seen on his chin, she couldn't have a life with him. Something shorter might have been an option, except she didn't trust herself that much, not with the way she felt drawn towards him.

Not to mention he'd never even once shown anything but a professional interest in her.

Trying to shake off the useless desire that rose, she placed the cases in the back of the Jeep. Lacey moved back a few feet with Shane, leaning in to whisper something to him.

'Do you need extra cover over the weekend to make up for cutting this trip short?' Hale asked, voice a soft rumble at her back. When had he got so close?

'This was the last one,' Sam said, turning back towards him.

He'd stopped a few feet back from her, watching her with those intense brown eyes flecked with gold. For a man who was barely taller than her, he had a presence that made people turn and stare. Or, if he wanted to, have everyone forget he was even there. She'd never met anyone like him. She'd have said it was part of being an alpha, but the previous Highland Rift Scar's alpha had never had that kind of presence.

'There aren't any more results due until next week,' Sam continued after a slow breath. It did nothing to soothe the butterflies fluttering in her stomach.

'I'll make sure we get a full patrol to check for any other stragglers before then,' Hale said, running a hand through his short black hair as he glanced back towards the border.

'Sounds good,' Sam said, feeling uncomfortable as she noticed Lacey's eyes on her. But not enough that Sam turned and got in the car, even though she knew she should.

'Good,' Hale said, but he didn't make a move to leave either as he continued to watch her. 'I'll see you tonight?'

'Yes.' Sam swallowed against her dry throat. Every month, she'd wait for him to arrive before she left to go to the hotel. That's all he meant. Yet her body seemed to think it was more.

Lacey must have decided that was her dismissal because she moved towards the passenger side of the Jeep and unhooked her gun so she could get in.

It took Sam another minute before she managed to tear her eyes away from him and move to the driver's side door. No matter how much she told herself getting involved with him was a bad idea, it didn't make the attraction any less. But it was too much of a risk. Keeping her secret was hard enough without letting someone like a Shifter into her life.

No matter how much she wanted to wake in the early morning sunshine with Hale's arms wrapped around her and children laughing in the hall. That wasn't to be her life.

Sam tried to shake off the image as she got in the Jeep and closed the door. She risked a single glance back, telling herself that she didn't want to run him over by accident. But really, she just wanted another look.

He was still watching her, face an unreadable mask. Then he turned and walked away with a predatory grace, all tense watchfulness that made goosebumps dance along her skin—for all the wrong reasons.

Hale couldn't be her future. No matter how much she wanted it.

WATCHING SAM DRIVE AWAY was both a relief and a frustration. Hale wanted to be with her, but even if he was willing to give in to that foolish desire, he'd another job to do first. Track where the scorpion had come from and make sure there weren't more.

Hale headed back towards the corpse without a word, Shane at his heels. It was time to bring the patrol together. Though he really didn't want to have to send a flare off if he didn't need to. But if they were close enough, maybe Hale and Shane could go to them.

Opening the pack bonds, Hale sensed Shane first, his frustration now anger, though what had changed, Hale couldn't tell. It was a problem that needed to be sorted soon, but he couldn't think of any way to have it out with him that wouldn't end up with them fighting. Something that they didn't have time for.

Pushing past the bundle of emotion, he sought the rest of the patrol, finding them a lot closer than he'd expected. An edge of worry came through the link. Communications might not be possible, but somehow Hale suspected he knew exactly where they were and what they'd found.

Hale saw Lance first as the border came into view. He was in his wolf form, as he moved in circles around the dead scorpion, four paws puffing up dust. He had armour strapped to his back and underbelly, making his tawny fur stick out in odd tufts. The gear was light enough to still allow him to manoeuvre. They'd a heavier-duty version of the kit that extended out to the legs and neck, but it was too cumbersome for scouting. They only used it when they went deeper into the Rift Scar.

Lance paused to look at Hale, inclining his head, before he put his nose back to the ground. The Rift Scar was one of the very few locations exempt from the law that banned shifting. Not that many would choose to run here if they had the choice.

'Is everyone okay?' Oliver asked, eyes showing the amber of his wolf as he looked Hale up and down for injuries. He was the tallest in the group at six and a half feet, with wide shoulders and light brown hair. He was one of the more dominant wolves in Hale's pack, though he often seemed to forget. 'We heard the shot,' Oliver said, the amber fading back into his normal grey.

Hale nodded. 'Everyone is fine. As far as we can tell, this scorpion was alone, but I'd like to track it to be sure.'

Oliver let out a relieved breath and shifted his focus to Amelia, the last member of their patrol. The woman was six feet tall and slim, with a square jaw and honey-blond hair. There was a neutral expression on her face as she stared at the carcass.

'What else do we need to do, other than track where the scorpion came from?' Oliver asked her. She was the newest member of the pack, having not even been here for two full months.

She'd come, like most did, with just the basic training they'd put everyone through before they sent them to work at the Rift Scar. He'd assigned Oliver to help train her, but there was no easy introduction to the job. It was very much a trial-by-fire experience. From what Oliver had said, she'd done well so far. This wasn't the first question-and-answer session Oliver had done with her in the field.

'Remove the body,' Amelia said, rolling her eyes as she answered his question. The answer had been an easy one, likely something they'd have learned in training before coming here.

'And why do we remove it?' Oliver said, raising his eyebrow.

Amelia cast a look at Oliver that matched the icy colour of her eyes. There was a reason that Hale had chosen Oliver to train the prickly woman. Not many of the pack would have tolerated the attitude, but Oliver seemed to have endless patience.

Not need patience. She not pack, Fang said with an edge of a growl. He didn't like the attitude that Amelia was giving at all.

Amelia is a pup and needs to learn, Hale said, trying to put it in terms his wolf would understand even though Amelia had to be nearly twenty, if not older. But all his wolf saw was a new and fragile connection. There were too many wolves coming and going that it was sometimes hard for the wolf to keep up.

As for Oliver, well, that was up to him to let her get away with the attitude or not, and since he didn't comment, Hale didn't get involved. There was a time and place to press his presence as alpha but micromanaging the pack structure wasn't it.

'I don't know,' Amelia said begrudgingly. Her irritation seeped away as she thought about his question. 'Maybe to stop other predators from coming to eat it?'

Oliver nodded. 'Any other reason?' he said, patience wearing her down and reducing the attitude. He treated Amelia like she was family, a little sister who needed guidance and protection. Though Hale imagined if they had actually been related, Oliver wouldn't have been quite so civil.

'Scorpions don't hunt solo,' Amelia said, sounding sure, but then she hesitated, looking at the ground again. 'The rest of its group might be looking for it?'

Oliver smiled and nodded, opening his mouth to continue his lecture, but Shane must have had enough because he stepped forward, interrupting him.

'As interesting as class time is, I imagine dealing with the body might be a better use of your time,' Shane said, looking between the group like he was scolding bad behaviour.

Hale had to suppress a growl at the challenge. Because deliberate or not, that's what Shane was doing by inserting himself like that. Challenging Hale's authority. Unlike Amelia, who'd only challenged Oliver.

Not his place. Pup training important, Fang said, which contradicted his earlier insistence that Amelia wasn't pack. Though Hale agreed with his wolf.

But Shane was also right. They needed to keep moving before others in its group decided to come looking for it. If there were more.

Oliver gave Shane a cool look, but he didn't say anything as he then turned to Lance, who had been circling back and forth throughout the entire conversation. 'Lance was trying to track which way the scorpion had come from,' Oliver said.

Lance raised his head at his name and moved to stand next to Oliver. He was large enough that his wolf's head came up above Oliver's hip. Lance scratched the ground once, then pointed his nose west. His leg and paw were hairless where it was twisted with scars. The history behind those scars was something that Hale had only heard second-hand. But it didn't affect Lance's ability to work, and if he wanted to keep his past private, that was up to him.

Hale nodded in the direction Lance had indicated. 'We found a dead imp out there and a trail for a single scorpion. I'd like to make sure that there aren't any others close to the border,' he said.

'That's a waste of time,' Shane said, and this time Hale did growl. The entire group grew still, watching Shane, who stiffened but didn't back down. 'What are the chances of two solo scorpions out in the Rift Scar? We should move the body, then continue with the patrol as normal.'

If Shane hadn't been in a foul mood, Hale might have had a longer discussion, found out why he thought that, then found a middle ground. But the attitude was making it impossible to think in nice, polite terms like 'discuss'.

At this point, if he spent much more time with Shane, Hale would snap and say or do something he regretted, but that wasn't a solution that would help with Shane's underlying issue. Hopefully, space would help smooth his attitude.

'Take Amelia and Oliver and trace our steps back to the dead imp. You can dump the scorpion there,' Hale said, letting a trickle of power leak out around him as the younger man moved to argue. 'I'll walk the border with Lance, and we can meet back at the cars at the end of the patrol.'

Shane had no choice but to swallow back whatever he was going to say, and he all but stomped to the body. Oliver watched him go, a flash of amber in his eyes, but Hale wasn't worried about a fight there. Oliver had no desire to climb the pack structure and fighting with Shane would put him right near the top.

Amelia didn't say anything but looked uncomfortable as she followed Shane to the corpse. Hale left them to it as he turned back to Lance.

'Lead the way,' Hale said to the tawny wolf.

Lance trotted out in front of Hale, head swivelling as he searched for tracks as much as scent.

Behind him, he heard Shane telling Amelia to carry the scorpion and Oliver giving her a safer set of instructions. Hale really hoped that some time away would calm Shane down. With the full moon tonight, he didn't want to drag this foul mood into their hunt.

SAM DROVE IN SILENCE down the dirt track. Lacey was still watching the treeline as she'd done on the way in, but she was less tense now that they were done for the day.

'What are your plans tonight?' Lacey asked as they reached the turning to the main road. The question held more force than it should have as Lacey turned to look at her.

'Movies, junk food, and a cheap hotel,' Sam said, glancing at the other woman. Sam's plans were always the same on the night of the full moon. Her hotel had a regular slot blocked off for her every month like clockwork. They'd even started bringing in her favourite sweets.

'You know you could stay at home. We all have excellent control. No one will go near your house during the hunt,' Lacey said, but she'd turned back to the woods, surveying the very edge of where she'd be running tonight.

Sam gave Lacey another glance. It wasn't like Lacey to ask her to stay. 'I'm good. You guys don't need an extra non-Shifter wheel in your pack party,' Sam said. Though being on her land when the pack shifted had less to do with the danger and more to do with secrets that Sam couldn't risk getting out.

'Then there's the next morning.' Lacey shivered, continuing as if she hadn't heard Sam's previous answer. More than one person travelled to town just in case some frustrated Shifter took a liking to them the morning after the full moon. 'You really should try it. There really is nothing like Moon Fever sex.'

Sam was glad Lacey wasn't looking at her as the image of Hale came back. Funny that of all the Shifters searching for other ways to burn off their excess energy, only Hale gave Sam pause. But images aside, it wasn't like Lacey to push.

'Maybe another time,' Sam said, pleased her voice came out smooth as she tried to ignore the vision of Hale in her mind. Him walking out of the forest, naked, and looking for just her. Not that it had ever happened. Sam timed her return for after the pack had left.

'When are you going to finally cave and just have sex with Hale?' Lacey said, suddenly giving Sam her full attention.

Sam coughed, turning to the woman before jerking her eyes back to the road as her face heated. She'd not thought she'd been that obvious. But then she remembered the looks Lacey had given her earlier when talking to Hale.

'Hmm,' Sam said, pretending to focus on the road. Which required a lot of attention as she scrambled for an answer.

'It's obvious you both want each other,' Lacey said, leaning forward. 'Even a human couldn't miss it, and trust me, my nose is anything but human.'

Sam's face moved to scorching as she squirmed in her seat, wishing Huntly was a lot closer than the twenty-minute drive she knew it was.

'Are you saying no because he's a Shifter and you're human?' Lacey asked, tone indicating that while she might be offering it as an option, she didn't really believe it.

'No,' Sam said automatically, then wished she could take it back. That would have been a perfect excuse. A lot of people were still prejudiced or uncomfortable with Rift Bloodlines and humans mixing. But she also didn't want Lacey to think that was the type of person she was.

'Then what? Coz right now all I'm seeing is two people torturing each other.'

'It's not that simple,' Sam said, evading the answer. 'Hale has never once shown any interest in me, and even if he had, I'm not looking for anything complicated in my life right now.'

'Complicated? I'm not asking you to marry him, Sam. I'm saying you should let loose and have some fun,' Lacey said, but she backed up a fraction, no longer pressing quite so close. 'Give him a chance.'

'A chance to do what?' Sam asked, forcing a laugh.

Lacey looked at her, face closing down, humour leaving her. 'Forget I said anything. What you do with your life is your own business,' Lacey said, turning away.

Sam tried to get Lacey to talk to her, but all she got for the next twenty minutes were grunts and hmms. Whatever Sam had said, it had struck a nerve, but Lacey wasn't giving her a clue as to what it was.

'I'm sorry,' Sam said as a last resort when she pulled up outside the pack's base of operations in Huntly. It was an old gym that they used to store their weapons and train. From experience, Lacey would drop off her gear and then grab her car from where it was parked nearby.

Lacey finally looked at Sam, giving her a small smile. 'Don't worry about it. Forget I said anything. I'll see you later.'

She got out and closed the door before Sam could say anything else. Sam sighed, but she didn't know what was wrong, so she didn't know what to say. She waited for a car to pass, then pulled away to head home. Shifters were strange near the full moon, but normally that meant high energy, not this odd sadness.

Sam would talk to Lacey again tomorrow. See if she could find out what was wrong.

When Sam got home, she shoved all the samples and CDS equipment into the secure space in her large garage. She'd converted it to hold all the equipment she'd need to process the samples and readings. But since no one was going to be looking for the data this late on a Friday, she didn't bother doing more than storing it all.

Once everything was away, she headed inside for a much-needed shower, wishing she knew what was wrong with Lacey.

CHAPTER FOUR

AMELIA DROPPED THE SCORPION a few feet away from the dead imp. It had been easy to follow the trail of torn-up dirt from Shane's and Hale's sprint, even for her, and she had little to no tracking skill.

She inhaled slowly, trying to even her breathing. The scorpion hadn't been heavy exactly, but dragging it hadn't been comfortable, or simple, as it caught on every rock. There were worse jobs for the junior rift ranger, though not by much.

Neither Oliver nor Shane asked her to move the corpse elsewhere, so she assumed that was where they wanted it. Though, going by how they were surveying the area, she wasn't sure they'd noticed. Except, of course, Oliver always noticed.

Amelia turned back to the dead imp. Its short muzzle was frozen in a snarl, showing off stained black teeth. She'd seen them alive, even during her short time here, but this was the first time she'd really had the time to linger and see one up close. It was another experience she could have done without.

'Can you tell me why we don't bury the bodies?' Oliver asked her, his frustratingly even and patient tone somehow short of condescension as he turned to her. The ongoing quizzes seemed to be Oliver's favourite pastime. She imagined this was how annoying it would have been to have a brother.

Hale had really known what he was doing assigning him as her mentor. It was so bloody hard to stay mad at Oliver. He seemed to have an endless amount of patience for someone who was the same age as her.

'Because it's a wasted effort,' Shane said, shaking his head as he turned away from them. Amelia wasn't sure what his problem was, but it was obvious why Hale had switched to Lance. Shane wasn't exactly pleasant at the best of times, but normally he was at least civil.

Amelia decided it was probably best to ignore him. Besides, his answer didn't sound exactly right. 'Is it to stop anything else that comes along from lingering?'

Both imps and scorpions had a pack mentality, and they rarely travelled around solo. If one was lost, they'd actively look for it. But neither of them were above eating their own kind if they were dead. Meat was meat, and it wasn't always easy to get in the Rift.

Oliver smiled at her, again somehow just missing being condescending and instead making her feel good that she'd got the right answer. She hadn't come here by choice, and she refused to enjoy it. She really needed to figure out how he did it. But until then, she satisfied herself by forcing a scowl in his direction that did not affect him at all.

Though there were certainly some benefits of being here. The topmost of which was that she was nowhere near the man who thought she was destined to be his mate. She wasn't. But convincing him had become complicated, and she'd been the one to be punished and sent here.

'Let's get on with it. I want to get a shower before the hunt tonight,' Shane said, already heading away from the body to continue the patrol.

Oliver motioned for Amelia to go ahead of him, then took up the rear. Despite him using this as a teaching moment, he'd never let his guard down and was constantly scanning the hills and gullies for anything else that might have been out there.

Amelia tried to mimic him. There were two constants: the stench of the Rift Scar and the sound of their footsteps on the sandy ground. After five minutes of walking, Amelia's thoughts wandered, her mind going to tonight's hunt and the need to shift. So much for paying attention.

Need more running, Luna, Amelia's wolf, said. *Need four paws.*

But they weren't likely to get that here. She was less than two months in, and being limited to one shift a month was already driving them both crazy. How the other Shifters managed, she didn't know. The full moon tugged at her like it was already in the sky, pressing on her to let go and run free. But she couldn't do that yet unless she wanted to be stuck in the Rift Scar for the full moon.

No, Luna said, huffing. *Woods. Hunt deer.*

Soon, Amelia said, shivering as her wolf backed off. It would only be temporary, but the reprieve was a relief.

The rest of the patrol was uneventful, with Oliver only occasionally asking her questions. All their talking was about the job, but Shane's shoulders hunched tighter as he walked in front of them. She could feel it from his wolf too, tiny tendrils of his annoyance seeping out. By the time Hale and Lance re-joined them, Shane looked about ready to explode.

The tension made her wolf pace in her head.

Not like, Luna said, letting out a whine. *Challenge or not challenge. Not like game.*

They'll figure it out, Amelia said, though she didn't know any of them well enough to be sure. It didn't help that both of them were stronger than she was; it was like she was stuck between two battling storms.

When they finally reached the cars, Amelia let out a breath of relief despite the fact the next patrol hadn't arrived yet. They were almost done. Just another couple of hours, and then it would be the full moon. She'd shift and run with clean air in her lungs. Hopefully, after the full moon, the tension would ease.

She was carpooling with Oliver while she tried to get a car of her own. When the next patrol arrived, he'd drive them back to the rangers' lockup to drop off the weapons, then give her a lift home. Normally they'd also clean their gear and guns, but because of the full moon, they'd go back tomorrow instead.

Hale unhooked his rifle, then nodded at Lance. 'Go ahead and shift back. No point in waiting for the others to arrive first.'

Lance shook out his tawny coat and moved behind his truck, where he'd left his clothes. Oliver followed to help Lance out of his armour before moving back to lean against his own car. She didn't envy Lance trying to shift back to human with the full moon so close. The pull to change was already strong enough that her skin tingled like her fur was trying to push through.

'You two can head out as well,' Hale said, nodding at Oliver and Amelia.

'You sure?' Oliver said, waiting until Hale nodded before he moved to the boot of his car to open it. Amelia didn't argue as she stripped off her body armour and weapons so they could lock them inside. It was a relief to be free of the weight, even if the air wasn't really any cooler.

'The next patrol is late,' Shane said, kicking up the dust as he moved to lean against his car. The fact Hale had not dismissed him wasn't lost on anyone.

'We're early,' Oliver said, voice sharper than normal as he slammed down the lid of the boot.

Shane's energy rose in the car park, needle-sharp as it stabbed at her, his eyes flashing to yellow as his wolf shone through. Oliver's wolf reacted in kind, rising so close to the surface that Amelia stepped away, her wolf whining at the weight of the two powers.

Oliver never let his power out like this, and the strength surprised her. She'd known he was strong, but this was so much more than she'd imagined. Shane's attitude must have really been wearing on Oliver for him to react like this.

'Enough,' Hale said. That single word cut the energy off like a switch had been flipped.

Powerful, Luna said, sounding almost nervous. *Alpha.*

That was a bit of an understatement. She'd never experienced an alpha being able to shut down people as dominant as Shane and Oliver with a single word like that before. It was terrifying.

'Oliver, take Amelia home,' Hale said again, never looking away from Shane. 'Shane can wait with me for the next patrol.'

Even though the command hadn't been aimed at her, it wrapped itself around her mind until her feet moved of their own accord, heading towards the passenger side of Oliver's truck and getting in. Her wolf didn't even complain, like she couldn't even consider saying no to Hale.

By the time Oliver had got into the car and started driving, her head was pounding as she fought to get free of the command.

They were two miles away before the deep primal need to follow Hale's instructions faded. She shivered, seeing the same motion from Oliver.

Alpha, Luna said, barely a whisper in her mind as it processed what Hale had just done.

How powerful was Hale? Back home, she'd been frozen in place when her alpha had stopped her from hitting his son. At the time that had terrified her, but the control had been brief, and as soon as he'd walked away, the command had dissipated. This was something else altogether. Hale had barely even been trying.

'It's not always like this,' Oliver said as he took the turning that would take them towards Huntly.

'Which part?' Amelia said, giving Oliver a look. 'The part where Hale made you get in the car without argument, or the fact that I'm not sure he meant to do it.'

'Shane just pushed the line,' Oliver said, his eyes flashing to the bright amber of his wolf. 'Hale is good people. He'd never deliberately hurt anyone in the pack.'

'But he could,' Amelia said, shivering. She imagined what her life might have been like if her family pack's alpha had that kind of strength. Or his son. The thought made her feel sick. That kind of power was dangerous.

Oliver was silent for a minute. 'I can only tell you my experience and from what I heard from those who were here before. Hale has never stepped beyond the boundary of rift warden.'

'But Hale is our alpha,' Amelia said. Hale would never just be one. He always had to be both.

This time, Oliver smiled, expression changing to the one he used when he was teaching. 'He's not your only alpha though, right?'

Amelia frowned and nodded. Her family's pack link was still there––even though it was muted to almost nothing due to the distance. Hale only held a small sliver to her in comparison. It allowed them to exist as a pack. Albeit more loosely.

'He runs the hunt on the full moon, but the rest of the time, he influences us only to make sure we aren't running around as wolves in town.' Oliver shrugged, rubbing at his wrist. 'Everything else he does is related to our jobs in the Rift Scar, our training, our patrols.'

'Except for tonight, when Shane challenged you,' Amelia said.

'You'll see what I mean over time. When Shane's not being a dick and challenging Hale,' Oliver said, eyes flashing amber again. Though, unlike Shane, there was no aggression in the look. It was more like the two were talking to each other, like she did with her own wolf.

Amelia shrugged noncommittally. She didn't want to argue with him about it more because it was obvious that Oliver had made up his mind. The silence held until he pulled up outside the small old gym in Huntly, where they stored the guns.

'I promise it's not always like this,' Oliver said again, smiling at her.

'I hope you're right,' Amelia said as she got out of the car. If this is what it was like, it was going to be a long year. She moved around to the back of the car to grab the weapons so they could put them inside and get home.

She wanted to get a shower and change before her lift arrived to take them out to where they'd shift tonight. From experience, it would take a couple of washes to get the stink out of her hair.

HALE STAYED QUIET AS Lance shifted back to human and left. Normally, Hale would have had more of the patrol group stay until the next one arrived, but this was the only chance he'd get to talk to Shane before tonight's full moon. The last thing the pack needed was Shane ruining the mood of the hunt.

He wished they weren't so close to the Rift Scar so he could pull in Shane's scent. What he was getting was so tainted by the Scar that it told him nothing. Instead, he had to rely on what little Shane's body was telling him, which was just anger.

Ask pack, Fang whispered, tugging at the pack bonds.

No, Hale said. He'd already pressed too hard on Amelia and Oliver as he'd sent them away. He'd sensed her spike of fear. There was little he could do about that now, but pressing Shane through the bonds as well was only going to make matters worse.

'Being angry at me is one thing, but you can't take it out on the rest of the pack,' Hale said.

'So now you care about how the pack feels?' Shane said, but he didn't turn around. He'd had his back to Hale ever since Oliver and Amelia had left.

Hale growled, unable to stop himself as his own anger rose. 'Everything I do is to protect the pack.'

'Who did you ask to give us more time to shift?' Shane said, turning around, eyes still more yellow than their normal hazel.

'The prime alphas have said there isn't the budget for more time this year,' Hale said carefully, not liking Shane's question.

'So, you didn't ask Sam? Try to negotiate a rate with her?' Shane said, eyes changing colour to his wolf, then turning back. 'How do you know it's too expensive if you didn't even ask?'

Bloody prime alphas and their pack politics.

'It's not that simple,' Hale said, wishing he could just tell Shane the truth. But somehow, Hale doubted that the truth would convince Shane since he was this angry. Hale needed something else to calm the man, though he'd no clue what would help.

'You have the chance to change everything,' Shane said, all but spitting out the words. 'All you have to do is take it. You and Sam are clearly into each other. She'd let us have more time on her land if you just took what was offered. Hell, she'd probably do it for free.'

Not wrong, Fang said, almost smugly, despite the tension in the air.

Hale ignored his wolf. Whether Sam was interested wasn't the problem. Her being human was. But it was irrelevant when the prime alphas weren't going to accept any changes to the land agreement.

'Even if you were right, changing the contract isn't just Sam's decision to make. It needs to be agreed by the mayor,' Hale said, his wolf slipping into his voice with his frustration. Not that Hale imagined the mayor would have any issue signing it, especially when reminded how much the pack did for this town.

'We have to do something. We get one day a month to become our wolves. One. Damned. Day. It's not enough, Hale. It's never going to be enough. Why do you think no one chooses to stay?' Shane said, eyes flashing yellow. It was hard to tell whether it was a challenge or just poor control. This close to the full moon, keeping the wolf at bay was always harder.

'Do you think I don't know that?' Hale took a step closer until they were only a foot apart. Hale hated releasing the bonds. Hated the wolf's relief as they finally got to leave. 'I'm the one who has to let them go. Do you have any idea how hard that is?'

Hard was such a poor word for how much it hurt to have a member of his pack ripped from him. To know that every time a new member of the pack joined, it was only ever going to be temporary. Hale had to suppress his wolf's rage at the memory of it. Of the pain.

But there wasn't any other choice. Without the pack lands, the wolves wouldn't stay. But to get the pack lands, Hale had to change how the prime alphas saw the Highland Rift Pack.

Ignore, Fang said. *Not our alpha. Not need them.*

Hale couldn't answer that without starting an argument with his wolf.

'Then do something about it,' Shane said, almost desperate as he echoed Hale's wolf's sentiment.

But unfortunately, short of challenging the prime alphas, there was nothing Hale could do. And dominant or not, Hale didn't have the numbers to make that challenge and survive.

Hale was saved from the need to find a reply as he heard an engine in the distance. The next patrol.

Shane spun away and stalked over to his car. He didn't even wait for the rest of the patrol to get parked and geared up before putting his gun in the boot and speeding away. Hale let him because the alternative was to start a fight, and he really didn't want to put Shane down like that. Not right before the full moon. But if his attitude continued tomorrow, Hale might have to do something.

Protect pack, Fang said, though whether Fang wanted to protect the pack from Shane or protect Shane, Hale wasn't sure. When his wolf didn't clarify, he suspected that his wolf didn't know either.

Hale turned towards the approaching car. The confrontation with Shane had left his skin itchy with the need to shift and run. To hunt. But some things had to be done before he left.

The car that pulled up was an old Land Rover, the battered green colour more chipped than not. This patrol would be made up entirely of Elementals this time. No sane wolf would spend the full moon in the Rift Scar if they could avoid it, and it was too dangerous for humans to attempt it.

Five people got out of the truck, already dressed in heavy armour. Four of the five circled around to the boot and started pulling out guns. The Elementals might have been able to use magic, but why waste energy when enough bullets can kill most of what lurked in the Rift Scar?

'Shane was in a hurry?' Patrick said, shielding his eyes to look over the grey wasteland as the sun drew lower. He was tall and lanky, with brown hair and mismatched eyes. He'd been here longer than most, almost two full years, and had quickly become one of the senior rift rangers like Shane.

The Elementals suffered from many of the same problems as the pack. Few people wanted to be this far north, though they didn't have pack politics or government restrictions on using their magic to worry about.

'We ran into a few solos at the eastern edge,' Hale said, hiding his annoyance. He liked Patrick, but Shane's problems were pack business, not rangers. 'This close to the full moon, it's made everyone a bit restless.'

'Ahh,' Patrick said, though it was obvious he didn't really get it. But he didn't ask any more questions, and that was the main thing.

Hale talked Patrick through the details of the patrol. He listened without comment until Hale had finished.

'Strange to see two solos, let alone that far out?' Patrick said. 'You expect us to run into any others?'

'Unlikely, there were no signs of anything when I searched with Lance, but it might be best to circle tight to the edge and see if we missed anything,' Hale said. He didn't like how both creatures had been heading out of the Rift Scar.

'Will do,' Patrick said, accepting his gun from one of his team. They were a mixed bunch in gender, age, and Elemental type. 'You go, enjoy your hunt. I've got us covered.'

Hale gave him a small smile. Somehow, considering Shane's mood, he doubted the hunt was going to be quite as enjoyable as usual. But maybe a good run would help settle him.

SAM PULLED HER SHOWER-DAMP hair into a messy bun as she entered her kitchen. It was a relief to be clean, even if the sweat would be back soon enough.

The stink of the Rift Scar had finally faded from her nose, and she could smell the pine trees even before she opened her back door to step out onto her veranda. The trees started a couple of dozen metres back from her house, and if not for the road, they'd have the whole place circled.

It was quiet here, miles away from anyone else. No traffic, no people. Just the birds as they chirped, swooping lazily in the faint breeze, and the crickets buzzing out in the woods. She wanted to linger in the peace, settle down into the old wicker chair beside her front door, and let the heat of the day lull her to sleep. Then in the morning, she'd wake up to an all too dark-haired alpha's lips on hers as the dawn rose.

Sam shook her head, reminding herself that staying wasn't an option. Nor had a kiss ever been something Hale had offered.

Besides, she had things to do if she wanted to save the infected tree before the pack arrived. Which would be soon going by the way the sun was nearly at the treeline. It wouldn't be long before everything was in the shade, and the pack filled the front yard, cramming in their cars, all energy and power.

Pulling in deep breaths of clean air, she stepped down off the veranda, letting her bare feet touch the dirt. The Land rose around her, buzzing loudly in her ears as if it knew she was planning on doing something and it already wanted to help. She ignored the temptation to connect for now. There were certain places on her Land that made it easier to focus than others, and given her distraction earlier, it was probably best to use one of those.

She took a well-worn path into the woods that was so old and broken; it was more of a series of markers. Grass poked through the cracks and wildflowers grew along the edges, both looking wilted from the recent lack of rain. Each step made new sweat prickle her skin, but even so, she was glad to be outside.

The last of the day's tension drained away as she reached the clearing. An old gnarled yew tree sat in the centre, creating a canopy with its broad branches and thick leaves.

As a child, she'd come here to play in the tree's shade. Back then, she'd not understood what she'd become or how much her life would change.

For those born an Elemental, their powers didn't manifest until somewhere around thirteen to fourteen. When Sam had shown signs of having the magic, her mum had taken her aside and explained what was happening. That had been when the secrets had begun.

Her mum had forbidden her from telling anyone she was an Earth Elemental. Including her father. If she'd been paying attention back then, she'd have seen the subtle signs that showed how much he hated the Rift Bloodlines. But Sam had been young and careless, and her mum had paid the price.

Both of them had.

Sam knelt in front of the tree with a sigh, struggling against the sense of loss that rose. She couldn't change the past. Couldn't undo what she'd done. But she could do this small thing and help the tree.

The power in the roots under her knees trickled into her, that awareness trying to connect. But she didn't welcome it yet. Not because she didn't want to, but because the last thing she needed was to bring her worries to this space.

With a calming breath, she reminded herself why she was here and that she was rapidly running out of time if she wanted to get this healing done today. She let go of the day's worries and stresses, then reached out and placed her hand on the tree. The bark was rough under her fingers and cool when everything else was too warm.

The Land's energy pulsed around her with an edge of excitement. It was like it knew the pack was coming and was looking forward to it, which was ridiculous because the phases of the moon had little sway over the Land.

This feeling was why she couldn't risk being here when the pack was hunting. There was too much she didn't understand about the Land and Shifter magic. Lacey might not have sensed her earlier, but the energy changed when the whole pack was here. The Land changed.

Sam lowered the mental walls she'd built to block the Land; the connection sharpened from a hum into a storm of new sensations. That same overload from earlier threatened to overwhelm her, drag her under, and make her forget who she was.

She struggled to pull back. To hold on to herself in the chaos. Pressing her other hand into the dry earth around the roots, she focused on that sensation. The dryness on her fingers, the coolness of the ground.

It helped, at least a little, but there was still too much information, and she couldn't filter any of it out. She was bombarded with all the conflicting instincts from the creatures on the land: to run, to hunt, to fly, to swim.

This was always the hardest part of the connection, and the most exciting. It was too easy to forget who she was. The Land wasn't human; it didn't understand individual identity. It was instinct and sensation.

Pulling her thoughts together, she searched for the words she needed to direct the Land.

Show me the gap.

The Land grew calm, taking the idea, processing it, deciding if it wanted to show her what she was looking for. A child torn between the new toy and the old one. Sam couldn't help but smile at the sensations it brought in her.

She wished she knew more about how the Land worked, how it connected to her. There were a lot of things she wished she knew more about. But there was no one left to ask.

The Land's awareness darted away from her, doing as she asked. Sam let herself float in the chaos, letting the

Land search for that spot of nothing. It didn't take long to find it. A dull spot of darkness in the web of energy around her.

The tree was sicker than she'd first thought, the fungus seeping deep into the wood. Left alone, it would destroy the tree and spread to others around it until nothing was left. She wasn't going to let that happen.

Reaching out to the tree itself, she let the energy of the Land flow through her into it. The tree grew brighter, the energy working to heal the damage and give it the strength to fight a little longer. It wouldn't last much more than a day, but that would be enough for her to get down and clear off the fungus itself.

Her head throbbed, each beat of her heart ringing in her ears. The energy used to heal and protect had to come from somewhere. Something she'd forgotten in her hurry, and she'd given more from herself than she should have. She should have linked through the other trees and spread the cost. Now she'd have a headache all night.

Sighing, she pulled back from the connection until she was back in the centre of the chaos once again. It was tempting to linger here, but experience told her that would only make the headache worse, even if she had the time, which she didn't. The pack would be here soon.

Sam pulled all the way back from the Land, gently fighting its renewed excitement. It wanted her to stay. But that wasn't happening.

Raising her walls again took effort, making the headache grow sharper. Or maybe it was just the loss of the extra senses, leaving the world dull and dark in a way that had nothing to do with the setting sun.

She stood, brushing off her knees. Tomorrow, after the pack had left, she'd be able to go down to the tree when no one was watching and remove the fungus. Since she'd taken the samples today, there shouldn't be anyone down there for another week.

Plan firmly set in her mind, Sam turned back towards the house.

CHAPTER FIVE

SAM WAS SITTING ON the veranda steps, watching the night close around her when Hale finally arrived. He parked in the furthest corner of her yard, leaving plenty of space for the rest of the pack.

As he got out of the car, he tucked his keys and phone into his pocket and scanned the treeline. He looked like he was already searching for tonight's hunt, eyes flickering to gold.

Part of her wanted to get up and go to him, like a string of energy was tugging her towards him. It would have been so easy, but she kept her arse firmly on the wooden veranda step. Getting together with Hale was a bad idea, despite what Lacey might think.

After a moment, he turned and headed in her direction, eyes fading back to brown. 'Sam,' he said, nodding at her as he settled his hip against the wood at the bottom of her steps.

He'd changed into a thin black T-shirt and dark jeans that clung to him. Heat radiated from him, and unlike the lingering heat of the day, she wanted to bask in it. On a chilly night, she could imagine him curled around her, keeping her warm in more ways than one.

'Looks like you're in for clear skies and a warm night for the hunt,' she said, swallowing to clear a suddenly dry throat. Not that she cared about the heat, or how the sky was lit with a red glow of sunset in full bloom above the treetops. Not a single cloud to be seen.

'I don't think anyone will care,' he said as he scanned the woods again, eyes flashing to the gold of his wolf as they searched. He drew in a deep breath and focused back on Sam. 'It's just good to be able to shift somewhere with clean air.'

Sam pulled in her own breath. The sweet pines were the strongest scent, but there was a hint of Hale——a spicy musk that made her want to inhale again. But his words gave her pause, reminding her what Lacey had said about wanting more time to shift.

The Land buzzed in Sam's head as if sensing her thoughts, pulling at her to connect. But that was too risky with Hale so close.

'Are you staying tonight?' Hale asked, eyes settling to brown again as he turned back to her.

Her heart skipped a beat at the thought of sunrise with Hale. Of getting lost in the raw need of the Moon Fever, as she reminded him what it was to be human again.

But that wasn't what he was offering. No matter what Lacey might think.

'No, I'm staying in town,' she said as she stood, brushing away imaginary dust while she let that reality check get her hormones under control. Her body might want him, but her mind knew better.

She stepped down from the veranda, and despite her earlier resolve, enjoyed the heat that radiated from Hale. It tingled against her skin as that line of energy between them grew tighter. She wanted to linger there, but Hale drew in another sharp breath, making her face heat. The pine trees wouldn't be all he could smell.

Cursing silently, she took a step towards her Jeep. She hated how little of her reaction she could hide. And how, even knowing what she wanted, he'd never offered more. Even if it was stupid to wish for that.

She forced a smile, trying to pretend her blush wasn't happening. She'd put her overnight bag in the Jeep already, which was probably why he'd asked if she was staying in the first place. 'I've plans to meet some friends,' she said, even though it was an outright lie. She wasn't meeting anyone.

Hale let the distance increase as she took a few more steps, and Sam immediately missed the heat.

'If you ever change your mind, you're always welcome to stay,' Hale said, voice holding no hint of what he thought of her reaction. But that was Hale. Ever the practical leader. 'I—' Hale cut off, head snapping towards the driveway.

The Land prodded at her senses, trying to show her what had caught Hale's attention, but she pushed it back. It wasn't hard to guess that more of the pack were arriving. She didn't need the Land to tell her that. But what she hadn't expected was the speed.

A car barrelled into her yard far too fast, sending a spray of dust and stones towards her as it skidded to a stop. Hale moved so fast she barely tracked him as he jumped in front of her, shielding her from the spray with his body as he pulled her flush against him.

Sam froze, but not from fear. The car could have been about to smash into her for all she cared. Hale stole all her awareness like a black hole as that line of energy between them snapped tight. Heat and power ran through her like an electric shock, drawing her in much like the Land had earlier. But where the Land had been chaos, this was different. It was wildness and power. Freedom. His wolf.

Hale's growl broke through the overload. It was a low, feral sound that vibrated through her body. She couldn't stop the shiver that ran through her. Again, it should have been from fear, but that was so far from where her brain was at, she wasn't sure it was possible to be afraid.

It took more effort than she wanted to admit to step back out of his protective grip. Hale's fingers tightened around her arms for a heartbeat, eyes a solid gold, no hint of his brown. That instinct to protect was an almost visible aura around him. An alpha's instinct.

Then he let her go, stepping away as he turned towards the car. Brown dirt and a few pieces of grass spotted the back of his T-shirt from what the car had sprayed at them. But there was nothing more serious than that.

Without Hale blocking her view, she finally saw the car. In the front seat, Shane was waving his arms animatedly to Lacey, who was in the passenger seat. Another woman sat in the back. It looked like the newest Shifter in the pack, though Sam had only met her once. She was blond and in her early twenties, if not younger.

'How's your new wolf settling in?' Sam asked.

Hale glanced at Sam. Something she couldn't place passed across his face, then he turned back to the car as Shane opened the door. 'Amelia is doing well.' There was nothing in his tone to indicate what he thought of her.

Amelia got out of the car, showing off long, delicate limbs, moving like a dancer even though she was obviously angry. She shoved her straight blond hair back with one hand and walked over to Hale, not even looking at Sam.

'Hale, I need a word,' she said, jaw tight as she almost reluctantly registered Sam's presence. 'Alone.'

Sam fought the urge to close the gap between her and Hale again. To stake her claim on him. Except Hale wasn't hers. Not if she wanted to protect her secret. She'd no right to be angry or jealous. And she was definitely both. Which only annoyed her more.

'Amelia,' Hale said, voice low as he used her name like a warning. Amelia stiffened, but she didn't back down.

Sam shivered as a sense of power rose, more an echo through her Land than something she felt directly. But it was yet another reason to avoid getting involved with Shifters, especially an alpha. There was an entire set of culture rules that Sam doubted she'd particularly like. If Hale tried that on her, she was more likely to slap him than do as she was told.

Shane and Lacey both got out of the car and headed towards Hale. Lacey had changed into a loose summer dress but still looked serious. She nodded in greeting but didn't speak as she settled into the space beside Amelia.

Shane was now wearing loose knee-length shorts and a white T-shirt. He gave Sam a passing glance but didn't even bother with a greeting. Which was pretty much normal for the grumpy Shifter.

All of them together were making Sam feel like an intruder as the energy from the Land grew more excited. It always changed as more of the pack arrived, growing wilder somehow.

'What the hell was that?' Hale said, focusing on Shane. Sam practically felt the anger as they faced each other. It was hard not to reach out and touch Hale, offer calm. But that wasn't her place here, and quite frankly, Shane had been here often enough that he should've known better than to be going at that speed.

Shane stiffened but didn't slow his steps. 'It's been a long day,' Shane said, giving Amelia a cool look. 'I forgot how short the last stretch of road was.'

Hale let out a low growl, and this time, Shane stopped, lowering his head. Sam didn't miss the fact that there was no apology.

'Amelia, why don't I show you around? I don't think we got a chance last time you were here,' Lacey said, offering her arm to Amelia.

Amelia mumbled something unintelligible, then lifted her eyes just long enough for Sam to see a shift in colour, blue growing brighter as her wolf peeked out. This woman might have been acting cowed, but she was anything but submissive.

'You should check the stream out that way. It's beautiful just now,' Sam said, giving Amelia a tight smile. It was beautiful, but Sam would have sent Amelia to a manure pile and claimed it was stunning to get her away from Hale right then.

'That sounds like a good idea,' Hale said. Again, that neutral tone was back, and Sam couldn't get a read on what Hale really thought of Amelia. But even so, the idea that Hale was sending her away at all sent a thrill through Sam. Which was stupid.

Lacey hooked an arm around Amelia, not bothering to wait for an answer, then headed towards the stream. Shane, who'd been standing silently beside them, shook his head and gave Hale a look that Sam couldn't interpret.

Hale's eyes flashed gold, forcing Shane to look away. Clearly, something else was going on. Something that was none of Sam's business. Even if the need to stay and protect Hale settled into her gut like lead.

'I'm going to head out before more cars arrive,' Sam said, turning towards her car. 'Enjoy the hunt.'

'For the one day we get it,' Shane said, just at the edge of her hearing. The bitter words made her pause and turn back to them. It echoed Lacey's from earlier.

Hale growled, the deep bass vibration echoed through the Land, and although there was no doubt that he was angry, she once again felt the tug to go to him. To soothe his wolf. Also, to smack Shane for daring to upset Hale in the first place. But she did neither. It wasn't her place.

Shane flinched back a step, then stalked off after Amelia and Lacey without another word. Hale never let pack business spill into the public. Whatever was going on must have been pretty serious.

Hale turned back to her, some of the tension easing from him. 'Sorry, it's been a tough week,' Hale said, voice soft, like he was afraid of scaring her.

'Is everything okay?' Sam asked, but the Land tugged at her before he could answer. Probably wanting to show her that more of the pack were arriving.

Hale straightened, the mask closing back down tightly as he heard it too. The change made Sam's chest grow tighter.

'It's fine. Enjoy your night, Sam,' Hale said, glancing towards the driveway.

'You too,' Sam said, wishing there was something else she could say as she turned back to her car. The string of energy between them stretched thin, and she wanted nothing more than to turn around and run back to him. Screw her past, screw the pack. Screw everyone else.

But she didn't.

She got in her car and drove until the tug to go back to Hale faded. But no amount of distance would help the gut-twisting fear that she'd abandoned Hale when he needed her.

Except, Hale didn't need her. He was an alpha, with a pack behind him.

HALE GRITTED HIS TEETH as he watched Sam drive away for the second time that day. He wanted to follow her. Ask her to stay. Ask her to wait for him and the sunrise. For him to be human again.

Ask. Stay, Fang echoed.

But it wasn't that easy.

She wasn't his. She was human, fragile, and would never accept pack life. Even if it felt like part of himself was being stretched thin as the distance grew, until it finally snapped, and he was left feeling bereft.

He took a deep breath, but it did little to help as he caught Sam's scent. Normally it was a subtle smell of sweet honeysuckle and fresh, clean earth, almost lost in the scent of the land. But there was a lingering sharpness of anger from the challenge she'd aimed at Amelia, as well as the layer of concern.

It would have been so easy to just tell her everything. About the prime alphas' games, about the frustration from his wolves. How they wanted more, but he couldn't give it to them. But she wasn't pack. None of these were her problems.

Nor was a human likely to understand.

Hale's father had been an alpha covering the area around Whitehaven, reporting to the prime alpha of the North-east England Pack. It had been a quiet job, with barely a dozen wolves living in the small town and no Rift Scar at all. But even that had been too much for Hale's mother to handle. If she'd not been able to deal with that simple life, how was any human expected to deal with Hale being a rift warden and an alpha of a pack that changed almost entirely every year?

Hell, some days, Hale wondered how he managed.

Hale forced himself out of his own head as Oliver arrived with Lance and two other members of the pack, tucking his car in behind Hale's. Even as big as Sam's yard was, there was no way to fit all the pack's cars in it. Most would double up on their rides or more.

Oliver took one deep inhale and picked up the tension without needing to be told. All the wolves would. It was setting up to be the poor start that Hale had wanted to avoid.

It was hard enough as it was to balance the temporary pack bonds without this added stress. Especially this close to the full moon when all Hale wanted to do was pull the pack closer and open the connection wide. Hunt and run like they were one unit.

Our pack, Fang said.

Hale wished that was true.

Trying to get a hold of his frustrations, Hale let out a slow breath. Which was, of course, when Amelia returned with Lacey and Shane at her heels. As did another carload of wolves.

'Can I please have a word?' Amelia said, voice low and less demanding than last time, as she reached out and put her hand on his arm.

Hale suppressed the growl that settled in the back of his throat at the touch. It didn't help that his wolf wanted a different hand on his arm. But what made it worse was he didn't know Amelia well enough to feel like she was pack and not an intruder. This was only the second full moon she'd run with them. Neither of which was her fault.

She dropped her hand almost immediately. Either sensing the anger or the tension, Hale wasn't sure.

'We'll talk tomorrow,' Hale said at last. She started to object, so he raised his hand, this time keeping the pack energy to himself. Something was clearly bothering her, but this wasn't the time or place to deal with it. 'Tomorrow.'

Amelia closed her mouth, then nodded reluctantly. Submitting. Though the scent of her anxiety didn't seem to lessen.

Protect pack, Fang whispered.

But there was no danger to protect them from. Not here on Sam's land. Not from Amelia. Not even from Shane, though he wasn't any happier as his eyes flashed yellow, energy buzzing around them like flies on a manure pile. Despite his position near the top of the pack's rank, he wasn't strong enough to challenge Hale.

Hale had always assumed Shane was aware of his limitations, but he was beginning to wonder if Shane understood how outclassed he was. How long before the younger wolf tried his luck? Before this week, Hale wouldn't have even considered it, but now? It seemed like a matter of time rather than a question.

Shane turned away without a word and began stripping his clothes off and throwing them onto the veranda. Then he knelt in the dirt and called to his wolf. The change started slowly, muscles and flesh twisting unnaturally un-til bones snapped, moving into a new shape. Tawny fur spread out over his skin in a wave, doing nothing to hide the process as Shane was ripped apart and put back togeth-er. Nothing would remain the same when it was over.

Shane's change took ten minutes, but Hale didn't watch the entire way through. No matter how many times he saw it, the process never got easier.

When he'd been a teenager, freshly come into his new form, he and his friends had dared each other to watch the shift all the way through and not join in. Few had managed it back then, making for interesting lunch breaks where the teachers had to round up half a dozen pups. His school had set a detention policy for any kid stuck as a wolf. That way, no one would be tempted to miss class.

Those had been simpler times.

The anger dissipated from Shane's scent as he finished shifting and shook out his fur. The wolf didn't understand human emotions quite the same way, and the change in energy made it very clear the man part of Shane was upset with Hale, not the wolf.

But regardless of what Shane's wolf wanted, at some point soon, Shane was going to tire of being second and challenge Hale.

But Hale wasn't willing to step down.

Our pack, Fang said again.

Hale didn't argue with his wolf. Instead, he tried to soothe him with the promise of the hunt as more of the pack grew closer.

Lacey joined Shane in shifting, tossing her clothes into a pile on the veranda as well. She was slower than Shane but no more elegant. There really wasn't a pretty way to shift. But despite the pain and ugliness of it, the change tugged at Hale, calling for him to follow. But he couldn't just yet. At least not until all the pack was here.

Hale moved to lean against Sam's veranda again, pulling in the last remnants of her scent. The old wood was warm from the sun, and it soaked into his skin, making him feel like he was home. Which he wasn't, no matter what he might wish for.

Is home, Fang said, tone implying that he thought Hale was being stupid.

Hale wished his wolf was right as he watched Lacey finish her shift. But this would never be their home. Not while the prime alphas refused to listen.

Lacey scratched at the brown fur on her neck, then trotted over to sit next to Shane, who towered over her by half a foot. They sat together, waiting for the rest of the pack to shift and join them.

It took time for them all to arrive. There were normally around thirty people in his pack, all of them fit and trim from working in the Rift Scar. Five of them had gone home for the full moon, making tonight's group smaller than normal. All of them, except Lance, had been there less than a year. Every time they gathered for the full moon, it always brought home how much this pack changed. How much he'd lost.

Not want pack to change, Fang said, voice a whisper. Hale wished there was something he could do to ease his wolf's pain, but after seven years, he didn't see the prime alphas changing their policy now.

When the last Shifter had finished their change, Hale stripped and knelt on the grass, loosening his grip on his wolf. The change came quickly as his wolf leapt forwards.

Muscles twisted in on themselves, halfway between a cramp and a sprain as they tried to slide into a new position. Bones twisted, cracking as they found their new shape. Skin flowed to fur, making everything itch.

All of it came with pain. Fast, sharp, and deep, but short-lived as the moon sped up what was normally a much slower process. Unlike Shane, Hale's shift was only five minutes.

Hunt, Fang whispered in his mind, sending him the faint hint of wild deer in the wind.

Hale howled, calling to his wolves through the pack bonds. The connections sprung up around him, bringing him their excitement and hunger.

Others joined him in the howl as the pack came together as one.

He padded forward, tasting the air, searching for the trail he'd scented earlier.

Deer.

It was time to hunt.

EVERY TIME FANG'S PAWS hit the ground, dry dirt puffed up to make his nose itch.

But he ignored it, pushing harder, reaching for more speed as he ran through the woods.

The deer had scented them early as the pack had tried to close in around it, and it had bolted. But the pack wasn't giving up.

Hale said it was useless, that the deer was too far away, but he was wrong.

The full moon cast enough light to easily see the white flash of the deer's tail ahead of them. With all the pack hunting, there were more than enough wolves to trap the deer. They were faster.

Not going to be enough, Hale said, but Fang ignored him again.

Fang could feel the pack all around. The distance got larger as they spread out wide, moving to block the deer's exit. Shane ran just behind Fang, his breath coming in short huffs. But Shane couldn't match Fang's speed. None of the pack could.

It felt good to hunt here. This was home. Not like the hunts in the Rift Scar.

Not home, Hale said.

Fang didn't argue with his human half. He would figure it out, eventually.

Shane whined a breath, slowing further.

Fang glanced at Shane, considering slowing, but he yipped, veering off to the side. It looked like they were going to cut a shorter path and stop the deer from going to the right.

Because Shane couldn't keep up.

Fang tried not to gloat. The human word was heavy in his mind, but it fit the feeling well. The satisfaction of the win. Of beating another of the pack. Fang didn't like how the human emotion settled in his mind, but it was there regardless.

Pulling in a deep breath, Fang pushed for more speed. But instead of clean air, his nose burned, the sharp scent of aniseed searing as it erased all other scents.

Fear tightened in his chest as he skidded to a stop, pine needles digging into his paws.

Whining, he scratched at his muzzle. But it was too late. The aniseed was all Fang could smell. Fang struggled to pull in enough air. To breathe through the scent. But every breath was like a fire in his nose, pulling the scent deeper.

The pack sensed Fang's confusion and abandoned the chase as they changed direction, moving towards Fang instead. The deer would get to live another day.

Hale tugged at Fang, warning him to be careful.

But Fang didn't need the warning. He felt the wrongness of what had happened, too. He searched for the source of the scent, blinking away tears as his eyes watered. But there was nothing obvious.

Birch trees filled this section of the forest, pushing back the pines. There was deep heather, the purple flowers in bloom, but Fang could scent none of that. Not under the aniseed.

He hated not being able to smell. If Fang had been able to pick up scents, he would have known what was out there.

Trap, *Hale whispered.* **These woods don't have anything like aniseed in them. Someone had to have put it down.**

But who would attack Fang on his own land? Fang circled slowly, trying to hear and see what he couldn't smell, but he didn't know what he was looking for.

Fang pressed out a sense of warning to the pack. It would make them stay back. They wouldn't like it. But they didn't have to. Fang was their alpha, and they had to do what he said.

Everything was silent around Fang; there were no birds. No animals. Wolves were enough to scare off a lot of wildlife. But not everything. Yet there was nothing to be seen. Not even twitching leaves.

Fang took a step back, hackles rising. He didn't like this. Hale pressed at him, trying to pull back control. Like Hale didn't trust that Fang could keep them safe.

Not true. *Hale added more complicated sentiments that Fang couldn't follow.*

Before either could win the argument, the pain came.

Sharp searing fire hit Fang like a blade had sliced through his hind leg. Snarling, Fang spun, snapping behind him at whatever had caused the pain.

His teeth just missed a hard scorpion shell as it darted out of reach. Fang took a step back, too, watching the scorpion's tail sway back and forth over its head, Fang's blood dripping from its stinger. It was small for its kind, and a dark mottled grey.

Fang howled a sharp warning note out to the pack. Though it didn't translate to words, it would warn the pack to stay back. The bonds vibrated with the pack's worry and confusion, but they slowed their approach.

The scorpion chittered, claws twitching as it tried to get closer.

Let me help, Hale said, prodding Fang to let him in. But human instincts were not as good as Fang's.

No, Fang said, **I fight.**

Fang backed up a step, careful about how much weight he put on his leg, giving himself space to find an opening to attack. Hale didn't argue. Now wasn't the time, but Fang knew he would be annoyed later.

Every step sent a burning wave through his leg as he moved back, the poison burying deep into his blood. But Fang had been stung before. Most had during their time at the Rift Scar, though it never got easier. This one sting was enough to stop him from shifting form. But enough stings and it would kill them. Not that one scorpion would get the chance.

If the scorpion is on its own.

Fang tried to search the underbrush without taking his eyes off the scorpion. The heather was thick but not tall. It wouldn't have been able to hide more scorpions unless they were small like this one.

Fang didn't want to find out, so he lunged forward, testing the scorpion's reaction. It stabbed with its stinger, moving so fast it only just missed the spot where Fang had been.

The pack was slowly growing closer despite his warning. But there were no returning howls, meaning no one was finding more of the creatures. That gave Fang hope that this was a scorpion out on its own. An easy kill. Easier with more of the pack coming.

Get it away from the scent, *Hale said, this time not pressing for control.* **If others are coming, we need to protect their sense of smell.**

Fang backed up a step, wanting to attack, not retreat. But his human was right. Protecting the pack came first. Though how he was going to know they were far enough, he didn't know.

The scorpion took the bait, stabbing at Fang, then scuttling back. But not as far back as it had been. Fang repeated the process a few times until he was back among the pines. The scorpion's chittering grew louder the more times it missed.

Shane appeared behind and to the left of the scorpion, creeping through the heather. Oliver was on the other side, brown fur lost in the backdrop of a tree. Both were silent and behind the scorpion so it wouldn't see them.

Bracing, Fang moved to lunge again, hoping to draw the scorpion back one step to let the pair attack from behind, but he landed wrong. Fire tore up his leg. He tried to keep their footing, unwilling to show any signs of weakness.

Not in front of Shane.

The wrongness of the thought, along with the pain, broke through Fang's focus, pushing Hale forward.

He stumbled, unused to four paws or the pain in his hind leg. The scorpion took the chance to dive forward, taking advantage of Hale's weakness.

Oliver moved lightning fast, his teeth closing around the thick lower shell of the scorpion and his paw pinning its tail, avoiding the stinger.

Shane came from the other side, teeth tearing into its upper body.

The shell cracked, the sound loud in the quiet space. Black blood oozed out between from where teeth had broken the shell. The creature tried to twist away, but it had nowhere to go. No way to recover. The two halves ripped apart, splashing guts and blood over the ground.

Hale was glad his sense of smell was lost for that part. Scorpion blood smelled as vile as the rest of the Rift did. Shane and Oliver dropped their halves, careful of the stinger even with the beast dead.

Shane's muzzle twitched as he backed away, clearly smelling the stench. That was good, Hale must have pushed them back far enough from the aniseed. That meant no one else would be nose blind.

Not like, Fang whispered. *Scorpion not welcome. Our home.*

Hale ignored the part about home, but he agreed about the scorpion. This was supposed to be their safe place. Somewhere they didn't have to be on guard and could relax. But there would be none of the latter tonight.

Shane let out a loud howl, signalling success. However, this hadn't been the hunt they'd planned.

Hale felt the pack move closer. They weren't celebrating just yet. Experience had taught them caution. They might not know exactly what had happened, but they'd know it wasn't a deer that had been brought down.

Oliver circled Hale, sniffing his leg to check the damage, but didn't get too close. No one wanted to be unable to shift, even if it was unlikely there was enough venom around the wound to affect anyone else. Not that they could do much to treat it in this form, except maybe walk through some water.

Two dozen wolves gathered around Hale, slipping around the moonlit trees, nervous energy rising like needles on his skin. As wolves, their conversation was limited, and with the full moon high in the sky, having the pack change back, or at least some of them, wasn't an option.

Hale stepped forward, pressing his paw on top of the dead scorpion. They'd killed it. He'd take that win.

But the mood had been ruined, and he already knew the rest of the night was going to be a long one. And there wasn't much chance they'd be able to catch a deer now.

CHAPTER SIX

AMELIA ROLLED HER STIFF neck, trying to release some of her tension. She wasn't sure she'd ever had a full moon go so badly. She'd had rubbish morning afters like the one that had caused her to be sent here in the first place, but never the actual hunt.

As the sun had risen, it had almost been a relief to know it was nearly over, even if shifting back had been harder than normal with Hale still being a wolf.

She risked taking a glance at Hale where he stood, waiting for her to try to treat his wound in the stream. Sam had been right yesterday when she'd said the area was beautiful. The water ran through the bottom of a small gully, with wildflowers growing along the banks and large pine trees shading the area. But it was hard to enjoy that view when your alpha's blood was dripping into the water, turning it pink before it ran lazily away.

He stood with all his weight on his injured back leg despite the deep slash. He'd never let his guard down for the rest of the night. Even now, his ears twitched as he watched the forest around them.

Be safer if stayed wolf, Luna said, still unhappy at changing back.

There are rules, and I doubt the owner would appreciate us staying another day, Amelia said, remembering how Sam had looked at her. That woman might have been petite, but she'd not looked remotely afraid when facing off against a Shifter. Unusual for a human.

Amelia tried to shake off the memory as she stepped into the ankle-deep stream. She had to focus on helping Hale.

The cool water flowed over her bare feet, helping ground her, even if it was only a little. She ran the storiform cup she'd been given through the water, trying to get rid of the residual coffee. It wasn't ideal, but it was the best chance she had of washing Hale's wound. If part of the stream had been deeper, she could've soaked it, but no one had known if there was an area like that.

Nor had anyone got anything remotely like a first aid kit, even though there were around two dozen Shifters here and nine different cars. She would've given anything for some scissors, disinfectant, sterile needles, thread, and a dressing that would stay on even over Hale's fur. Even though she hadn't finished medical school because of prejudice against Shifters, she still knew enough to be able to stitch Hale up. She'd just have to do it with what she had.

Which wasn't much. A half-empty bottle of vodka, numerous old coffee cups, a needle and thread from a sewing kit, and half a dozen rags and old clothes.

Amelia pulled the cup out of the water and checked it. It was as clean as it was going to get, so she filled it with fresh water and turned to Hale. He was still watching the treeline.

'This is going to hurt,' Amelia said, drawing his attention to her while keeping her eyes on the top of his muzzle. It was easier that way, especially when every time she looked into his eyes, it was like a part of her got lost in the angry power he was pumping out.

Not lost. Connected, Luna said, huffing a breath in annoyance at Amelia.

But it was more than that. Hale's pack bonds were so different from what she was used to, stronger and more binding. Like how he'd commanded her to leave yesterday. He'd promised to talk to her today, but now he was stuck as a wolf.

Waiting until tomorrow should have been fine, except her stomach churned every time she thought about how easily the command had overtaken her. She'd enough worries about control without Hale taking more of it from her.

Hale dipped his head and turned to watch her. She took that as consent, even if she couldn't tell what he thought about her treating him. It had been Oliver's idea. He'd known about her medical background from when he'd decided to introduce her to the best pubs in Huntly. It had been a short trip, but one that had ended in them both drunk.

Amelia placed a hand on Hale's back, well clear of the wound, so she could hold him still if he tried to move. Her connection to Hale grew sharper until it was like his pain and anger were seeping into her. But also his distrust of her. He closed the link quickly, but it was too late. She'd already felt it. Not that she really blamed him. She'd not even been here two months, and at the end of her year term, she'd not be staying.

Would trust if was full pack, Luna said, unconcerned with Amelia's plans to leave. Her wolf was growing more attached every day despite the frustrations around shifting. *Halfway bad.*

His control would only be worse if we were full pack, Amelia said, because being tied closer to Hale didn't exactly seem like such a great idea, considering how much control he already had.

If trusted would not need control, Luna said, ignoring Amelia.

Amelia let the argument go. She needed to focus on what she was doing. She poured the water carefully over Hale's wound. The stream was mostly a bright red, but there were streaks of black there too. Rift poison. Hale stiffened under her hand but didn't try to move away.

It took a few rinses before the water changed to a hazy pink. Only then did she take one of the old rags that looked clean to press down on the areas around the wound, careful to keep her hand clear.

Pain flared through the bonds like it was her own leg on fire, making her gasp. The link between them grew hazy and dull again as Hale tried to shut her out, then slowly it closed altogether.

She exhaled slowly, trying to ignore the lingering sensation of searing. During training to go into the Rift, they deliberately infected everyone with Rift venom so they knew what to expect. But it had been a small dose, and the pain had been nothing like that.

'Are you okay?' Oliver asked, making her jump. He'd been so quiet where he stood at the top of the slope that she'd forgotten he was there.

Amelia nodded, taking a slow breath. Hale hadn't even flinched despite the pain he'd been in.

'You're worried about her? It's Hale who was stung,' Shane said. She'd missed him returning, and he stood on the other side of the slope to Oliver.

She gritted her teeth against the need to snap back. He'd been throwing his authority around left and right ever since turning back to human. Taking advantage of the situation as Hale tried to keep a little distance between himself and the pack to allow them to shift back more easily.

'Screw you, Shane. Of course I'm worried about Hale. I'm worried about all the pack,' Oliver said.

'And you think I'm not?' Shane said, taking a half step toward Oliver.

She tried to ignore the boys' argument, focusing instead on working her way around the wounded area, pressing out as much of the Rift venom as possible. It would still be tomorrow before Hale could shift back to human, but it would help it heal faster and reduce the pain. At least that had been the theory she'd been taught.

Hale barked. The deep bass sound cut through their argument. Amelia froze as the pack energy washed over her, lashing out at the two boys equally. They took a step back from the power of it. Hale wasn't able to argue with Shane, but he could still put him in his place.

Amelia shuddered even though it hadn't been aimed at her. She hesitated, not sure if she should keep tending Hale's wound, not wanting to upset him further. Before she could decide what to do, he solved the problem for her by moving a few paces away. He was clearly done with letting her treat his wound, and she was certainly not sad about that.

She let the rag drop into the river, not bothering to wash it. It was, at the very least, blood stained, even if it didn't have Rift venom on it, and no one would want it back. Hale shook out his fur, sending a spray of water into the stream. Thankfully, he'd moved far enough away that he didn't cover her.

The pack bonds sparked to life, sending through the sensation of running and the freedom of four paws. Then it was gone, and Hale trotted out of the gully and into the woods. Amelia exhaled in relief as the bond fluttered closed almost as quickly as it had opened.

'What the fuck is wrong with you, Oliver? You think that now is the right time to challenge me?' Shane said almost as soon as Hale was out of hearing range, giving Oliver a disgusted look. 'The pack needs stability? Unless you think you're better placed to keep two dozen wolves calm?'

Oliver curled his lip, but he looked away, submitting. Or at least refusing to outright challenge. Amelia didn't understand why. Oliver was clearly stronger than Shane. But Oliver always seemed to back down.

'I didn't think so,' Shane said, eyes flashing yellow as he glanced at Amelia. 'Why don't you help Amelia gather up her shit, and hopefully, by then, Sam will be back? Once I convince her she needs to let Hale stay, we can get everyone the hell out of here.'

Amelia shivered as Shane turned on his heel and headed back towards the pack. She didn't like the way he'd said 'convinced'. From what she'd seen of Sam, it was doubtful she was going to take to that well.

'You shouldn't let him win,' Amelia said quietly so her voice didn't travel. 'If he ever gets full control of the pack, you won't like what you get.'

'A lot is going on. Shane isn't normally like this,' Oliver said, making excuses. In the short time Amelia had known him, this wasn't the first time Oliver had backed down from a fight she knew he'd win. Not just physically.

'What? Domineering, arrogant, rude, or full of himself?' Amelia said, gathering up everything but the stained rag.

Oliver came down the hill and took half the small load. 'Angry,' he said, looking towards where Shane had gone. 'He's always been the rest, but the anger is new.'

Amelia grunted, picking the side of the slope that wasn't steep to climb up. She suspected it was more that Oliver hadn't noticed, rather than the anger was anything new. Despite his position near the top, Shane hadn't endeared himself to many in the pack. But from what she'd seen, Shane normally contained his anger around Hale, so maybe he'd been doing the same with Oliver.

'Let's just hope that he sugars his tongue a bit before Sam gets here,' Amelia said, taking a deep breath, trying to erase the scent of the Rift poison from her nose. The woods were alive with creatures waking for the day, and she smelled rabbits and mice in the wind. It made her stomach growl. They'd never managed to get to do much hunting with the need to stay close together and protect the pack.

Oliver winced and let out a sigh. 'He's already asked Lacey to smooth those waters. She knows Sam the best. I'm sure it will be fine.'

'If you say so. Stopping the pack from leaving until she agrees to let Hale stay seems counterproductive to protecting the pack to me,' Amelia said, keeping her voice low. She might have been happy to say that to Oliver, but there was no need to advertise her opinion to everyone.

'That's why people like Shane get to be in charge,' Oliver said, giving her a twisted smile that didn't really have any humour. 'They get to make the hard choices.'

Amelia didn't answer this time. She didn't think this had anything to do with hard choices, but this wasn't the time to convince him. Hopefully, he'd figure it out on his own.

SAM KNEW SOMETHING WAS wrong as soon as she pulled into her yard. Dawn was hours past, but there were still cars lining her yard. The pack milled about in front of them, oozing a feral nervousness that set the hairs on her arm to attention. She knew the change took time to wear off, but they were usually focused enough to drive home on their own by now.

For the entire drive towards her house, the Land's energy had purred in the back of her mind, content, at peace. It was an odd contrast to the wolves in front of her now.

She parked close to the house, trying not to block anyone so they could leave, then got out of her car. Every eye fell on her with an intense focus that was unnerving. Hale was nowhere to be seen. It wasn't like him to leave before the others.

'Sam, finally. You're late.' Shane's voice was low and hoarse. He looked half wild with dirt smearing his chest and his T-shirt tucked into the back pocket of his shorts. His eyes were yellow with no sign of his human colour at all.

'I'm not late,' she said, attempting not to sound defensive as she looked around at the pack again, trying to figure out what was going on. No one seemed hurt, or at least no one looked to be bleeding. Though with Shifter healing, who knew? 'What's wrong?'

Sam searched the group again, looking for something other than injuries that would help explain what was going on. The new girl from last night stood next to Oliver, slightly apart from the rest, her arms wrapped around her waist. Oliver's eyes were the amber of his wolf, but interestingly, Amelia's were her normal human colour. She was one of the few that were.

Lacey was at the front of the group, her dress inside out. She moved closer to Sam, mouth opening to speak, but then paused, turning to stare out into the woods.

What the hell was going on?

'We have a problem,' Shane said, bringing her attention back to him as he ran his hand through his hair. A small leaf fell to the ground. He shook himself, taking a deep breath. 'It's Hale.'

'What about him?' Sam asked, looking for Hale again, fear rising. Had he been hurt? It wasn't like him not to be here with the pack so agitated.

The pack grew still as leaves rustled behind Shane. She moved slowly so she could see past him, expecting to find Hale stalking out of the trees. Instead, a large black wolf stood at the edge of her yard. It tilted its head to one side as it watched her with intense golden eyes.

Sam swore, taking a step backwards towards her car. Her instincts were conflicted. The Land told her it was safe, but every other part of her--back from when humans lived in caves and wolves were the things in the dark hunting them--was screaming at her to run. It wasn't that she'd never seen a wolf. She occasionally crossed paths with them at the edges of the Rift Scar. But this wasn't just any wolf.

This was an alpha.

This was Hale.

Hale stalked forward with long, powerful strides, fur rippling with each step. The pack energy surged around her, echoing up through the Land at the edge of her senses. It pressed against her walls, and she struggled to keep it at bay.

Then Shane grabbed her wrist.

Her walls crumbled against the wave of energy that hit her. The Land might have been calm and sated, but the pack energy was anything but. It overlaid the link to the Land, making her skin tingle with the power of it. It was almost like she was connected to the wolves; she could feel the wild energy of the pack as it soaked into the Land around her.

'Let us explain,' Shane said, voice level. But there was an edge under it. Anger. She hadn't heard it in his voice. She'd felt it through the Land.

Fear made her try to pull her hand back, but Shane wasn't letting her go. Until Hale growled. The sound vibrated through her like Hale had been the one touching her, though he was still a few feet away. She felt the touch of his power and warning as he pushed it towards Shane.

Shane let her go, stepping back. Lowering his eyes. The connection to the Land snapped like a dry twig, leaving her breathless and shaking. She threw up her walls quickly before it could creep back in. Fear curled in her gut as she rubbed her wrist.

Had Shane sensed her through that link as well? He kept his eyes down and away from her, not giving her any sign that he had. Nor was there any reaction from the rest of the pack. If they'd sensed something, surely, they'd have said so?

'There was a scorpion in the woods,' Shane said, exhaling slowly. His eyes slipped back ever so slowly to their human shade as he looked back up at her.

Sam struggled to get herself under control as she processed Shane's words. She couldn't afford to let years of secrets be torn apart by one arrogant wolf. Or her own fear.

'Another one?' Sam said, turning to Hale. He watched her with those gold eyes, one of his back legs slightly up. Her previous fear shifted direction, and the need to check that he was okay rose so strongly, she almost stepped towards him before she stopped herself. Her stomach dropped as she suspected she knew what Shane was going to say next.

'It was deep in the woods, and we killed it. There aren't any more,' Lacey said, looking at Hale, and added almost unnecessarily, 'Hale got stung. He can't shift back to human.'

Sam wanted to curse. The damned council and their rules. They couldn't transport Hale off her land. He was stuck here.

As a wolf.

'There aren't supposed to be wolves on my Land outside the full moon,' Sam said, feeling trapped. She couldn't afford for the council to investigate her and find out the truth about what Sam was. But she couldn't let Hale risk being arrested for being in his wolf form off her land. Or send him into the Rift Scar edge that butted up against her land. She wasn't that cruel.

'So, you want to throw Hale out on the council's mercy?' Shane said, raising his eyes to meet Sam's. There was defiance there, a challenge. The pack rumbled, a series of growls and shuffling feet flickering through the clearing.

The reason the whole pack was here crystallised in her mind. Shane was using them as leverage to make sure she did what he wanted. The pack would never let anything happen to its alpha.

Hale growled, one massive paw scratching the ground, tearing up the dry mud. Shane looked down again, shoulders tight. But he hadn't backed down. Not really. But the rest of the pack grew still again.

'What Shane meant to say is that no one will know if you allowed Hale to stay here and recover,' Lacey said, giving Sam a tight smile, not quite meeting her eye. 'Once we know Hale is safe, the whole pack can go home.'

The last part was added in a much milder tone than Shane's, almost embarrassed.

Sam turned to Hale, trying not to let her frustration through. It was stupid to challenge a creature that could tear her apart before she blinked, especially in front of his pack. But he was letting Shane do this. If the roles had been reversed, would Hale have done the same to force her to protect Shane? She was pretty sure he would have. Hale didn't react to her look as his gold eyes continued to watch her unblinking.

'One day,' Sam said, raising her finger towards Shane, like that would help emphasise her point. She didn't tell them that she'd have let Hale stay, even without their little game. That was ammunition she'd cast at Hale later. 'Then he's out of here.'

Shane's eyes flashed at her, turning yellow between one blink and the next. 'Of course,' he said, then turned away, heading towards the pack without another word to Sam.

Her acceptance created a ripple in the pack––a relief so strong she almost felt the weight of it even without any connection to the Land. Shane might have been playing bully, but the pack had been genuinely worried for their alpha.

Oliver caught her eye. He'd been in the pack for about six months, and Sam had worked with him on patrol many times before. He nodded at her, mouthing a thank you as his amber eyes flickered between wolf and human, then he turned back to the newest member of the pack. Amelia didn't even look at Sam as her eyes followed Shane, a wariness that seemed strange amongst all the others' relief.

'Thank you, Sam,' Lacey said quietly, closing the gap between them. She reached out like she wanted to touch Sam's arm, then thought better of it. 'I'm sorry. I didn't want him to ask like that.'

Apologising wasn't going to help much. It wasn't going to let Sam go down and scrape the fungus off the tree. Or allow her to connect to the Land. Or any of the multitude of activities that involved being outside. Nor would it change the fact that Shane thought he'd beaten her. Something that sat poorly with Sam.

But she forced a smile. 'You don't have to apologise. You haven't done anything wrong,' Sam said, giving Shane a brief glare. He ignored it. She sent a fraction of the look towards Hale for good measure, and he ducked his head slightly. A human nod on a wolf's body looked bizarre.

'I'll hang around just in case Hale needs anything. If that's okay? I won't get in the way, I promise,' Lacey said, smoothing her dress, hand catching the seam. She scowled like she'd just realised it was inside out.

Sam's smile froze. The last thing she needed was a babysitter. But before Sam could argue, Lacey gave a huff of annoyance, then pulled her dress off. She seemed unconcerned about flashing her bare breasts, and more, as she untangled her dress and then pulled it back on the right way round.

Embarrassment made Sam too slow to react as Lacey fluffed out her hair, offering Sam a quick smile. 'It will be fun. We never get to hang out outside the Rift Scar.'

Sam nodded, still struggling to keep her smile wide as she realised she was too late to argue. Now she had a wolf outside and a babysitter inside. She wasn't going to get anything done today.

'Sounds great,' Sam said, hoping it didn't come out strained as she struggled to find her manners. 'Do you want something to eat?'

Lacey's eyes flashed yellow, and her nose flared. 'I'm starving. We never got to finish our hunt.'

Sam glanced back at the nearly two dozen Shifters who were listening to something Shane was saying. Hale sat at the edge of the clearing, his eyes on her. She considered making him the same offer, then changed her mind. After how Shane had asked for Hale to be allowed to stay, she was feeling more annoyed than helpful.

'I think I've some burgers in the freezer,' Sam said, turning away to head towards the house, Lacey following beside her.

HALE LOPED THROUGH THE woods, sticking to a tight circle around Sam's house, ignoring the pain that sliced at him with every step. It was a reminder that he should rest, even if that was the last thing he wanted to do.

Make pack stay, Fang snarled in his head.

Hale ignored his wolf. He'd been repeating the same words over and over since the sun had risen, trying to convince Hale to keep the pack here with them. But that wasn't possible, and certainly wasn't practical, not when he was struggling with his own control. The pack had barely shifted back as it was, even with the distance he'd been putting between them.

Shane's voice came through the trees as if to taunt Hale. The thud of a palm on the roof of a car followed it as he sent more of the pack away. Shane had taken charge and made sure everyone could change back, which was just as well. Sam might have agreed to let him stay, but there was no way she'd make an exception for half the pack. Not when she'd been furious with them over the way Shane had asked.

Something else Hale needed to speak to Shane about just as soon as he had his voice back. Though part of him feared he may have done the same thing if it had been another in his pack that had been stuck.

Our pack, Fang said, tugging at Hale's control over the pack bonds. He wanted to pull the pack closer again.

Not helpful, Hale whispered as he pushed his wolf back again. Trying to convince Fang that Shane wasn't stealing the pack or challenging Hale hadn't been going well. Because that's exactly what it felt like.

Hale pulled in a deep breath, trying to catch Sam's scent, filling his lungs with it until he was sure she was okay. Which was a stupid thing to wish for right now, given she wasn't hurt. But he hated the look she'd given him. Her anger breaking through her fear. Which was fair. He needed to fix things with her.

But there was nothing but the bitter scent of aniseed. He felt blind without his sense of smell. Even smelling the Rift Scar would have been better than this. None of the pack had got close enough for it to kill anyone else's nose, thankfully.

Frustrated, he reached for the centre of himself where the balance between one half and the other existed. What was usually a clear path back to his human form was simply not there. Like there was no other part of him. Even knowing the Rift poison only blocked the change temporarily, the idea that he'd be stuck forever as a wolf still scared him.

When the moon was full, their wolf halves were at their strongest. But even then, there was the choice to remain human. It wasn't easy, but it was possible. Now there was no choice. The longer he stayed as a wolf, the less he'd remember his human instinct. The less human he'd be.

Without the human instinct, the world would be right to treat them like any other creature from the Rift Scar, something to be hunted and killed. When the first Shifter had been created, that was what had happened. Even now, some people still believed that was the way they should treat Shifters.

Hale gave up running circles and moved back to the front of the house, staying inside the edge of the woods. He was breathing hard, tongue lolling out of his mouth as he struggled to cool down. Almost all the pack was gone now, so he forced himself to lie down in the hard dirt and watch those who were still getting into their cars. Thick tree roots jutted out irregularly, digging into his side. Even if his leg had been healthy, it wouldn't have been comfortable.

He should have let Amelia look at the wound properly and stitch up the gash. If it had been anyone else in the pack that had been hurt, he'd have made them stay until it had been done. But between Oliver and Shane challenging each other and Amelia feeling like an outsider, he was barely able to stop himself from snapping at someone.

Some alpha he was if he couldn't even control himself.

Protect pack. Make stay. Safer, Fang growled in his mind again.

Enough, Hale said, but a growl vibrated through his throat as if to prove that Hale wasn't as in control as he wanted.

Danger, Fang said. Then it sent him the rancid scent of the Rift scorpion, along with the taste of its bitter, acidic blood.

It wasn't like his wolf to keep pushing like this. Not when there was nothing left to protect the pack from. The threat was gone now. The scorpion was dead, and they had already loaded the carcass into the back of Oliver's truck to be thrown back into the Rift Scar. He and Amelia were going to do it before they cleaned yesterday's guns.

We killed it, Hale said, trying to show his wolf the image of their win. *It's dead.*

Frustration came through their connection. Communication between them wasn't always easy. Not when their instincts ran so differently. More complicated ideas got lost in translation.

Danger, Fang said again. More images of hunting came to him from his wolf. Tracking the scorpions. The thrill and challenge of the hunt. The need to prove their strength and power as they took down an entire group of scorpions.

Hale huffed out a breath that stirred the dirt and made his nose itch, about ready to tell his wolf enough again, but he wasn't done yet.

Fang sent him more images. Last night's hunt. The forest. The deer. The chase. Then the aniseed hitting them without warning.

Danger, Fang said.

Hale shivered, remembering the moment before the aniseed had wiped out his sense of smell. There had been no hint of danger. No scent of the scorpion. But surely there had been something? The scorpion had to have come from somewhere. The wind had been blowing towards him, bringing him the scent of the deer. He remembered thinking that it had been a trap at the time, that the aniseed wasn't natural. But keeping the pack safe had become his first priority. But why would someone put a trap out with a scorpion in it, and how would they have made the beast stay there?

Where rest? Fang added, showing images of hunting in the Rift Scar again, fighting against half a dozen scorpions. *Beast alone.*

Which was also strange. Two solo scorpions in one day were unheard of. Was that why the scorpion from earlier had been heading towards Sam's land? Was it trying to find the one who had already wandered in? Except, how did it just happen to be next to an aniseed trap?

'Hale?' Shane's voice made Hale jump to his paws. Shane backed up a step, watching him with caution, but he didn't take a second step. 'That's everyone away now. Do you need anything before I go?'

Hale needed answers, but Shane didn't have them, and even if he did, Hale wasn't able to ask for them. If someone had laid a trap for the pack, he wanted to find out more about what had happened first before pulling anyone else in. He shook his head slowly, the exaggerated motion unnatural in this form.

'I'll be back tomorrow. Until then, I'll get the patrol to recheck the border and make sure nothing else got out,' Shane said, looking past Hale into the woods. Clearly, his thoughts had followed a similar line to Hale's.

Shane didn't wait for an answer this time as he turned to go to his car.

Protect pack, Fang said again, almost longingly.

But it was too late to make the pack stay. They were all on their way home. Besides, sending them away was more likely to protect them since the danger seemed to be here.

Hale huffed a breath as he turned away from the clearing. He needed to find out what had happened last night, and since he was stuck here for the rest of the day, he might as well make the most of it.

Which meant it was time to go hunting.

CHAPTER SEVEN

'THIS PLACE IS MASSIVE,' Lacey said, looking around Sam's kitchen. This had been the last room on the slightly awkward tour that Sam had taken Lacey on.

Massive was stretching it, but it was a decent size. Wooden cabinets lined the shorter back wall from floor to ceiling, and a hardwood counter ran most of the way down the long wall, stopping at the door. A stone sink took centre stage under a massive window that looked out into the front yard. On the second short wall was an old stone fireplace. As far as Sam remembered, it had never been lit, but it was soot-stained enough that she knew someone had used it in the past.

The cottage's rustic style look was somewhat spoiled by Sam's cheap laminate table she'd added so she didn't have to use the dining room.

'I wish my flat had something half this big,' Lacey added, stepping further into the room as she took in the large window. 'And all that view.'

'The bigger it is, the more you need to clean,' Sam said, remembering the day she'd come back after she was finally old enough to live here on her own. That had been a big job, one her grandparents had been happy to help with, though neither had been fit to do much. Three years' worth of dust had taken months of work to remove. At the time, she'd welcomed the distraction from the memories.

'I think I've burgers, if you don't mind waiting for me to defrost them?' Sam said, pulling a stack of burgers out. She'd been lazy when she'd frozen them and not separated them. Now they were welded together, and she'd never had enough people round to make it worth defrosting them.

'Burgers sound fine...' Lacey said, '...but first, can I use your bathroom?'

'Last door on the right, down the hall,' Sam said, offering Lacey a smile as she shoved the burgers in the microwave and turned it on to defrost for a dozen minutes.

Sam let out a slow breath as Lacey disappeared down her hall. It wasn't that she didn't want to speak to Lacey, it was just that there were other things she'd rather be doing. Like sitting under the yew tree.

The Land brushed her mind as if it'd heard the thought, the connection weak and shaky with her being indoors and no longer touching the earth. It tugged at her, wanting her to come outside and connect. It didn't understand why she was ignoring it, like a puppy who wanted cuddles all the time.

Sam glanced out the window. She couldn't see the cars from this side of the house, so she wasn't sure if everyone had left yet. There was also no sign of Hale. Not that she expected to see him. He was probably enjoying himself in her woods, which was where she wanted to be. Then she could sink her hands into the earth and let the Land fill her. But she couldn't risk that. She had to stay in control. Had to wait until Hale and Lacey were gone. She couldn't let anyone else find out her secret, not after last time.

As she turned away, her eyes settled on the old photo on the fireplace mantel. She moved closer before she thought better of it.

It was the only photo on the shelf and one of the few she still had of her mother and father. The quality was poor, but her parents looked happy in it. The slight bump of her mother's pregnancy was just noticeable if you knew what to look for. She'd only been four months along with Sam when the photo had been taken.

Looking at the photo was always a double-edged sword. A reminder of what she'd lost, but also a reminder of how happy her family had been once. Until Sam ruined it.

Her mother had always told Sam to be careful, to never let anyone know she was an Earth Elemental, not even her father. But magic had been something Sam had been proud of, even if, back then, she'd not understood how prejudiced people were against the Bloodline Elementals. Especially Earth.

Her father had been growing flowers in a little greenhouse on the veranda. He'd been planning on entering them into the local flower show, but the weather had changed unexpectedly, and the frost had got to them. They were on the edge of dying despite everything her father had done to save them. It had felt like such a small thing to fix it for him at the time. To make him happy again. She'd been so damned naïve.

She'd checked to make sure she was alone, then she'd told the Land to fix it, but she hadn't been specific about her intent. The flowers went from wilted to full bloom. In the middle of a winter storm.

Her father's horror as he'd found out had made her stomach twist. Then her mother had come out. She'd taken one look at the flowers, and she'd known what had happened. There had been screaming, voices strained to the edge of their capacity as they'd argued. Sam didn't remember their words anymore, only the result.

Her dad had packed a bag and left.

The snow had started at some point while her parents had been fighting, a sleety wet flurry that had already been freezing as it hit the ground. Her mum had grabbed the other car keys, told Sam to stay inside, and then she'd left too.

That was the last time Sam had ever seen either of them.

Less than an hour later, both were dead. They'd been going too fast for the road conditions, and they'd come off. No one had ever said that to her specifically, but it wasn't hard to put it together on her own. They'd died because Sam had let her father find out the truth.

Sam always remembered them the way they'd been that night. The tears, the pale faces. The yelling. The police on her doorstep. No matter how many times she looked at photos of them smiling, the other memories overwrote them.

'They look happy,' Lacey said, making Sam jump. 'Your parents?'

Sam turned away from the photo, wiping away a tear that had escaped so Lacey wouldn't see it. 'They were,' Sam said, clearing her throat. If Lacey noticed, she didn't comment.

'How long have they been gone?' Lacey asked, like the passage of time made a difference. It didn't.

'Almost ten years,' Sam said, rubbing her arms. She'd moved in with her grandparents on her father's side until she had enough money to move back here, to her home, to the Land that waited for her. Not that she'd ever been away from the Land for long. Even then, she knew she needed to come back regularly. To connect with it and keep it alive.

That need to reconnect rose today, as it always did anytime she was away from the Land for more than a few hours. She wanted to sink her hands into the dirt, become part of the Land until there was only one. Not doing it wouldn't hurt Sam, but it would hurt the Land if she ignored it long enough.

'I'm sorry,' Lacey said, but there was a hesitation that came when someone didn't really understand loss. Like she wasn't sure 'sorry' was the right word. She'd yet to learn there weren't any right words.

'It's okay.' Sam offered Lacey an awkward smile. 'I'm going to set up the data upload for the CDS scans while the burgers defrost.' Maybe that would help distract her, at least for a few minutes, while she got her head in order.

'I'll come with,' Lacey said, a little too quickly as she moved ahead of Sam to the back door. Maybe Lacey was as restless as Sam.

Or maybe she just didn't want Sam outside alone with Hale running around as a wolf. Not that it was far to go to get to her garage.

Either way, Sam had little choice but to offer another awkward smile and follow Lacey.

Sam was starting to remember why she didn't have people over.

HALE SLIPPED THROUGH THE thick ferns, following what he thought was the same path he'd run last night. Just at a much slower pace. With the aniseed blocking his smell, he was forced to rely on other markers, but thankfully none of them had been careful of their trails last night as they'd run after the deer.

Scent better, Fang huffed. Hale didn't argue. His wolf wasn't wrong, but they'd make do with what they had.

A rabbit darted ahead of him, heard but not seen, making his stomach rumble. The pack had not managed to catch anything after the deer had escaped. Between the lack of sleep and the way his leg was slowing him down, there was no chance of him catching anything now, either. Then there was the heat.

Hale shook out his fur and let his tongue loll out of his mouth, trying to cool down. The temperature had never really dropped much overnight, and with the sun breaking through the cover of trees above, the heat was already growing again.

Hopefully, it wouldn't take long to find what he was looking for, and then he'd find some cool shade to take a nap.

The forest changed from pine trees to birch as he neared the area where he'd been stung. Scratching away some of the undergrowth with his claws, Hale found spots of red blood. His blood. Tendrils of fire trailed down his leg at the reminder. He shook out his fur again, trying to push the pain aside as he stepped over the bloody ground. He was close to where he'd first seen the creature.

Though he couldn't smell any change, his nose burned as he passed where he'd first scented the aniseed. It took a bit of back and forth, but he eventually found the place where the burn was strongest. Not that he saw the source.

The sun cast dappled shadows over the small clearing. The trees here were thin and young, the silvery bark unmarked, and the undergrowth a mix of ferns and brambles. It looked just like a dozen other spots in Sam's woods. Except for the burn in his nose.

Hale limped further into the clearing, searching the ground for anything that stood out. There was nothing obvious on the ground level. Nor was there any sign that anything but him had recently passed through, but the aniseed scent had likely deterred most creatures.

Turning in a slow circle, Hale took in the trees themselves, looking beyond the surface. Nothing seemed out of place. The young birches swayed in the faint breeze, branches dancing, all undamaged.

Except for one.

One of the lower branches had been bent back so far that it had splintered. It might have been damaged by passing animals. Except it was higher than most animals could reach. Hale circled the tree, ears twitching as he tried to compensate for the lack of scent. There was nothing but the sound of birds chirping nearby and the rustle of leaves in the wind.

A flash of silver caught Hale's eye as he rounded the back of the tree. It looked like a small silver thread, fluttering in the breeze. It was too high up for him to get to it, almost invisible among the leaves. Not that the height mattered. Without human hands, there was little he'd be able to do even if he could reach it.

He traced the thread instead, guessing the line of sight from the item to the forest floor, searching for anything it might have connected to.

It didn't take long to find it once he'd widened his search.

A metal cage about two feet square, with nothing but a few small breathing holes, had been hidden in the ferns.

It was dented on the inside, with deep scratches and black smears. It didn't take a genius to figure out where the scorpion had come from.

On the ground in front of it were shards of glass and more of the silver thread. That, plus the furnace his nose had become, Hale was pretty sure he'd found the source of the aniseed as well. The deer they were chasing must have set off the trap, spilling the scent and releasing the scorpion. That was why Hale had never scented it.

But why had someone gone to so much effort?

Attack pack? Fang snarled, his anger so sharp that it stole Hale's breath. Edges of fear closely followed it.

We are safe, Hale sent, trying to soothe them both. Their attackers hadn't hurt anyone but Hale. But more importantly, a single scorpion wasn't going to be more than a painful inconvenience to the pack.

None of that helped his wolf calm down. They'd been targeted and attacked on their own land. Sam's land--Hale corrected in his own head, huffing out a breath. Now his wolf had him saying it.

But how did someone know where to set up the trap? There was no way to know that any of the pack would come here. They'd been chasing a deer, and it could have taken any path through the woods.

Unless this hadn't been aimed at the pack, or it wasn't the only trap?

Snarling, Hale spun. Not that it did him any good. He'd already set off this trap. There was nothing more to see, and by the time the aniseed cleared the area, the scent of who laid it would be gone.

He needed to find out if there were any more traps out there.

By the time an hour had passed, Hale had found another three traps similar to the first. Once he'd known what he was looking for, he'd been able to hear the beast in the cages, quietly chittering and calling for the rest of their buddies. Each cage was connected to a trip wire in the tree, likely where the aniseed was coming from.

They'd been lucky last night. It would have been too easy for one of them to have stumbled onto more of these traps.

Call pack, Fang said.

No, Hale replied. Calling the pack here, with no way to warn them, would only cause more panic and might risk setting off more traps.

His wolf grumbled, anger still a vivid spark across Hale's mind. But it grew silent, hopefully agreeing that it was best to keep the pack away from here.

At least for now.

Hale hated leaving the creatures where they were, but he needed hands and help to kill the beasts. Even his wolf wasn't foolish enough to want to trigger the traps if they didn't have to. Though if they didn't get back into the Rift Scar soon, they'd be an easy kill. The longer they spent outside the Scar, the sicker they'd get.

He'd have to keep circling the cages and make sure no passing animal triggered the traps. Though most seemed to be sensing the creatures and steering clear.

Hopefully, it would stay that way.

SAM SLAMMED THE SIDE of the monitor as the screen flickered off and on. The computer was almost old enough to have been around in her grandfather's day, and it needed a little extra encouragement to display the results.

'What has the PC ever done to you?' Lacey said, giving her a look from where she was poking around the collection of machines Sam used to test the dirt. Those tests would take longer than uploading the CDS scans, so she'd do them tomorrow.

'Today? Or do you want a full list?' Sam said, giving a fake smile. Her cheeks were starting to ache from forcing it. If Lacey noticed, she didn't say anything as she snorted and went back to studying the machines.

Sam let the smile drop, searching for something to say that would make the woman give her some space. Which she knew was stupid because it wasn't like the garage was cramped. One wall held all the basic lab setup, and another held the PC and an area to do paperwork. The rest of the room was all open space with nothing but a concrete floor and an old roller door that Sam had never used. Half the pack would fit, providing no one wanted to move much.

But despite the space, she felt like she was trapped somehow.

'You can head inside if you want. It will only take another few minutes to upload the files. I'm sure it would be cooler there,' Sam said, trying to make it sound like she was suggesting it for Lacey's benefit as she wiped sweat from her forehead. It wasn't even a lie; it was already roasting in the garage, even though she'd left the door open to let the air flow in. Not that there was much of that.

Lacey opened her mouth to speak, but her phone rang before she had time to get any words out. She grabbed it from her pocket, face going serious as she checked the screen. 'I'll be right back,' Lacey said, slipping past her to go outside.

Sam sighed, torn between worry for the pack and relief at finally being alone. Not that she expected to be that way for long. But right now, she'd take five minutes. She shook her head, turning back to her computer.

The monitor no longer showed random hazy lines, proving that hitting it had worked. As expected, the CDS scans showed the baseline remained the same, just like the last five scans. There was a spike in some of the other readings, most of which was due to the exceptionally hot weather. Sam added an extra paragraph to her email with the readings to explain why, so no one in the Institute of Rift Studies & Defence got their knickers in a twist. Something the IRS&D was prone to do.

Satisfied everything was right, Sam closed the files, attached them to an email, then pressed Send. The ancient machine chugged away, thinking about processing her request.

'All done?' Lacey said, popping her head back through the doorway, making Sam jump.

That sense of claustrophobia came back almost immediately. Sam seriously needed to work on her social skills. 'Yep, and the burgers should definitely be defrosted now,' Sam said, trying to sound cheerful as she turned off the PC.

'About that,' Lacey said, wincing. 'I'm sorry. I've to go help one of the rangers.'

'Oh no. I hope everything is okay,' Sam said, trying not to let the relief show.

'It's all good, just a small thing,' Lacey said, giving a quick smile. 'But I'll be back later, and we can have a proper chat.'

'Sounds great,' Sam said, feeling the strain on her cheeks again as she stood and flicked the lights off to follow Lacey out. The Land buzzed loudly in Sam's mind as soon as her feet hit the patchy grass outside the garage.

'You should stay inside until I get back,' Lacey said, looking at the treeline. 'Just in case.'

Sam shivered at Lacey's tone. Yesterday she'd been saying how good Hale's control was, and now today, she was cautioning Sam to stay inside? Lacey couldn't have it both ways.

'I hope everything goes okay with the rangers,' Sam said, avoiding Lacey's comment altogether.

Lacey nodded, heading towards the two remaining parked cars and pulling out her keys. She said another goodbye, then drove away, still wearing that serious expression that Sam couldn't quite read.

Sam glanced back at her house as Lacey disappeared. The thought of going inside didn't appeal. But she also didn't particularly want to meet Hale as a wolf alone.

The Land surged in her mind, picking up on her thoughts, bringing her an image of Hale running. She should have pushed it away, but he felt distant, and curiosity got the better of her. She let her walls drop a little.

Hale's muscles worked hard as he ran through the woods, every step sending a line of fire through his back leg. He was focused, following something through the woods. Hunger clouded the edge of his mind, niggling at him. It wasn't all that was in his mind. Another presence ran in tandem with Hale, instincts different. His wolf.

Sam shoved the connection away and slammed her walls back up. Had Hale sensed her?

Fear crawled at the edge of her mind. She'd not felt anything from him that indicated he had. But that connection had been deeper than anything the Land normally showed her.

Stupidly, even with her fear trying to strangle her, part of her wanted to go back and reconnect. To enjoy the sense of freedom that Hale's running had brought. Even with the pain in his leg, it had been like nothing could hold her back, like she could run forever. Except running had never brought her that sense of freedom and power before. That had been all Hale's emotion.

Cursing at her own stupid, conflicted brain, she took a step towards the house. The Land tugged at her again, swirling around her, bringing images of trees and rabbits this time. She should ignore it and go inside. But it hadn't seemed like Hale had known she was there, and he'd been quite a distance away. She might not get another chance to connect to the tree and give it some more energy to last until tomorrow.

But did she dare take that risk? What if Hale found out what she was? What if he told others? She'd lose every-thing.

Yet the Land pulled at her, telling her it was safe. Of course, the Land had the foresight of a hyperactive puppy. It didn't see Hale as a threat.

Dammit, why'd this have to be so hard? She hated this fear and indecision. She didn't want to live in fear every time the pack was on her land. She wanted the freedom she'd felt in Hale. The freedom the rest of the Elementals had.

The forest danced around her as the wind picked up. She should go back inside; it was too big a risk. She should wait until tomorrow. The tree would probably survive an-other day.

Probably.

But it wouldn't take long to give the tree a boost. Hale wouldn't even notice she was outside. And even if he did, he wasn't some feral animal that might attack her. As long as he wasn't near her when she used her magic, it wouldn't matter.

With a shake of her head, she kicked off her sandals and stepped onto the dirt path that led out to the yew tree. The energy zipped through her in little sparks that made her skin tingle. She'd spend five minutes down there, give the tree some more energy and then come back to the house.

Everything would be fine.

HALE STUMBLED MID-STRIDE AS the unfamiliar connection broke off.

Sam.

It was almost like she'd been part of the pack, but different. Like the thread that always seemed to tug him in her direction had been pulled tight, binding them together closer than any pack bonds. Like she'd been part of him.

Then she'd just been gone.

Breath heaving, he spun, testing the air in a wasted effort to see if she was close. Nothing but aniseed came back to him. What had happened to Sam? What had caused the connection? Was she okay?

Protect mate, Fang snarled, tugging at him to turn back to the house.

Hale listened to his wolf this time, not bothering to argue that she wasn't his mate. Right now, it didn't matter. That connection surged back in fits and spurts as he ran, but this time it wasn't exactly Sam, but like something was watching him.

Fear made him press for more speed, chest burning. The sharp sting in his leg had become a familiar enough pain that he could almost tune it out. Almost. But he didn't dare risk slowing down. Not when he didn't know what was happening.

The house came into view all at once as he broke free from the under bush. The sprawling building was quiet. He searched for Sam, but she wasn't conveniently sitting outside on her veranda and there were no sounds except for normal forest animals. There was no sense of danger, nothing that had changed since he'd watched Shane leave. But something had happened.

He circled the house twice, searching for any sign of her. A pair of sandals lay at the base of the veranda, and the door to the garage was open now. He was sure it hadn't been earlier, but she wasn't inside. Neither door to the house was open, and there were no lights on, but with it being the middle of the morning, that wasn't a surprise.

Where was she? Dammit! He needed his sense of smell. With it, he'd be able to trace her scent. Follow her, and know she was okay. Without it, he felt blind.

The connection fluttered again. It was like a current running under his feet, leaving fleeting touches against his paws that made him shiver. He preferred the sensation of Sam running with him, like a part of her was inside him. He wanted her to do it again, though he wasn't sure exactly what she'd done the first time.

But first, he had to find out if she was safe.

Follow old trail, Fang sent, showing him images of a familiar rough stone path.

The pack had been coming to Sam's land for years, and there was one path that always sang with her scent. Turning away from the house, Hale followed the broken stones into the forest, where it turned into hard-packed earth and pine needles.

As he moved further into the woods, the tingling energy under his paws grew sharper, changing from an intermittent current to a live wire. But it still didn't feel dangerous. There was no sound, no screams. But without his sense of smell, he was missing so much information.

He hesitated as he neared the end of the path. It would empty him out into a large clearing, but he didn't want to scare Sam if everything was fine. He turned and padded into the thick heather instead, slipping through the ferns that were tall enough to brush the top of his back. It was as hidden as he was going to get. His black coat didn't exactly blend well against the bright green ferns and purple heather.

When he was sure he'd found what was hopefully the thickest part of the underbrush, he moved to his belly, crawling the last few feet to the clearing. He wasn't sure what he'd expected to see, but it hadn't been Sam kneeling in front of an old yew tree, its gnarled branches spread out like a canopy above her. She was calm, shoulders relaxed, and head bowed forward, one hand on the ground, the other on the tree.

There was nothing else but Sam and the tree. No sign of a threat. Nothing that looked like it was dangerous. He took another useless breath, pulling in nothing but aniseed.

He focused on Sam again, checking her in more detail. She was wearing the same strappy summer dress from earlier, the material fitting to her body in a way that showed off all her curves. The dark green making her look like she was part of the land. She'd pulled her golden curls up into a messy bun on the top of her head.

But if everything was fine, why did that vibration of power still echo up his body? And why was it stronger the closer he got to Sam?

It was almost like he was inside one of the old pack lands, the ones that radiated their own power. Those territories had been created when the first alphas had claimed land for themselves during the war. There were only two in the UK, and anytime he'd visited them, he'd been left longing to go back for months later. No one knew how they'd been created, and there had been a lot of wolves over the years who'd tried to figure it out.

But there had never been that kind of power here before. Though he had to admit there had always been something different here. He'd just put it down to the proximity of the Rift Scar.

He'd clearly been wrong.

But how was this possible?

Hale looked again at the way Sam's hand was buried in the ground. Like she was connected to it. He'd seen Water Elementals do similar when they passed anything larger than a puddle. But Sam wasn't an Elemental, and this wasn't water.

Except, what if he was wrong? What if she was an Elemental? But what? No Elemental had ever made the land feel like this?

Hale shivered. The land. Earth. An Earth Elemental?

Was that possible? He didn't know much about Earth Elementals, except that the government regulated them heavily. He'd never met one. Never seen their magic, though some people theorised they had none and the government was just trying to find something they could control.

But what else could it be? No other Elemental Magic had sunk into him like they were part of the pack. It would explain a lot. Her refusing to be on the land for the hunt, no matter how much he told her she'd be safe. How the land thrived so close to the Rift Scar.

Hale's gut twisted as he realised what else that meant. What it would mean if others found out. She'd lose everything. She'd be made to leave. He'd lose her.

Protect, Fang snarled. *Ours.*

Hale wanted to argue with his wolf. Sam wasn't theirs. But he couldn't find the words. It didn't matter whether she was Hale's or not; he wasn't going to let anyone hurt her. The strength of that decision should have scared him, but it didn't.

He tried to imagine what it must have been like for her to live in hiding. To never be able to show the world what she was. Shifters might be treated poorly at times, but they never had to hide what they were.

All because the government was afraid. For what? For land that thrived and felt like home. What right did the government have to decide where Sam could live?

Funny, these were never questions he'd asked before today. Hale decided to ignore that thought, at least for now. He'd dwell on his own unwitting prejudice and ignorance later.

A bird cried out, its squawk breaking the quiet of the clearing, making Sam open her eyes and follow its flight. She smiled as she watched it. Then the smile fled as her head shot round, staring straight at where he lay.

He tried to make himself as small and harmless as possible. But it didn't help as Sam jumped up, scrambling backwards over the roots that spread out around her feet.

Safe, Fang whined in the back of his mind, unhappy with her fear. He didn't understand why she was afraid of them. They'd done nothing to frighten her.

Hale tried to send images of what it must be like for her to live with this secret, to hide what she was. The concept was beyond his wolf; all he saw was fear. They'd never had to hide what they were. They'd been born into the pack, out and public their whole lives as Shifters. Though that didn't mean they'd always been accepted, they weren't treated like the Earth Elementals were.

Sam didn't run. He wasn't sure if that was a good sign or not. He wanted to tell her that he wouldn't hurt her, that it was safe. A breeze grabbed her hair, tugging at it. He wished he could smell her.

'What do you want?' Sam asked, crossing her arms across her chest as she watched him.

Hale huffed out a breath. He tried to keep himself low, say with his body what he couldn't say with words. But she wasn't a wolf to understand the body language, and even if she was, there was a limit to what he could share.

'You were far––' Sam cut off before she finished the sentence, taking a slow breath before biting her lip.

She'd sensed the distance when she'd connected to him. That was why she'd come out here. Because she'd sensed he wasn't close and had thought it would be okay. Except he'd ruined it.

He lifted his head, tilting it to the side with his ears raised. Every movement went against his wolf instincts. Damned venom. He needed to be able to speak, to talk to her. Though, to be fair, he wouldn't have even been there without the venom.

Pack, Fang said in his mind. Images of running in the woods, of lying next to her in the leaves.

Hale pushed the images away. Sam wasn't pack. Even if she were, it wasn't like he could talk to her in words through the pack bonds. The way she was looking at him, she was a heartbeat away from running and never looking back.

The clearing was quiet but for him and Sam. No birds, no other animals. That bird squawk had been the last time Hale had heard any sign of anything. What had sent it away?

Something felt wrong.

Hale tilted his head, listening, searching for signs of something he couldn't see or smell.

Something he'd have been able to smell if his nose had been working.

Like he should have smelled the scorpion.

SAM'S QUESTION HUNG UNANSWERED in the air. Not that she'd expected one. It wasn't like Hale was able to reply. He was almost invisible in the waist-high ferns, black coat somehow blending into the greenery. If not for his power as it danced across her awareness, she might not have seen him at all.

She didn't know how much time had passed, minutes or hours, but it had clearly been long enough. She'd been stupid to come here, to risk it. How was she going to explain this? Had Hale already figured out the truth? The memory of her father's face hovered in her mind; she pushed it away. Hale wasn't human; he had no reason to be afraid of what she was.

But even if he didn't fear her, she didn't know if she could trust him.

Hale stiffened, nose in the air, head swivelling like he was trying to catch a scent. He held the rest of his body rigid.

Her throat grew tight as she watched him, a different fear rising as she remembered his hunger, the gnawing weight of it. She fought to keep herself from bolting; she couldn't outrun him even if he was in his human form, let alone as a wolf. The memory of him running through the woods made her shiver at the power he had. She couldn't match that.

His muzzle curled in a snarl, eyes focusing on her as he flashed his white teeth.

'Hale?' she whispered, stepping back, unable to stop herself, half reaching for the Land.

Hale lunged towards her.

Her foot tangled in the roots of the tree as she tried to back away. The connection to the Land slipped from her as she fought for balance and lost, falling to the ground hard. Air exploded out of her lungs as a black blur filled her vision.

Then continued past her.

Sam fought to get to her feet, hip screaming at her from the ungracious fall. Hale snarled, the sound vibrating through her body like thunder. Then something very different screamed, an inhuman sound piercing her ears.

She turned to Hale. His black fur was puffed out as he stood between her and something Sam had only ever seen in books.

The Rift imp was a little over four feet tall, with grey hairless skin that held a slimy sheen. Its arms were so long that its razor-sharp claws reached the ground. It stirred the dirt almost idly. The odd limbs might have looked ungainly, but she knew from her school lessons that the creatures were fast and strong.

She'd no illusion of outrunning it any more than she'd had of outrunning Hale. It would easily rip her apart before she'd taken a dozen steps, likely less. Hale would fare better, but he was already injured, though you wouldn't have guessed it by the way he'd leapt over her to face off against the imp.

How the hell had it got here? There were miles of forest between her and the Rift Scar. She'd heard stories of them taking livestock or humans stupid enough to venture too close to the border. But neither had happened for years, and from what she remembered, they didn't hunt alone. Unless it wasn't alone?

That thought made Sam's heart skip a beat as she searched the clearing for signs of anything else being here. But there was nothing. Not that she was sure she'd know what to look for.

Stomach churning, she turned back to the imp. It swayed side to side, overly large eyes tracking Hale. The wind changed direction, making her gag at the stench that hit her. It was worse than the Rift Scar. Worse than week-old rotted meat, putrid and covered in maggots. She didn't even have words to describe it.

Then the imp looked past Hale, focusing on her, sensing her fear and disgust. It gave a small hissing sound, then threw its head back and let out a high-pitched cackle that made her ears ring.

She flinched and reached out to the Land, pulling it as close as she dared without getting lost. It couldn't see the imp, couldn't do anything to it. Hale, however, was a different matter. He flared to life in her mind, power, and grace. It wasn't like when she'd slipped into him as he ran.

This time it was more distant, like there was something between them.

Not that she thought a connection to him would be better. Or help her figure out what she was supposed to do. She couldn't leave Hale alone to face the beast, even though every part of her wanted to run. But neither did she have any way to help him.

Hale lunged towards the Rift imp. No sign of the pain she knew he must be in. The imp jumped back a step as it let out a high-pitched squeal. Hale didn't follow it, moving back to a position between her and it again.

The imp snarled at Hale, then let out another cackle, calling for others in its clan. Sam froze as she waited for a return call. But there was nothing.

The creature hesitated, its black eyes moving to her as its nose scented the air. Hale snapped at it again, and the imp snarled, taking another step back. But its eyes didn't leave her.

Sam swallowed, wishing for the first time in her life that the government was right about Earth Elementals. That the magic was dangerous. Then she'd have some way to help Hale kill this beast. But instead, she was forced to watch as Hale lunged again, unable to do anything as the imp didn't back up this time.

HALE JUMPED BACK AFTER his lunge, growling at the imp. This time it hadn't backed away, which wasn't a good sign. Its eyes kept moving towards Sam, hunger shining in them as it drew in her scent.

Sam's fear would be filling the clearing. He didn't need to scent it to know it was there. He'd heard it from how quick she was breathing and had seen it in her eyes as he'd jumped past. He hated that some of that fear had been caused by him. If she ran, it would chase her. Imps liked to play with their food, liked to hunt and torment their prey like a cat playing with a mouse.

But even with her fear tempting it, Hale's attacks should have been enough to force the imp back. They were cowards at heart and hated fighting solo. Except it wasn't backing down. If anything, it seemed to shake itself and settle into a more solid position.

Even if Hale had been a hundred per cent healthy, attacking it head-on wasn't ideal in this form. It was nearly as fast as Hale and had a longer reach. The best way to hunt one was to flank it as a group. Or attack it from behind as it ran. Neither seemed to be an option here.

Hale lunged again, this time not stopping short of the imp. His teeth scraped slippery grey flesh as the imp flinched away at the last moment, squealing. It leapt back out of reach.

But the attack had worked in a way. It finally put all its focus on Hale, snarling and sending a spray of black saliva over the ground. Though it would have been better if it had run. It glanced at Sam again, desperation in that look. Not just the need to hunt, but starvation.

He thought about the scorpions in their traps out in the woods. Had someone brought this creature here too? Bound and caged it until it was wild with hunger and savage. Right onto Sam's land, where she'd be an easy target.

Hale growled again, shoving the thought away before his wolf caught it. He was already angry enough without adding more fuel to the fire.

Attack. Kill, Fang snarled, trying to pull control away. Whether he had caught Hale's thought or he had just grown tired of waiting, Hale couldn't tell.

Slow. Patient, Hale said. But his wolf didn't want to be either, not when Sam was at risk. But they couldn't afford a mistake. The Rift imp wasn't some defenceless deer. It was vicious, and even if it wasn't as smart as a human, it was certainly beyond animal instinct.

Protect mate, Fang said, not backing down. His wolf might have been better placed to fight in this form, but with Fang's fear driving him so deeply, Hale couldn't afford to give his wolf control.

The imp let out another piercing cackle, then launched itself towards Hale, long arms reaching out to tear into his side. It was fast despite the awkward, gangly movements.

Hale dodged to the side, pain spiking through his leg as he forced it to take too much weight. The imp's razor-sharp claws only just missed him, leaving deep gouges in the ground.

Without waiting for it to pull back, Hale twisted, narrowly missing taking a chunk from its arm.

The imp backed up a step, hissing, sending more black spit in Hale's direction, eyes flickering to Sam again. The look sent a chill through him. He had to end this quickly. They were too close to Sam. It might decide to try to slip past him and go for her. She was what it wanted.

Snarling, Hale feinted at the creature's legs, forcing it further away from Sam. The imp squealed and leapt back, swiping at where Hale would have been if he had followed through.

The imp growled, growing frustrated. Black saliva trickled from its muzzle, dripping to the ground as it launched forward again. They danced back and forth, attack, retreat, feint.

Inch by slow inch, Hale pushed it away from Sam. The imp's chest heaved, every breath wheezing through its teeth, but Hale wasn't in much better condition. His leg burned worse than before, no longer something he could ignore as his chest ached with the need for more air. Even before the imp, he'd been running low on energy. He'd not put enough back into his body to keep this up much longer.

The imp slashed at him again, but the attack was slower than before. Seeing his chance, Hale waited until the last second, then ducked under the arm coming towards him, and snapped after it. His teeth sunk into flesh, the wet, slimy texture tearing easily, filling his mouth with vile-tasting blood.

The imp squealed so loud Hale's ears rang. He expected it to pull away, but instead it threw itself at Hale, throwing them both off balance and closer to Sam.

Hale felt something tear deep inside his leg, and it gave under him, sending him to the ground. He howled, unable to fight the pain. The imp pulled its arm free, spraying blood over Hale.

The imp reared back, getting back to its feet. It spread its claws wide, slashing towards Hale's throat.

Hale tried to get his paws under him, but it was too close, moving too fast.

It was going to win.

He was going to fail Sam.

Then the imp stumbled off balance as something struck it. It spun away from Hale to face its attacker, then froze.

Sam held a long branch in shaking hands. She looked fierce and wild as she refused to back up. But that defiance wouldn't save her.

Hale scrambled to get up, wanting to howl as he watched the imp take a step towards Sam. It let out a short cackle, arm reaching out towards her lazily as it seemed to forget about Hale.

Sam screamed, trying to back away, almost tripping over the tree roots again.

Hale's leg barely held his weight as he launched himself sloppily towards the imp. His teeth sank into the side of its neck.

The Rift imp gargled a scream, but it twisted, raking its claws deep into Hale's side. They stumbled as Hale fought to hold on to the imp's neck. He felt the warmth of his own blood as it ran through his fur, but he refused to let go.

The imp's claws pressed deeper.

Hale didn't howl his pain. He was afraid that if he did, he'd lose his grip, and the imp would get free. Slowly, the imp sagged to the ground, and Hale followed it, gnawing at its flesh until bone scraped against his teeth.

The imp's arm dropped away from Hale's side, but still, he didn't let go. He had to be sure. He listened for the creature's heartbeat. Waited for it to move. But there was nothing.

Slowly, Hale let go and stumbled back from the imp. His breath came in pained gasps as he waited, watching. Its eyes were open, looking at nothing as it lay still.

Dead.

Hale shuddered, body screaming at him. He'd won.

But was Sam okay? Had he been fast enough to attack it?

He tried to spin as new fear tightened his chest. He had to find her, but the pain in his side flared so brightly that he lost his balance, falling to the side. He tried to get up, but he couldn't move. Couldn't do anything but breathe through the pain in his side.

He wished he could smell Sam, be sure she was okay. But the darkness crowded his vision until he slipped into an abyss.

CHAPTER EIGHT

Bile burned Sam's throat as she watched the Rift imp go limp, and Hale let go. Its neck had been shredded, leaving nothing more than grey flesh hanging in strips smeared with black blood. A flash of white bone was visible through the mess.

That had almost been her throat.

If Hale hadn't... She let the thought go, unable to finish it as she shifted her grip on the useless branch that dug into her sweaty palms. It hadn't been as useful as she'd hoped when she'd pulled it from the ground at the base of the tree. She'd been useless.

She fought to pull in a deep breath, to loosen the tightness in her chest, and gagged. The rot that had been in the air before was stronger now, so strong she could taste it. She fell to her knees, vomit searing her throat as she lost everything she'd eaten that morning.

Her whole body shook as she tried to get her stomach under control.

I'm okay, she told herself. Hale had won. He'd protected her. They were safe now.

The Land hovered at the edge of her awareness, but she didn't trust herself to reach out and connect. Not until her fear lessened. Which might be a while.

When she was sure there was nothing left to come up, she pulled back to sit on her heels. It took two tries, but she made it. She wiped her mouth to hide how badly her hand was shaking as she searched for Hale. She expected to see him sitting on his haunches, watching her with those serious eyes. But he wasn't.

He lay a foot away from the imp, not moving, not even looking at her at all. She wanted to talk to him, to say anything, but the words stuck like glue to her tongue. What did you say to someone who'd saved your life?

'Hale?' Sam said, clutching the stick tightly as she stood.

There was no response other than a rasping breath. She closed the distance slowly, moving around him so she could see him better. A flash of red caught her vision. Blood. It spread out over the dry dirt, flowing faster than it could soak in.

She said his name again, louder this time, as her heart caught in her throat. He didn't react. Cursing, she took another step closer. There was a gash in his side, barely visible under his black fur. The imp had hurt him. She let the branch fall to the ground and moved as close to him as she dared.

She'd been warned during her training with the rangers that wolves could lash out if hurt. Instinct overriding everything else. Up until now, she'd never had to worry about that possibility. Their instructions had been to wait for someone from the pack to come and never to get too close. Shifter healing could deal with a lot, given enough time.

Except, she wasn't sure she had that kind of time as she looked at the blood again. At the rate the pool was growing around him, he'd be long gone by the time she got help, which wasn't going to be quick when she'd left her phone at the house.

Her stomach twisted, and she was nearly sick again at the thought of losing him. Risk of him lashing out at her or not, she had to help him. Basic first aid told her to apply pressure to a wound to stop the blood. That Hale was a wolf wouldn't make a difference.

'Please don't bite me,' Sam whispered as she placed her hand over his wound. He whined quietly, making her flinch and pull back. But he didn't attack her. Hell, he hadn't moved at all. Even with her basic first aid knowledge, she knew that was a bad sign.

She moved her hand back over his wound, this time ignoring the whine of pain. His chest moved, breath coming in small gasps as warm blood slid over her fingers. What had looked like a small slash under his fur was anything but. The flow wouldn't stop no matter how hard she pressed or how wide she spread both hands.

She choked back a sob, searching the clearing for anything that could help. But there was nothing. Moss, branches, leaves, and grass. Nothing large enough to stop the bleeding.

Hale needed the pack. Or a surgeon.

Or healing.

The thought stole her breath. Healing him like she'd healed the tree? Her mother had never told her if it was possible to heal people. But her mother hadn't told her a lot of things she should have.

The Land pressed at her walls as if it had sensed the thought. She fought to keep it back. She didn't know what would happen if she healed him. What if she made it worse? Hale wasn't a tree. He was a living, breathing person.

But really, how much worse could it get? If she didn't help him, he was going to die.

If she healed him, there would be no way she'd be able to convince him she was human. She'd lose her freedom.

Shame followed the thought. Her secret had already cost her both her parents. She wasn't willing to let it take another life. Even if this time it might cost her everything. It would be better that than losing Hale.

Sam took a shuddering breath, pressing her fingers harder against Hale's side as she let her mental walls down. The Land poured in with such intensity that she almost threw her walls back up again.

It focused only on Hale, like it knew exactly what she wanted. She couldn't feel him like she'd done earlier, but she could see how close to death he was. Feel it like she'd felt the tree dying.

If she had any chance of saving him, she'd have to move fast. She focused on the massive yew tree, pulling its energy towards her, then into Hale. Just like she'd done to heal the tree, remembering this time to bring in more than just herself.

But nothing happened.

Sam swallowed back another sob at the thought of losing Hale. She had to save him. The realisation hit her so hard that her body shuddered under the weight of the fear. She didn't want to lose him.

She remembered the first time she'd seen him standing in the shadow of the council hall building, waiting for her. That thrill she'd felt at seeing him. The heat that had flowed off him as she'd sat next to him to sign the contract for the land. How she'd felt drawn to him even then.

Hale's chest rattled as he struggled to pull in a breath. She needed to do something soon or there wasn't going to be anything to save.

Tearing herself away from the fear and pain, Sam tried to focus. Tried to be practical. She was a scientist. She needed to think logically.

Why wasn't the energy working?

Hale wasn't a tree. He was flesh and bone. He wasn't part of the Land. But she'd felt him, felt his hunger and pain as he'd run through the woods. Except she couldn't feel him now.

Sam hesitated. She hadn't sensed him through the fight at all, not even once. Why had she felt him running, but not now? Had he let her in the first time?

But if he had to let her in, how was she going to get him to do that when he was unconscious?

She needed a way to talk to him, to convince him to let her in. A way to make him listen.

That tug between them shuddered. It was as tiny and delicate as a spider's web. One wrong move and the thread would break apart. How long had she ignored this connection? Pushing it aside, afraid to let anyone close. What would happen if she followed it?

Did she have a choice?

Hale's breath slid out of him in a rattle.

But this time he didn't take a new one.

Panicked, Sam reached towards that thread, not caring about being careful as she wrapped her energy around it, not even bothering to use the Land to bridge them.

The connection slammed into place. Hale jerked under her hand, his body seizing.

She screamed as pieces of her flowed into Hale, bringing back an echo of what he felt. The deep burning pain in his side, his blood loss. It felt like her body was on fire.

Then something pulled her under, and darkness flowed over her.

THE DARKNESS AROUND SAM grew hazy, then it cleared between one blink and the next. She was standing in an unfamiliar hallway. Hale's limp wolf form had disappeared from in front of her, along with the forest. There was no blood on her, or around her.

She searched for something she recognised, for Hale, for anything. But there was nothing. Had something gone wrong? She looked down at her hand. She almost felt the wet blood on her fingers. But she couldn't see it.

Shuddering, Sam took in the hallway in more detail. It was painted white, with several doors, most of them closed. It ran a couple of metres away from her, then turned a corner.

A teenage boy around fourteen appeared in a doorway. He had dark hair cut short and was somehow familiar, though she couldn't figure out why. He wobbled on his feet as he made his way down the corridor, one hand on the wall to steady himself, being careful of how much weight he put on one of his legs.

'Hello?' Sam asked, gut tightening. Where the hell was she? The boy didn't turn to her at all.

'He can't hear you,' Hale said, voice making Sam jump and spin to look at him. He was human now, wearing a dark T-shirt and jeans, skin pale, and looking far thinner than she remembered. Even though he was speaking to her, he never took his eyes off the teenager.

Hale had been right. The boy didn't seem to see Sam as he walked straight past her. It was like she didn't exist.

'What's happening?' Sam asked, looking around her again.

'It's a dream,' Hale said, taking a slow step to follow the boy. 'Maybe a memory.'

Sam watched the boy turn a corner, then she looked back at Hale. They were so similar that they could have been related. A shiver ran through her. Not just similar, the same.

A memory?

Were they dead?

'Not dead, not yet anyway,' Hale said, looking back at her.

She hadn't spoken out loud.

He turned back to the boy, following him around the corridor. Sam moved to chase after him, but the world shifted and blurred, and she was standing in a large entrance room. An older man and woman with many of the same features as Hale stood by the door, bodies stiff as they argued. The woman was petite, and the man was tall. Both had dark hair.

Hale's hand came to rest on Sam's back, making her jump again as she turned to him. 'My parents,' Hale said. Sam couldn't read his expression as he stared at the couple.

'What's happening?' Sam asked again.

This time, Hale didn't answer.

A wolf brushed against her leg as it moved to stand between her and the older Hale. Its dark fur unmarked by blood or wounds. It leaned into her like a dog seeking comfort. She reached down and buried her hand in its fur without any clear intention of doing so.

'At least wait until he's woken up and has a chance to say goodbye?' Hale's dad said, tone low and frustrated.

'Why? So, I can look at him and see what I've lost?' Hale's mum said. There was so much anger there.

Teenage Hale appeared at the edge of the room. Neither of his parents had noticed him yet.

The older Hale tensed. Fingers almost painful where they pressed into her side. As soon as the thought registered, he loosened his grip, but he still didn't speak. All his focus was on his parents.

'You haven't lost anything. He's not dead, dammit, he's just a Shifter,' his dad said, all but growling.

'Him being dead would be easier,' his mum snapped.

The energy in the room changed. Sam felt it in a way she'd never done before. Like she could see the older man's wolf and feel the weight of it like a shadow filling the room. The teenage Hale's eyes shifted to yellow, and with the change, a new energy rose to join the first. It was smaller, like a child taking its first breath. The wolf at her side shivered.

The older man turned as soon as the energy formed. He moved almost between one blink and the next and was at teenage Hale's side, arm wrapped around him so tightly Sam worried the boy might snap.

The woman flinched back from the exchange, and Sam felt the fear and anger that came from her. Memories of her own father looking at her in the same way rose so close to the surface, she could smell the flowers that had bloomed.

'Mum?' Teenage Hale's voice broke in a way that had nothing to do with puberty. It snapped her own memory off before it fully formed.

'I can't.' His mum shook her head, then turned and ran, slamming the door behind her as she went.

Sam shuddered as the wave of pain made her want to double over. It hadn't come from her.

'I'm sorry. This is my past. You shouldn't have to see this,' Hale said, reaching out to wipe a tear from Sam's eyes. How his were dry, she didn't know. His wolf pressed closer into her legs, like it wanted to support her, too.

'Let me help you,' Sam said, trying to refocus on why she was there. The feel of the blood on her hands even if she couldn't see it.

The room shifted, and they went back to the hallway she'd started in, the teenager coming out of the doorway. A loop.

How long had Hale been reliving this? She couldn't even imagine how she'd cope watching her father walk away on repeat. Again, the world wobbled, and only the wolf at her leg kept her standing.

The older Hale was at the far end of the hallway again, watching. Letting it happen. The wolf nudged her, using his body to push her towards Hale. She looked into the wolf's eyes. The yellow glowed with a mirror of Hale's pain. He wanted something from her, but she wasn't sure what.

'You can't give me what he wants,' Hale said, once again somehow knowing her mind even though she'd not spoken.

'How about you let me decide that?' Sam said stubbornly, moving to block Hale's view of his teenage self.

'He thinks you can help me,' Hale said, but he shook his head. 'But you can't. We're already dead.'

Bile burned Sam's throat. But he was wrong. He wasn't dead. If he was, surely neither of them would be here. She certainly wasn't dead.

Hale frowned.

'Why can't I sense what you're thinking?' Sam asked. She half expected the corridor to shift again and follow the boy, but it remained stable. The memory followed this Hale, not the teenager.

Connection not completed.

The voice came from all around her, or maybe inside her head. She wasn't sure. But she didn't have to look far for the source. Hale's wolf stared at her, yellow eyes sparking brightly.

'She isn't a wolf. You saw how my mother reacted to what I was. She thought she knew what she was getting into when she married my father. She regretted every moment. I won't put that on anyone else,' Hale said. The argument had the tone of something he'd said before as he glared at his wolf.

'I think that should be my choice, don't you?' Sam said, not letting any of her doubts show. She wasn't committing to marry the man, just save him. Though a small piece of her couldn't argue with the image that the idea inspired.

'You were afraid I was going to attack you at the yew tree earlier. Afraid of me. Tell me that I'm wrong?' Hale said, looking away from her.

Hale was right. She'd been afraid. 'You lunged straight at me. What did you expect me to do?' Sam asked, annoyance sharp enough that she stepped straight into his personal space. Something she knew better than to do with any wolf, let alone an alpha. 'Am I afraid now?'

Hale's eyes flashed gold as he dragged in a deep breath. He didn't answer her.

'Let me help you. If you don't let me in, you'll die,' Sam said, voice breaking at the thought of losing him, though she wasn't sure where her certainty came from. Hale's wolf pressed into the back of her legs, shaking. He felt it too. Felt the danger.

Hale still hesitated.

'Unless you want to abandon your pack?' Sam said, keeping her chin up high as Hale's anger washed over her. It had been a low blow that she'd known would hit hard.

He closed the small gap between them, body pressing against hers. She was sandwiched between him and his wolf, but again, there was no fear. Nothing but the certainty that this was her only chance to save him.

'Don't think I can't see what you did,' Hale said, voice low. But his eyes dipped to her lips, and the anger was already gone.

He was so close to her height that it would be barely any effort to pull him towards her. But he was the one who needed to let her in.

'As long as you live, I don't care,' Sam said, reaching up to wrap a hand around his neck. How many times has she imagined this moment?

A rush of pleasure filled her as she got a hint of Hale's thoughts for the first time. She'd not been the only one to imagine it. Surprise almost made her back away, but she wasn't done yet. He hadn't let her all the way in.

'I'm not sure I know how,' Hale said, voice a bare whisper. But he didn't wait for an answer as he leaned into her, pressing his lips to hers.

It was enough of a choice.

A fiery heat and energy flowed between them like a floodgate had opened. She wanted to linger in the sensation, to soak it up, but she barely got a taste of him before the darkness grabbed her and dragged her under.

SAM SHUDDERED AS THE world around her shifted, and she found herself in the clearing once more, Hale's wolf form under her fingers. She felt the fragments of his thoughts. His satisfaction that he'd won the fight. That he'd protected her. The pain of reliving the memory of his mum.

The connection was no longer just a tug towards Hale. It was something new. Something more. Something she'd figure out later. But right now, she had a way to help him. If she had enough strength left. Her eyelids dropped, barely wanting to stay open, and her body ached.

With effort, she pushed aside her doubts and buried one of her hands in the dirt. His blood had started to soak into the ground, turning it into a sticky mud. Suppressing a shudder, she focused on the energy flow pouring into Hale. Her energy. Which was probably why she was so damned tired.

Carefully, Sam reached out to the Land again, letting the energy flow through her from the yew tree. It didn't ease any of her aches. She couldn't heal herself with the magic. Something she'd learned the hard way after she'd broken her arm falling out of a tree.

Once she had the energy firmly in hand, she directed it into the new link to Hale.

Heal him, she thought. Imagining his wounds closed and his breathing unlaboured. Creating an image of him whole and healed.

The energy seemed to understand what she wanted because immediately the stream strengthened into a sharp slash of power. This wasn't a gentle flow, like when she'd healed the tree. This was a tsunami.

The claw slash on his side closed from the inside out, knitting muscles together, ripping a scream from her as she felt it like it was her own side. Nausea threatened to make her throw up again as his back leg came next. Old scabs fell away as new flesh grew under the fur, and something deep inside his leg reconnected.

But the magic didn't stop there.

She'd not been specific enough in what she'd wanted. The magic kept moving through Hale, healing everything. Wounds he probably hadn't even known he had. Then, finally, his blood. Acid burned through her veins. She didn't know if it was replacing the blood that had been lost, or clearing the venom, but either way, she'd never felt pain like it.

She could barely breathe as everything spun around her, threatening to pull her back into the darkness.

Then, finally, the pain eased, and she could pull in a full breath. But the relief was short-lived as something changed. Something deep inside Hale.

Sam screamed, fighting against the new pain, unable to escape as it raged through his body. Something was wrong.

Hale was being torn apart.

His bones shattered, then scraped against each other as they were remade.

His skin was on fire, as if he was being burned alive.

The air was too thin for him to breathe. His chest felt too small to pull in more.

She was lost in his pain, as broken as he was. The energy from the Land kept coming, pouring through her in crashing waves to Hale through the link.

Until it was finally done, and Hale lay under her, his now human skin slick with sweat.

She was in too much pain to hold the connection to the Land once the magic stopped and it slipped away from her without warning. There was no need for mental walls. The pain was enough of a barrier now that the flow had stopped.

She wanted to check on Hale, see if he really was alright, but without the magic to keep her awake, the darkness surrounded her and pulled her under again.

CHAPTER NINE

AMELIA FELL TO HER knees as pain tore through her. It was like a part of her was being ripped out. Her wolf howled, trying to steal control and shift. She fought against both the pain and her wolf.

What was happening?

Something bad.

Amelia tried to force herself to focus on the slight pain in her knees as they ached where she'd hit the hard tiled floor. That pain was easier than the deep shredding inside her chest, like her soul was being split down the middle.

Blinking away tears, she forced herself to look up. Oliver was bent almost double, white knuckle showing against the metal table where they'd been cleaning yesterday's weapons.

Not just her, then.

But what had happened?

It had felt like something had been rippe––

Hale! Luna howled, tearing at her mind.

Her breath caught as she searched for the bonds that tied her to him. They were nothing but tattered fragments, already splitting away from her. Hale was their alpha, and without him, the pack didn't exist.

There was only one way an alpha let go of the pack like this, with no transfer. Death.

'Amelia?' Oliver asked, voice trembling as he raised his head. His eyes were amber, his wolf shining through. Amelia didn't doubt hers showed the blue of her own wolf, too.

She still sensed Oliver as pack. Just. But it was fading. He staggered round the table. Their joint fear and pain was all she could smell. He stumbled to his knees in front of her, placing a hand on her shoulder like he could hold on to the connection. But he couldn't, not without an alpha to bind the pack together.

'Hale,' Amelia whispered.

Another wave of pain burned through her as something pulled at the tattered connections. Unfamiliar, aggressive, and impatient. At first, she was terrified it was her family pack. But they were too far away, the little knot of connection distant. No, this was something closer––something trying to take control of her.

'Son of a bitch,' Oliver snarled, head snapping back as he arched his back. 'Shane.'

Amelia screamed again as the new connection tore through her mind, not just pulling in the tatters but also ripping apart that link back to her family pack. Her stomach twisted, bile burning a harsh path up her throat as she vomited up the food she'd eaten only an hour ago.

It was like red hot wires were being used to tie the pack bonds back together. She'd never experienced pain like this, not when Hale had bound her or when she'd turned wolf for the first time and had joined her family pack.

This was messy. Clumsy. Reckless.

Never before had she realised how much care an alpha took over their pack. How much damage they could actually do.

Hurts, Luna cried, trying to twist away from what felt like an attack. But there was nowhere to escape. Not when she was still tied up in the shredded bond to Hale.

I'm here. It's going to be okay, Amelia whispered to her, trying to wrap herself around her wolf. To calm her. But she was beyond reason. She only knew pain.

Slowly, Shane settled into the back of her mind, taking Hale's place as alpha. But unlike Hale, this wasn't a subtle presence. No. Shane was a black hole rising to the east. Calling to her. Pressing on her to come to him.

Going by Oliver's groan, Amelia wasn't the only one being summoned.

She struggled to take a deep breath as her whole body ached like she'd been rolled down a mountain, hitting every rock on the way. She didn't think she had the strength to crawl, let alone walk. But the pressure built, growing sharper.

'Can you stand?' Oliver asked, gripping her arm like he wanted to support her, though he didn't look any better than she felt.

Amelia nodded, though she wasn't sure she could. She didn't think she was going to get a choice, though.

'I'll drive,' Oliver said, but with his wolf so close to the surface, she couldn't imagine how. But somehow, he forced himself to his feet and helped her up.

Amelia couldn't do much more than cling to him as they abandoned the half-assembled guns, out in plain sight, and limped towards the exit.

They found Lance in the lobby, slumped against the wall, skin covered in a sheen of sweat. He didn't speak as he looked at them, his wolf's energy licking at her skin.

'I'm driving,' Oliver said, that calm energy of his spreading out despite the pain.

Lance blinked slowly, like he was considering it, then nodded and pushed away from the wall. How either of them could stand she didn't know, because another wave of energy from Shane made her double up in pain.

'It will be okay,' Oliver whispered. Amelia wasn't sure if he was talking to her, or himself, as he kept one arm around her waist and led them toward the car. 'Once we get to Shane, the pain will stop.'

Amelia couldn't find the energy to argue with him. Shane was hurting them. Either he didn't know, or he didn't care. But it didn't make the hurt any less.

She wouldn't have made it to the car without Oliver, and she doubted Lance would have been able to drive either. Many of the pack wouldn't be so lucky to have that support.

They'd lost Hale, but if Shane didn't loosen his grip, that might not be the only member of the pack they lost today.

CHAPTER TEN

Hale struggled to grasp onto something solid as the world spun around him. There had been pain––a lot of pain––but that was gone now, leaving only a tingle of energy and the post-full-moon buzz of restlessness.

A weight pressed down on him, warm and comfortable. Sam. She breathed slowly, body relaxed against him. Her scent filled his nose with a mix of honeysuckle and fresh earth. Something he shouldn't have been able to smell for hours yet.

What had happened?

He remembered killing the imp, but he'd been sloppy. Its claws had torn into his side. Then Sam had been there, hand against him. But there hadn't been anything she could do. The wound had been too deep. He'd felt it. Felt himself dying.

Except he was still here. How?

'Unless you want to abandon your pack?' Sam said, chin lifted defiantly as she challenged him.

The memory rippled through him, like a dream, half remembered. He'd been with her in a white hallway. She'd seen his mother walk away. She'd seen him lose control. And still she'd stood in front of him without fear. His own wolf pressed against her, encouraging her.

Needed. You not listen, Fang said. It was a distant whisper, more so than after a normal full moon run. Not that this full moon had been anything like normal.

The pain from shifting to his human form had been worse than any shift in his memory. It had been like he'd been torn apart, then patched back together. Sam had been there with him, part of him, like she was inside him. He still felt the echo of her fear and pain.

Sam had saved him.

He let the feel of her soak into him. It wasn't the same as how the pack felt; it was deeper somehow. He had to stop himself from reaching out to her through it. She was tired, exhausted from whatever she'd done to save him.

From the Earth Magic.

Magic that could heal. But how? Hale had never heard that anything like that was possible. But why would he? The government refused to let Earth Elementals settle anywhere long enough that they could use their magic. But why would they fear healing?

Powerful, Fang said, tone filled with pride and respect. Both were rare emotions from his beast.

His wolf wasn't wrong, though. To bring Hale back from the brink of death wasn't a small thing. Was this something she could do to others?

Ours, Fang said, nearly snarling as he imagined anyone else having a connection to Sam.

Hale didn't bother arguing with his wolf. He was too tired. But just because his wolf thought she was theirs didn't mean Sam wanted him. But the memory of her lips on his rose in his mind.

Sam stirred against him, then woke all at once and pulled back from where she lay on his chest. Her emotions flickered too fast to follow as her breath caught.

Hale opened his eyes, fear spiking as he expected another threat. But Sam wasn't looking around her. She was looking at him, eyes travelling down his chest slowly, burning a fiery trail in their wake. Her desire flared, both in her scent and in her eyes.

His wolf nearly purred at the attention, the moon lust stirring through him, pooling in his groin. Naked as he was, there was little he could do to hide it. He wanted her to trail her fingers in the same path her eyes had taken. To get lost in her scent and forget everything that had happened. To wake with her in his arms as the sun rose tomorrow.

The thought made him freeze. Just because she wasn't human didn't mean that she'd want to be part of the pack. It didn't mean she wouldn't run. Wouldn't abandon a child.

Hale swallowed the painful memory. It was irrelevant right now. Sam had never wanted to be a part of his life before. There was no reason to believe what had happened had changed her thoughts on the matter.

Sam's hand rose like she was about to reach out and touch him. A sound, somewhere between a groan and a growl, slipped from him before he could stop it. Her hand shot back to her side as she met his eyes, flushing. She was cute when she blushed. But as Hale looked closer, there was more than the flush on her cheeks. Blood smeared down from her nose to her jaw.

He drew in a quick breath as fear hit him, but he only smelled his and the imp's blood. Not hers. The relief made his chest loosen like he could take a full breath again. She wasn't hurt. At least not physically. He could feel her fatigue still. It was the only individual feeling he could make out through the new bond.

'Thank you,' Hale said, his voice hoarse. He might not understand exactly what had happened, but he knew Sam had saved him. He knew it without understanding how.

Sam gave him a tired smile. 'You saved me first,' she said, pulling back a little further, moving to tuck a strand of hair behind her ear, but hesitated as she saw the blood on them. She lowered her hands, wiping them against her dress. Her fear hit him through the new link even before it soured the air. She shook her head, turned away, then immediately grew still.

He followed her gaze to the yew tree. Or what was left of it. The tree was a skeleton of what it had been. More leaves were on the ground than on the branches. The edges of the clearing were just as sickly looking, heather brittle and yellow, and the ferns brown and sagging.

She'd done this to save him.

He knew logically everything had a cost. When he shifted, it took energy from him, something that was easy to fix with food. But this was different. She'd saved him with the energy she'd taken from the Land. He hadn't even thought something like that had been possible. If she could take energy from the Land, what else could she take energy from?

Maybe this was why the government had been so afraid of Earth Elementals? If they even remembered themselves.

Sam pulled further back from him, breaking the connection. It was like he'd been dunked in cold water as she took the warmth with her. The little knot of her emotions faded as well, and it took effort to stop himself from reaching out to draw her back. She'd been sad and afraid, and he wanted to tell her it was okay. That everything was going to be fine. But he didn't know that for sure, nor did he know if she'd welcome him.

Ours, Fang repeated sleepily in the back of his mind. *Protect.*

But she wasn't theirs. Sam was her own person and would make her own decisions. Going by the scent of her fear, that wouldn't involve falling into his arms any time soon. Even if the rest of her scent screamed that she wanted to.

Hale shifted position, moving his arm to at least partially hide his attraction to her. It was a painful throb that he wasn't optimistic about resolving soon. The rest of his body protested loudly at the movement as well. Most of it was bone-deep weariness from the speed of the change. It wouldn't last long, but for now, he felt like a slow old man.

'Are you okay?' Sam asked, turning back to him. This time she never looked down his body, though part of him desperately wanted her to.

'Are you?' Hale asked, to avoid answering as he watched her.

Sam frowned at him, clearly unimpressed by his evasion. She turned and stared at the tree again, like she wanted to will it alive. He let her keep the silence, feeling something more under it. Another question she wanted to ask.

Protect, Fang whispered again, wanting Hale to wrap his arms around her. He wasn't a fan of keeping their distance.

'Are you going to tell anyone?' Sam asked at last, wrapping her arms around herself. She didn't turn around, but her voice held suspicion like she was waiting for him to do something that would hurt her.

'It's not my secret to share,' he said, wishing he had more than words to give her.

'I can't let them take this place from me,' Sam said, voice tight. 'It's all I've left of my family. Without me, the Land will die.'

Hale heard the emphasis on the word Land. It was the same way many of the pack referred to their wolves. A kind of acknowledgement that it existed separately to them. He remembered the feel of the ground under his feet as he had run to find Sam. Maybe it hadn't all been her like he'd first thought.

'I'd never do anything to hurt you,' Hale said. But it left him with the sensation that all he had was words, and words weren't enough. Not when it was her future on the line. She had saved his life knowing he'd find out this truth.

She stared at him, still afraid as she weighed him with her eyes, debating if she trusted him with this secret. He hated seeing that fear. She shouldn't have to hide. She shouldn't have been forced to be alone.

Hale leaned closer, gently placing a hand on her cheek to wipe away a smear of blood. The connection flared between them. Unlike the pack bonds, this one had no walls built up to keep his thoughts his own. He let her feel everything he did. Her breath caught, eyes growing wide.

'I promise I won't tell anyone what you are,' he said. The connection between them deepened now that he was touching her again. He felt her fear and suspicion like an old wound. He hadn't entirely convinced her, but his stomach chose that moment to growl loudly in the quiet clearing.

Her lips twitched, some of the tension breaking. He lowered his hand, pulling back to give her space. He felt the loss of the connection like a blow again but satisfied himself by inhaling her scent. The fear was less now.

'Would you like something to eat?' she asked.

Hale bit back a growl of pleasure at the offer. The idea of her feeding him was more than a little appealing. That was enough to tell him he should get dressed and walk away. Go home and stay away from people until the Moon Fever passed. But that wasn't the words that came out of his mouth.

'Yes,' he said. 'Please.'

Sam nodded, a blush colouring her cheeks like she'd sensed there was more to his hunger. Then she stood slowly, turning towards the house.

He forced himself to his feet, following her, scanning the woods just in case something else had approached while they'd been talking. That he'd only just remembered to check around them for that danger annoyed him.

The imp's corpse lay in the dead grass behind him, and there were still scorpions in the woods. Yet a sense of safety had settled into his gut like the warmth of the sun, and even his wolf seemed content to trust it.

Though *what* they were trusting, Hale wasn't sure.

Home, Fang said, pressing Hale to take in another deep breath. The forest filled his nose. Tangy pine trees, warm earth and the sweet honeysuckle scent that was just Sam. Like she was part of the land.

Hale turned the idea over in his head and decided it might not be that far from the truth. How many times had he thought her scent had surrounded him in the forest? He'd never questioned it. Maybe he should have. Though it was a little late to ask questions when he knew the answers.

But regardless of how it felt, this wasn't their home. It belonged to Sam. He doubted she'd appreciate him claiming it.

THE WALK BACK TO the house seemed more like miles to Sam, rather than metres. She was stiff and sore, like she'd run a marathon, though she knew she'd physically done very little. The connection, whatever it had been, had taken a lot of energy from her, as well as the yew tree.

Guilt flickered through her. The old tree was going to die. She'd taken too much from one place to save Hale. Thinking of the power that had ripped through her made her head throb harder, like someone was beating her slowly with a hammer, which was probably just as well because, without the pain, she might have been tempted to do something stupid.

Fun. But stupid.

Unless Hale had meant what he'd said about keeping her secret?

He followed silently behind her, energy a wall of heat pressing against her back. She remembered the way he'd looked on the forest floor. Covered in the residual dirt and gore, he'd seemed almost primal. All solid muscles, with not an inch of fat on him as he pulled up one knee to hide his obvious attraction.

To her.

That thrill set her stomach alight. Her fingers itched to reach out and touch him despite the throbbing in her head, but she kept them at her side. How much of his attraction was because of the full Moon Fever? Would he still feel the same way once he was back to a level head again?

Sam took a slow breath, not liking that she was even considering doing anything with Hale. She didn't need to make this any more complicated than it already was. It didn't matter if he wanted her or not; she was going to keep her distance, at least until she decided if she could trust him to keep her secret.

He'd sounded sincere. Hell, he'd felt sincere with his hand on her cheek, sending wave after wave of emotions through her. So many of her own emotions echoed his that she hadn't been sure where he had ended and she had begun. But could she trust it?

Her father's expression when he'd found out Sam's secret flashed through her head. The horror and disgust had been so clear that it made her stomach twist. He was her family, and he'd not been able to accept what Sam was. A new memory followed the old one. Hale's mum turning away from him. He understood the pain of rejection.

Except it wasn't really the same. It hadn't been his fault his mum had left, unlike Sam, who was entirely to blame. Her foolishness had not only made her father leave, but it had killed both her parents. Would Hale be so willing to keep her secret when he found that out?

She didn't know. Another reason why keeping her distance would be safer. No matter how much her whole body vibrated with the need to have Hale touch her again.

It was an effort not to sigh in relief when she entered the house, like it offered safety. But Hale wasn't something the house could protect her from. Not that she needed protection. Just a cold shower.

She'd taken Hale through the back door, straight into her kitchen. The room was stuffy from the heat outside, but the burgers she'd defrosted for Lacey earlier sat in the microwave still, the timer long since gone off.

Forcing a smile, she turned to Hale. Every intention of asking him if he was okay with burgers. But the question died on her lips as she found him closer than she'd expected. She tried to step back, but her own feet tangled her up and she tipped backwards. Hale grabbed her, stopping her from falling on her arse.

The connection that sprang up washed over her mind like fireworks. Lust, need, desire. It tugged at her own needs, whispering how easy it would be to just close the distance. Let herself give in. But it was more than just that. There was the need to protect and defend. To keep her safe.

Hale's nose flared wide as he helped her stand. She flushed, though it wasn't like he'd need to smell her to know how much she wanted him. The connection between them would broadcast it loud and clear. But even though he must have felt her desire, he didn't press her, leaving it up to her to close the gap.

She wanted to, wanted to step into his arms and forget everything that had happened today. Forget all the reasons she'd thought it was a bad idea only a moment before. How many times had she walked away from him in the past seven years? Each time, it had been to protect herself and her secret. But he knew it now and had said he'd keep it.

Dammit, why couldn't she make up her mind still? Stop this loop. The facts didn't change, yet they repeated over and over in her head.

'Why would you want to keep my secret?' Sam blurted out, heart skipping a beat as the question hovered between them.

'It's not my secret to share,' Hale said, like it was that simple. But it couldn't be. No one kept a secret like that for nothing.

Not when there was something Sam had that the pack wanted.

'But you want more time on my Land?' Sam said, wincing as his expression closed. The link swirled with emotions, but they moved so fast that she couldn't figure out what they were.

He was silent for a long minute, but Sam didn't retract the question. Lacey's words yesterday, and how Shane had acted to get Hale to stay, had put Sam on edge. She had to know if it had come from him.

'That's not something that's being asked for,' Hale said, phrasing odd. She sensed anger rising above the chaos in the connection between them, but it wasn't aimed at her. Then who?

'Lacey seemed to think that someone was supposed to be asking me about it,' Sam said.

This time, Hale's flash of annoyance made it on to his face. 'She only has half a story,' Hale said. He looked down at his hand on her arm, like he was considering if he wanted to keep the link open, but then he sighed and continued.

'The prime alphas have refused to allow any conversation around extending the land rental,' Hale said slowly.

'Why would they do that?' Sam asked, then nearly pulled her hand away as Hale's anger hit her. Again, it wasn't aimed at her.

'There's stability in a regular place to shift and run, a comfort in it. They're afraid that Shifters would want to stay here if they had it. Then being sent here wouldn't be a punishment anymore,' Hale said, reining back that anger with a slow exhale. 'The harder their experience here is, the less likely they are to misbehave again and want to come back.'

Sam shivered. She'd known that Shifters didn't choose to go north, but that the prime alphas outright considered it a punishment was news to her. Lacey's frustrations were making more sense, but why didn't Hale just tell her the prime alphas had said no? There was more to it that he wasn't saying.

'Why not just tell the pack that?' Sam asked.

'After a Shifter serves their year here, they'll go back under one of those prime alphas,' Hale said, lips twisting into a weak smile. 'It's better if they dislike me and think I'm blocking the land than knowing the prime alphas are responsible. As it stands, few want to come back here for a second visit. If they don't like me, it's not a big deal.'

Sam didn't know much about the prime alphas, but she wasn't impressed by what she was hearing. But something else registered. Hale had given her a secret. One he'd kept from the pack. One that could change everything.

'Why didn't you ask me, anyway?' Sam asked as she felt the echoes of his frustration. 'I can't imagine they could do much once you signed the contract?' Even as she said the words, her stomach twisted.

'You never wanted to stay here even for just the full moon. It wasn't fair to ask you to spend even less time at home,' Hale said, giving her a small smile. 'Now that I know why, I know what your answer would have been.'

Sam looked away as she realised he was right. She'd never have said yes, and the question would have made every-thing awkward, especially when she'd never have been willing to tell him the truth.

'Why not try to get someone else to rent their land in-stead?' Sam said. 'Someone who wouldn't care about the pack being on the land more often?'

Hale was silent so long that Sam pulled her gaze away from the worn tiles on her kitchen floor to meet his eyes. They swirled to gold and back, his wolf dancing just under the surface.

'Because we wanted to run here,' Hale said, voice low. The 'we' in that sentence wasn't the pack. She felt Hale's wolf. He cleared his throat, then added, '...besides, as soon as the prime alphas found out, they'd pressure whoever had made the agreement and try to reverse it. The pack might end up with nowhere to shift.'

Despite his additional clarification, the energy between them flowed back to tantalising desire. Though in fairness, it hadn't exactly gone away, even if she'd nearly forgotten that Hale was naked in front of her.

Attraction had never been the issue for either of them, it seemed. But for once, that crushing fear of letting someone close had loosened. Hale already knew her secret, and now she knew one of his.

There was only one question left.

'What happens tomorrow?' Sam asked, heat flushing her cheeks as she fought her embarrassment. 'When the Moon Fever is gone, will you regret telling me the truth?'

Though the truth wasn't really what she was worried about him regretting.

Hale frowned, then shook his head. 'That's not how it works. The Moon Fever isn't some drug we ride on the back of. It's who we are but are always forced to suppress.'

'Really? You're telling me that you always walk around like that when we are in the same room?' Sam said, managing not to look down by some miracle.

Hale smiled, a tiny flush flaring across his neck. 'Attraction has never been the problem,' Hale said, echoing her earlier thought.

Sam blinked at him. That hadn't been the answer she'd expected.

'Pack life isn't for everyone,' Hale said, his thoughts clearly going to his mum, Sam realised, as he looked away.

'So, you think you get to make that choice for me?' Sam said, anger sparking.

'Like you made mine for me?' Hale said gently, though the two scenarios didn't exactly equate. He wouldn't risk his freedom by starting something with her.

Heat flared in Sam's cheeks again, regardless.

'But to go back to your original question,' Hale said, slowly letting go of her arm. 'I'm not under the influence, and I'm perfectly capable of making decisions. So are you.'

Sam inhaled sharply. She no longer felt Hale, and that loss left a small pit in her stomach. He stood still in front of her, body wire tight as he left it up to her, giving her the space to make her own choice. Without the connection feeding her his emotions.

That she might not have known the difference wasn't a thought that had even crossed her mind. But her desire didn't lessen with the break in contact. It just settled to almost painful levels in her stomach.

She felt like a teenager waiting for her first kiss, though it wasn't like Hale would be her first lover, or even her second. The need to keep her secret close had meant she couldn't have anything long term, but there were plenty of people out there looking for nothing more than a one-night stand and a release.

This was different, though. She'd felt it every time she'd been near him. This wasn't a brief encounter between two people who needed to let off steam. There was something more here that she'd been running from for a long time.

And she was very tired of running.

Sam took a deep breath, then let it go sharply as she stepped forward, closing the gap between them. Hale reached out to her, wrapping an arm around her waist as her lips met his.

HALE GROANED AS SAM'S lips finally met his. How long had he wanted to do this? To have her in his arms? Since the day he'd met her? The desire to taste her had been in his head for so long that he was almost afraid that the reality wouldn't meet the expectation. But he was so very wrong about that.

She tasted like she smelled. Like the forest and honeysuckle, of the wildness of the hunt. Of anticipation. Or at least that's what the half of his brain that was still working told him.

All that separated them was the thin cotton of her dress. It rubbed against him, creating friction with every movement. Sam wrapped a hand around the back of his neck, pulling him closer, fingernails scraping against his skin, making him shiver. Her tongue darted into his mouth, tasting him in turn.

Hale pulled back to draw in a deep breath. He could smell their arousal in the air, but underneath there were less pleasant smells, a reminder that they were far from clean. Leaving her even for a minute to deal with that wasn't an option he wanted to consider. But maybe they could kill two birds with one stone?

'Shower?' Hale said, moving to kiss the side of her neck.

'Upstairs,' Sam said through a shuddering breath, but she made no move to head in that direction. 'Bigger.'

Hale smiled, lowering his hands to her butt and lifting her in one smooth motion. She gave a small squeak as she wrapped her legs around his waist and tightened her grip around his neck.

He stood still, enjoying the feeling of her in his arms. She wasn't heavy, but the weight felt good against him. His wolf felt it too, the connection.

Mate, Fang whispered to him, almost asleep after the strain of everything that had happened. *Pack.*

Hale didn't have the presence of mind to argue with his wolf as Sam ran a series of kisses along his jaw. Her bare legs felt like a furnace against him. If she was just a little lower…

She wriggled against him, making his hips jerk forward, like his body was trying to complete the connection without him. She gasped, dropping her head back, tightening her legs around his waist.

Hale groaned, pressing Sam against the kitchen wall so he could slide his hand under her dress, enjoying the silky feel of her skin under his fingers. She might not have been as strong as a wolf, but there were muscles there. Strength that came from hard work and hiking around the edges of the Rift Scar.

Moving his hand higher, he ran his fingers around her hip, finding the waistband of her panties. He followed the edge of the material, making Sam squirm at his light touch, but he stopped before he reached her inner thigh, then just as slowly moved his hand back over the same path.

Sam moaned and squirmed against him, creating more friction. Her panties ripped between his fingers, the material falling away on one side.

Sam laughed, clearly having heard the sound. Her breasts strained against the dress as she dragged in a deep breath. He wanted so badly to rip the dress away as well and slip inside her right here.

But in the corner of his eye, he could see black specs flake off the material and fall to the tiles under his feet. Very little of it was mud. Sam saw it too. It cooled the lust between them a little, leaving them both panting for breath. It was the reminder he needed that he'd been heading towards the shower. Both of them needed to be clean.

Besides, this wasn't how he wanted their first time to be. A few thrusts against a wall where he'd likely lose his shit long before she did.

'Shower,' Hale said again, gritting his teeth as he stepped back from the wall, easily balancing her weight. He forced his feet forward, never breaking contact with Sam, as he headed to the stairs and climbed. Every step was torture, yet he never wanted the stairs to end.

He followed Sam's directions to her bedroom and en-suite bathroom. Her bedroom was enormous, with wooden floors and pale cream walls. He had just about enough awareness to see the king-size bed and a balcony door on the far side of the room. Then they were in the bathroom.

The massive shower took up one corner of the room. It was done in white with hints of red here and there to add colour. Even now, when they were near the shower, he didn't want to let Sam go. But the alternative was to step into the shower fully dressed and turn on cold water.

Sam seemed to sense his hesitation, and she loosened her tight grip around his waist and ever so slowly slid to the floor. He let her, enjoying the softness of her skin against his. She was just a little shorter than him, and she lingered there, pressed against his chest, dropping a single slow kiss to his lips, then she stepped back.

Losing the connection made him shiver like a cold draft had rolled into the room. It hadn't. The room had one small window that was closed, and it was as stuffy as the kitchen had been.

Sam pressed a button near the shower, and the water started, then she turned back to him. Her bright green eyes nearly glowed as she looked him up and down, biting her lip. He wanted to go to her and peel the dress off. But Sam beat him to it.

With one smooth motion, she grabbed the bottom of the dress and dragged it over her head, then let it drop to the ground along with the torn remains of her pants. Then she reached up to pull out the hairband, letting her hair out of its messy bun. Blond curls fell over her shoulders, covering her breasts.

Even without the bond, he felt her discomfort as he let his gaze linger on her. He hadn't experienced that kind of awkwardness since the first few years after becoming a

Shifter. You learned early to lose your inhibition when you had to get naked to change forms. But he did remember it.

'You're beautiful,' Hale said. The words weren't enough. He wasn't sure there was a word that could describe what he saw when he looked at her. How much he loved her sun-kissed skin and summer tan lines. Or the way the green in her eyes reflected the light like he was staring at emeralds. But it made her smile, and he'd take that above any flowery speech.

She reached out to him. He closed the gap between them again, letting her walk them back into the shower.

The water was a warm wash against his skin, making him close his eyes, enjoying the feel against his shoulders, and Sam's heat in front of him. Tension he hadn't known was there, started to fall away.

Hale opened his eyes to watch black and red streaks swirl under them. Most of it was coming from him. Another reminder that while sex in a shower sounded like an excellent idea, it wasn't the reason they were there. Not the first one, anyway.

'This isn't how I imagined this going,' Sam said, amusement in her tone, though it was layered over other emotions like a mask. She had one shoulder under the spray of water, her eyes watching the black and red swirl headed towards the drain.

The image of her standing with that stick in her hands, attacking the imp, rose in his head. A fierce fighter trying to protect him despite her fear.

Strong, Fang said, though the images that followed also spoke of never wanting to put Sam in a situation where she had to display that kind of strength again.

Hale couldn't argue with that. But regardless of what he wanted, she had fought for him. Fought to defend him when she should've run. When others in his life had run from less.

Mate, Fang said again, giving Hale a mental shove that said he was being stupid.

Instead of answering his wolf, Hale focused on Sam again, drawing her chin up with one finger so he could ask her a question. 'Have you imagined this often?' Hale asked, going back to Sam's original words.

Another flush flooded her cheeks and desire peppered the air again. He bit back a groan as it rolled around him.

SAM LET OUT A slow breath as she realised what she'd said, but she wasn't going to take the words back now. Not when he looked at her like she was the last drop of water in the desert.

'Sometimes,' she said, voice rough, as she ran her hand up his arm slowly, enjoying the feel of him against her. Though, in truth, every day might have been a better frequency for her fantasies of him.

His eyes widened in surprise. Clearly that hadn't been the answer he'd expected.

'And how do these fantasies start?' Hale asked, a smile playing on his lips, shifting his body further into the shower spray. She followed the trail of water that poured over him. But this time, she didn't follow any of those multicoloured streaks. No, she only followed the clean water as it rolled off his shoulders and down a little strip of hair on his chest like an arrow, drawing her gaze lower.

He let her look without any nervous shifting or awkward hesitation that had been her experience with previous lovers. Hell, she'd felt awkward as he'd stared at her, despite his words to her. *Beautiful*. Though the discomfort stemmed more from vulnerability than vanity. Not that she wouldn't welcome the compliment.

Hale knew who and what he was. Not from arrogance, or even because he liked her looking, though it was obvious he did. No, he was just comfortable. Being naked for him was as normal as wearing clothes, and he was more than happy to let her watch him. She felt it through the bond as he held her.

'You would come in behind me,' Sam said, dragging her eyes back to Hale's so she could make herself form words and answer his question. She hesitated, but only for a second, then turned her body away from him slowly, feeling his hunger grow through the link, until she was forced to drop her hand from his, and she was once again alone in her head. His reaction gave her a confidence that his compliment earlier had not.

'What did I do then?' Hale whispered in her ear, close enough that he could have run his tongue over the skin of her neck, but he didn't touch her. Not yet.

A tremor ran through Sam as she forced herself to stay still. 'You would run your hand down my body,' Sam said, breath catching. He moved behind her. She ached for him to press himself against her, to be inside her. But she knew the game wasn't done yet.

The water spray hit her head and shoulders, making her gasp. Never before had she thought her water pressure had been good, but with Hale just behind her, it was like every inch of her was being caressed.

When the touch came, it was softer than she'd expected. A cloth sliding across her shoulder. Sam's core tightened as the connection between them fluttered, the material blocking it from fully forming. Each stroke was a flash of his desire mingling with hers. Then it was gone again.

He moved slowly, almost painfully so, as he cleaned her back, arms, legs, and butt. Sam had to raise a hand to the tiles in front of her, her body shaking as she tried to keep herself from turning around. Her hair fell forward, giving her a clear space to breathe, which was just as well. She might have drowned and not even noticed.

When he was done with her back, he reached around her and ran the cloth over her stomach. Still never touching her with any more than just the cloth.

She wanted to scream her frustration at him.

But she also never wanted it to end.

By the time he was done scrubbing the front of her body, her heart was pounding in her chest, and she was panting. She heard the cloth land on the shower basin a second before she felt his fingers trail along her back.

She moaned and writhed, unable to hold still any longer as the connection burst up between them. He dipped his fingers lower, sliding down her hip. She raised her other hand to the tiles, legs barely holding her weight.

Hale's fingers brushed the edge of her sex, not even making full contact. But even that was too much.

The orgasm that rocked through Sam made her cry out and arch back against Hale. The connection between them solidified, and she felt him, felt how close he was. Then he followed her into bliss, hips jerking as he came against her back. Another orgasm hit her almost as hard as the first one had.

Then another.

Nothing existed except for Hale and the pleasure that knotted her body so tightly it almost hurt.

She couldn't tell where she ended, and he began.

And she didn't care one bit.

CHAPTER ELEVEN

HALE'S LEGS SHOOK AS he held Sam against him, the water from the shower caressing his shoulders and back. Feeling their combined pleasure had been an experience that he wouldn't soon forget. Hell, he was damned near ready to go again.

Which was when his stomach once again growled.

Sam chuckled, moving against him, her own hunger and tiredness rising. 'I seem to recall we had been planning something very different before we got distracted?' she said. 'Do you still want those burgers?'

He wanted to tell her no. That food could wait, and he had far more interesting things to do. Like pressing her against the wall and continuing what they started, but the shaking legs were a bad sign.

Between Sam's healing and the shift back to human, they were both running on empty. As much as he wanted it to be otherwise, they needed something to eat. Probably rest too, but he wasn't sure his willpower was that good.

Sighing, he loosened his grip where he had wrapped his arms around her. 'Burgers sound fantastic,' Hale said.

Sam turned in his arms. He was so close he could see the flecks of yellow in her green eyes. 'I'll go put them on,' she said, but she didn't immediately move away from him as she ran a hand over his shoulder.

'If you keep that up, neither of us are going to get to eat,' Hale said as his body stirred, wanting more. 'And I can feel how hungry you are, too.'

Sam flushed, desire trickling through the link, but it didn't quite override the hunger he sensed there. 'You're right,' Sam said, then paused as her stomach growled as if to echo her words. 'Some of my body even agrees.'

Hale smiled, dropping his lips to hers, tasting the clean water running over them. He'd planned on the kiss being light, but it quickly turned into something deeper. When he pulled away, they were both breathless.

Reluctantly, she stepped back, breaking the connection between them. He shivered at the loss, half raising his hand towards her before he got himself under control. She took the towel from the rail and wrapped it around herself as she looked back at him.

'I'll be down in a minute,' Hale said as he watched her, not trusting himself to move. She nodded, her arousal as strong as his. Then she turned away and left, closing the door behind her.

Hale leaned against the shower wall, already missing Sam's warmth even with the hot water pouring over him. He fought not to call her back, even though his stomach cramped, twisting itself in a knot as it reminded him of the reason she'd left.

Pulling back from the wall, he wiped the water away from his eyes. Most of the dirt and gore that had covered him had washed off while he'd been taking care of Sam, but there were still a few patches clinging to him. He took the cloth that smelled of Sam, even with the soap, and started washing himself.

It was a bad idea. Images of Sam filled his head. Her body pressed against his. Wet. Hot. Soft.

Biting back a groan, he threw the water to cold as his erection throbbed. But with Sam's scent all around him, the water barely seemed to cool him at all.

He reached up to scrub his shoulder. Pain flared down his side where the Rift imp had sliced him. It was like a muscle was being pulled too tight rather than a wound. He moved his hand to the area, tracing it carefully with his fingers. There was no scar, or any mark, to reveal how he'd nearly died. But he remembered the feeling of his muscles tearing as the claws had shredded him to the bone. This level of healing shouldn't have been possible.

He shivered and pulled his hand away. Even shifting straight away didn't heal a wound to nothing but smooth flesh. Was Earth Magic really that powerful?

Mate, Fang said again, like it was that simple.

It wasn't. Mates were a fantasy, a myth. No matter how much he was drawn to Sam, or how he sensed her somewhere out in the house like she was part of the pack, she wasn't his mate.

Wrong, Fang said, sending him a sense of amusement. *Our mate.*

Hale shook his head and gave himself one last once-over with the soap, then rinsed and turned the water off. Grabbing the clean towel, which also smelled like Sam, he dried himself.

He couldn't hear Sam in the bedroom next door, but he caught a faint whiff of cooking meat, which meant she'd started the burgers. He wanted to go down to her and wrap his arms around her waist and...

Sighing, he cut the thought off before he got carried away. He needed to be practical. There were things that had to be done. The scorpions needed to be removed, along with the dead imp. He needed to find out who had planted them there and check on the pack.

Hell, he still didn't know if the target had been his wolves or Sam.

His wolf snarled in his head, not even bothering to form words as Fang echoed Hale's displeasure at either being targeted.

It was tempting to open his connection to the pack. But he'd tied the link down so tight that he was no longer able to feel them, and right now, he suspected that was for the best. With everything that had happened, his head was all over the place, and he didn't trust that his emotions would send the right message. But even with his side of the link shut tight, he would've felt it if something had happened to them.

Bring pack home, Fang said.

No, Hale said, pushing his wolf back from the pack bonds. The attacks had all been inside Sam's land, so the pack was still safer elsewhere for now.

Whoever had done this had been organised. Getting an imp this deep into Sam's land couldn't have been easy. If they'd brought in one imp, what was stopping them from bringing in others? No. If they had, then they'd have attacked with the first one. Unlike a scorpion, a cage wasn't going to hold an imp for long.

Shaking his head, Hale wiped the water from his face. The how would come later. But the list had helped him focus, though it wasn't enough to deflate his new erection. He wrapped a towel around his waist and headed out in search of his clothes.

He didn't have to go far. Sam had brought his jeans and T-shirt inside and put them on her bed. With reluctance, he dropped the towel that smelled of Sam and dragged his clothes on. His phone was still in his pocket, along with his car keys.

He pulled out his phone to dial Shane and have him deal with the scorpions, then stopped himself, cursing. Hale was supposed to be a wolf. Being in his human form this soon was a neon sign to the pack that clearly something had happened. They'd want answers. Answers he couldn't give them.

Not if he wanted to protect Sam's secret.

He put the phone back in his pocket and dragged in a slow breath, trying to think of another way to deal with the dead imp and scorpions.

A gun would have been useful, except he'd dropped off his weapons at the rangers' headquarters. He hadn't expected there to be trouble here. Not that a gun would have been useful while he'd been trapped as a wolf. Or really all that useful against scorpions when they were in those metal boxes, and there was no way he was letting Sam anywhere near them to help.

The smell of burgers grew stronger, making his stomach growl. All of this would have to wait until after he'd eaten. Shaking his head, he left Sam's bedroom and headed downstairs.

Hale paused at the doorway to the kitchen. Sam had pulled on another dress. It was a light green and shorter than the earlier one. She was staring out the window, chewing her lower lip. She might have looked worried, but all he could smell in her scent was arousal. Apparently, both of them wanted more.

He wanted to go to her, but his stomach twisted, angrily reminding him of his hunger. So instead, he stayed at the other end of the kitchen. He'd have to close the gap soon as the burgers looked just about ready where they sat under the grill. Tiny sparks of grease flashed off the element.

'The burgers are pretty much done,' Sam said as she turned to the grill to check on them.

Hale's breath caught. Clearly, that new radar system went both ways. A thrill went through him at the idea, but the rest of him worried. He'd spent a long time keeping others out of his head, and now Sam had a connection he didn't understand. Could she sense him now? He couldn't sense her, just see her worry in how she stood, and smelled her arousal. He had to assume it was the same for her, without the scent part.

He wanted to ask her why she was worried, but after everything that had happened, he'd have been more surprised if she hadn't been.

'Thank you,' Hale said, taking a seat at the table so he could watch her.

She pulled the burgers out and loaded them onto plates on the table. Then sat opposite him. There were no rolls, but that didn't slow him down. He was on his third by the time Sam had made it halfway through her first. She watched him from under her lashes. Knowing to give him half a dozen burgers was one thing but seeing him inhale them was another. He tried to slow down, but he was starving.

'There's more in the freezer if you're still hungry?' Sam said, lip-twitching as he picked up the fourth burger.

'These are more than enough,' he said, offering her a smile. He'd need more food later, but his body needed time to process what he was putting in it now, first.

They finished the food in comfortable silence, though that might have been the tiredness that was biting at his heels now that he was getting food. Unfortunately, he wasn't going to be able to rest quite yet.

'I'm going to go out and remove the body of the imp,' Hale said as he took the last bite of the sixth burger. It was the easiest of the tasks that needed doing.

Sam's fear returned, peppering the air, making his nose itch. 'Is it safe?'

'It's dead. It can't hurt anyone now,' Hale said, though he knew that was probably not what she'd meant.

'Do you think there might be more out there?' Sam shook her head as she said it. Like she was trying to clear a thought she didn't like.

The opportunity to ask her to let the pack search or to tell her about the scorpions in their cages couldn't have fitted in better. But he hesitated. What if she said no? What if that made her more afraid?

When Hale didn't answer, Sam shivered, rubbing her arms though it was far from cold in the kitchen. 'Do you need to get the rangers to check?' Sam asked, fear touching her scent. 'See if anything else got in?'

Surprise and guilt twisted in his stomach, making the burgers churn. That was exactly what he wanted to do. 'If I call them, they'll know something happened to me. I should still be a wolf until sometime late this evening,' Hale said carefully.

Sam looked away. That taste of fear didn't change. She'd known the risk of making that phone call, and she'd made the offer, anyway. 'Call them,' she said, standing, fingering the plate, but she didn't pick it up. 'I don't want anything getting out if we can help it.'

There were no restrictions. No warnings about not telling the pack. But her fear choked him.

'I meant what I said earlier. I won't tell them the truth or about your secret,' Hale said. 'But if I call them, they'll ask questions.'

'I understand the risk,' Sam said, finally picking up her plate and putting it by the sink. He wanted to get up and wrap his arms around her, ease her fear. But if he did that, he doubted anything else would get done.

'I'll call Shane when I go down to remove the dead imp. I won't be long, and I'll make sure the pack doesn't come this far to your house,' Hale said, moving to stand. 'It would be safer if you stayed here.'

'Like hell,' Sam said, narrowing her eyes at him, chin rising. 'I'm coming with you. I've lived here for the last seven years, and I'll be damned if some imp will have me cowering inside the house. It's dead.'

'Absolutely not,' Hale said, but a quiver in Sam's voice made it hard to argue with her.

'I can help,' Sam said, straightening, giving him a cool look. That same fighter spirit he'd seen when she'd defended him earlier flashed through her eyes. 'This is my home, my land. This is my choice.'

'You're not trained to deal with an attack if one comes,' Hale said, trying to keep his voice low, even though he wanted to reach out and pull her towards him. 'If there's something else out there, I won't put you at risk.'

'You almost died once today,' Sam said, voice losing the sharper edge of anger. 'Your training didn't help you last time. I'll not sit inside like a spare wheel, waiting to see if you get yourself killed. Besides, you just said it was safe.'

Hale growled, unable to help himself. Sam just lifted her chin higher. She wasn't backing down. But dammit, didn't that just make his need for her burn all the brighter?

'Fine,' Hale said, trying to keep hold of the anger. Maybe that would help him keep a level head. 'We need a tarp or something to wrap the imp in.'

Sam paled a little, but still didn't back down. 'I've something that will work.'

HALE STEPPED OUTSIDE ONTO the veranda, tempted not to wait for Sam as she looked for a tarp. But he knew she'd just follow later, and then she'd be alone in the woods. Besides, he still had to phone Shane.

The afternoon sunshine was just as hot as it had been yesterday and sweat broke out on the back of his neck immediately. That sense of safety he'd felt earlier returned, though slightly more muted now. It was strange, the certainty of that feeling, almost like contentment. But he couldn't pinpoint why he felt that way.

He scanned the edge of the woods, letting the rest of his senses reach out, but there was nothing out here but the normal afternoon activity. Rabbits, birds, and a fox somewhere not too far away, skulking out of sight. There was no silence that came with an approaching predator.

He hoped the scorpions were still locked in their cages. The traps had been laid deep in the woods, far away from Sam's house, so no one should stumble over them by accident. But if they'd somehow escaped, they'd have broken the aniseed bottles. Between that and the rot, he'd be able to smell them coming long before he saw them. Though, they were more likely to head to another trap with another member of their group, or to the Rift Scar, than move deeper into Sam's land. They'd already sounded sick, and they had to have been here since yesterday afternoon, at least.

Taking his phone out of his pocket, Hale pulled up Shane's number. He'd already said he was going to arrange additional patrols when he'd left. If Shane changed them, or was more specific about location, the rest of the rangers wouldn't be suspicious. Hale just had to convince Shane not to ask questions.

Hale dialled the number. The ring was loud in his ear, unnatural against the backdrop of such beauty. He wanted to step down and bury his bare feet in the dirt and let go of his worries and stress. Which was a strange impulse. Not that he didn't enjoy being outside, but never like he wanted to become part of the earth itself.

Shane answered on the eighth ring. 'Hello?' he said, sounding annoyed.

'Shane, I need you to organise a team to go into the woods around Sam's house. I found another three scorpions locked in cages. You need to go in and remove them,' Hale said, taking a breath as he wished Shane was here in person so he could press the secrecy, then added. 'But you can't tell them I called or that you spoke to me.'

There was silence.

'Hale?' Shane said. He sounded suspicious.

'I'll explain later. Can you organise the team?' Hale said, guilt gnawing at him. He was outright lying; he wasn't going to explain. Nor had he mentioned the Rift imp, but that might have made Shane overreact, and that was the last thing Hale needed just now.

'How––'

'Shane,' Hale said, interrupting, trying to moderate his tone. 'There are Rift creatures here on Sam's land. I need you to organise a team.'

Something Hale had said broke through because Shane inhaled sharply. 'I'll sort it.'

'Good. Don't tell anyone I called you. I'll explain to-morrow. But call me if the team finds any sign of other borders being breached.'

'Are you...okay?' Shane asked, voice strained.

'I'm fine,' Hale said, glancing over at Sam's garage as she appeared with a large piece of plastic. It was more than heavy-duty enough to handle the imp's body. 'Call me if you find anything.'

Hale didn't say goodbye as he hung up the phone and tucked it back in his pocket. Shane would get it done, Hale was sure, and quietly. But it didn't make him feel any better.

He felt like he was giving away a piece of Sam's secret despite his promise. His wolf paced in his head, no longer sleepy, equally uncomfortable with the division of pro-tecting the pack versus protecting Sam.

It was hard to stop himself from reaching out to the pack bonds to reinforce the need for silence. But at this distance, that wouldn't have done much more than draw Shane to him, which was the last thing he needed.

Hale inhaled slowly, trying to get control over his emo-tions as he watched Sam move towards him. The most important thing now was keeping her safe and removing the imp. All the rest would come later.

'Do you have a gun?' Hale asked Sam softly as she placed the heavy material on the veranda beside him. While civilians owning guns wasn't technically allowed, a lot of people overlooked that rule this far north and this close to the Rift Scar.

Sam shook her head, fear spiking, making him regret asking the question. He might not have expected an attack, but there was no point in being under-prepared, especially after everything that had happened.

'That's okay,' Hale said, looking back at the kitchen. 'We will make do with what we have. Though I'm sure we won't need it.'

But regardless of whether he thought it was safe, he was going to make damn sure he had a way to protect her if he needed to.

AMELIA SHUT SHANE'S FRONT door as quietly as she could, then took a step down off the porch. The old cottage, complete with a real thatch roof and thick stone walls, was too small for the pack that had gathered inside. Two dozen wolves would take up a lot of space at the best of times, but with the pain of losing an alpha, it felt like Amelia was being smothered.

The walls didn't do much to block the anxious Shifter energy. Only distance would do that. A lot of distance. Something she wasn't going to get with Shane's house being at least two miles outside Huntly and with Oliver still having the car keys.

Not that she planned on running away. She just needed some air and a chance to breathe past the hurt the pack was projecting.

Protect pack, Luna said, voice small as it struggled against the weight of the pain.

It will be okay, Amelia said, wishing she believed her own words. But she couldn't see how the pack would make it through this in one piece.

She touched her chest, feeling like she'd been hollowed out from the inside. Though she knew the pack bonds weren't physically there, that's where the pain felt like it was coming from. The loss. The fear. The panic.

Not all of it was hers. Most of it, in fact, wasn't. She only knew for sure because she hadn't been all that attached to Hale before he'd died. She'd have been sad at his death, but not cripplingly so. This was the echo of what everyone else was feeling. What their wolves felt.

Something that Shane should have been able to stop from bleeding between the wolves in the pack. He was the alpha now, but he clearly wasn't strong enough to manage the pack bonds. Yet no one was challenging him, even though she was sure there were a few who were more than strong enough.

Amelia turned away from the door abruptly, her anger battering down the overload for a few short heartbeats. Oliver could have challenged Shane. But he did nothing, letting the pack suffer.

Hurt. Pain, Luna said, a very human feeling of reproach in the images that she sent her.

The anger subsided as quickly as it had come, and the overload of the pack's pain returned. Her wolf was right, she was being unfair. Oliver had been close with Hale; the loss had hit him hard.

She knew the pack needed stability, not more fighting, but that didn't mean they needed Shane. They needed someone like Hale, someone who was strong enough to lock down the bonds. The irony that she wished for the very control she'd been furious about yesterday wasn't lost on her.

So far, all Shane had done was to force them to stay put in a house that was too small.

Not want to stay, Luna said, snarling. *Want hunt.*

Her wolf wasn't the only one. The whole pack was angry under their pain. Ready to do something. Hurt something.

Answers first, Amelia said, but she was starting to doubt they were going to get any. Shane hadn't told them anything about what had happened to Hale or how he'd died. If Shane even knew himself.

But why not just tell them he didn't know? Let them investigate themselves?

After shutting down the last round of angry questions from the pack, Shane had slipped out to answer his phone. Without his presence in the room, Amelia had been able to pull away from the group and grab some air. Though the tug to return to the house niggled at her.

She ignored it.

All around the house were large open fields, with a few odd scatterings of trees and bushes, and a road to the left of her. There was a small front yard where a few cars were parked haphazardly, but most had needed to park out on the road itself. There was damage to the cars that hadn't been there this morning. Shane's reckless summons had made Oliver lose a wing mirror as well. Thankfully, no one had caused any serious accidents as they'd been dragged here. At least, not that she'd heard.

She took half a dozen steps down towards the road before she felt the niggle turn into a tug. Shane wasn't able to lock down the pack bonds, but he was doing this one command really well. She couldn't have left even if she had the keys.

Annoyed, she turned and moved parallel to the house instead. It was quiet out here in the afternoon sunshine. The house held the sound in pretty well, leaving her with just a soft murmur from those inside.

Distantly, she heard other animals, mostly crows, as they circled the bone-dry fields searching for food. The scents out here were mostly farm smells, like sewage and manure. Though after the Rift Scar, those scents barely bothered her at all.

Another sound came to her, a faint voice, but singular, rather than a group murmur. Shane. He'd come out here to answer a call.

She hesitated. Coming out to eavesdrop hadn't been her intention. But that niggle in her mind that told her to stay near the house seemed to be content with her moving towards Shane, so she let the voice draw her forward.

Ahead of her was a wooden summerhouse with a tar-lined roof. Its front held two large glass doors that were closed, but she saw Shane through them, his back to her. Unlike the thick walls of the house, the wood on this building did little to block sound.

'I'll sort it.' Shane snapped.

'Good. Don't tell anyone I called you. I'll explain tomorrow. But call me if the team finds any sign of other borders being breached.' Hale's voice came through the phone, just at the edge of her hearing. But there was no doubt that it was him.

Amelia froze, heart skipping a beat as the word sank in. Hale was alive?

That wasn't possible. She remembered the feeling of Hale dying. That wasn't something someone came back from.

Amelia missed the next few words that were exchanged as her wolf tore at her control. Hale needed them. Except she couldn't feel Hale, only Shane and the pack.

Protect pack, Luna said, writhing against her, trying to send her back the way she had come. *Protect alpha.*

Shane is alpha, Amelia said. The thought made her wolf hesitate, and her attempt to override Amelia slowed. They might not like Shane, but they weren't strong enough to challenge him.

But *how* was Shane their alpha if Hale was still alive?

Amelia backed away a step, turning towards the house. Had Shane challenged him and won? But if he had, why was Hale making demands?

Anger curled in her gut like a snake. She hated not knowing what had happened. Did Hale care so little for his pack that he'd abandon us like this? Her wolf whined, not willing to believe that. But what other explanation was there? Hale was alive, but he wasn't their alpha.

'What are you doing out here?' Shane asked, making her jump.

In her anger, she'd missed the sound of the glass doors sliding open. She should have moved faster. Amelia turned to watch Shane, his face closed and eyes narrowed. The pack bonds to him grew tighter.

'What did you hear?' Shane asked quietly, pressure building against her.

SAM FOLLOWED BEHIND HALE as they headed back towards the clearing. Somehow, he walked without making any noise, head swivelling side to side as he watched the woods. The confidence helped reassure her somewhat as her fear clawed at her with each step. It also helped that he was carrying the largest knife from her kitchen in one hand and an old shovel in the other.

In all the years she'd lived out here alone, she'd never felt like she needed a weapon before. But that knife was a reminder that all this time, maybe her safety had just been luck. How did she go back to that ignorance of yesterday where her only worry was Lacey trying to convince her to have sex with Hale?

The car cover she was dragging behind her caught on another root, making her curse. The thing was heavy, with a waxy coating on one side and a lined cotton on the other. It went over her previous car, though she rarely bothered to use it. It was the closest to a tarp she had, and it would work for what Hale needed it for.

Hale glanced back at her as she freed the material.

'I'm fine,' Sam said, annoyed as she saw his concern. It helped a little with the fear, even if part of her wished she had stayed in the house. But she was damned if she was going to let fear stop her from going onto her own land.

The Land swirled lazily around them, and despite her own nervous thoughts, it was content and at peace. She wanted to feel that, but she resisted creating a connection. The memory of the pain from healing Hale was still vivid. She didn't want to know if it would still hurt if she reached out to the Land.

As they moved into the clearing with the yew tree, Sam's breath caught. She'd forgotten how bad it had been. How the place had felt dead and empty. How easy it had been to drain it of energy and not even know. The leaves had almost all fallen from the tree now, and it blanketed the whole area. The dead body of the Rift imp was just visible.

Even Hale couldn't walk through those leaves in silence. They crunched and broke apart with each step. Sam followed, only stopping when she was ten feet from the body. She couldn't make herself take the last few steps. The smell was as bad as she remembered, and it took effort to keep the burgers down.

Why had she thought coming out here was a good idea? Oh yes. She didn't want fear ruling her.

Hale moved over to where the imp was and started pulling back the leaves. It looked worse than it had earlier, or maybe she was just seeing it more clearly. The ragged slash on its neck showed little pieces of white bone under the black blood and gore. Not a single bug went near it, as if even they knew it was toxic.

'Let me,' Hale said, coming back to take the car cover from her gently. This time Sam didn't argue as she swallowed back bile.

He dragged it over, laid it down beside the creature, then pulled on a set of gloves she'd picked up with the tarp. Without any hesitation, he leaned down, gripped the imp's slimy flesh, and started to pull. Sam turned away, unable to watch as he dragged it onto the plastic. She couldn't stop the sound from registering, though. The sickly squelch as it hit the plastic would forever live in her brain, she was sure.

Her stomach twisted, and she held her breath, desperate to stop the burgers from coming back up.

A lot of use she was being.

'We can take it back to my car to be removed later,' Hale said, voice seemingly unconcerned. 'That way, at least it won't rot here. I'll need to dig up some of the dirt, too.'

Sam nodded, looking down at her hands. She hadn't touched anything, but it was almost like the blood, dirt, and worse were still in the creases. The imp's blood. Hale's blood. The panic and fear in her gut churned as the memory of the attack flooded her senses.

Hale's hands closed over hers, hiding them from her sight. His were clean; the gloves gone. 'It's dead. It can't hurt either of us.'

Sam's hand shook as the connection between them pushed back the fear. Oddly, there was no desire this time, or at least it was little more than a background noise. She felt safe with him touching her. Something that she hadn't felt in a very long time. Not since her mum had died.

She took a slow breath, letting that safety wrap around her and steady her. There was something underneath it, fear that wasn't hers, she thought, but it was distant under his worry for her.

'I'm fine,' Sam said, an old habit, or instinct, throwing the words out of her mouth. But the panic had been very real, and Hale had seen it.

Hale raised his eyebrow at her, clearly not believing her. 'You don't have to be.'

Sam struggled to not automatically lash out at him. She wasn't some damsel in distress despite the near break-down. But he had helped, and she couldn't deny that. Why was it so hard to let someone in?

Because the last time she'd let her guard down, someone had died. But Hale was still here. He hadn't run away despite the dead yew tree behind them. Her father had been afraid of her, disgusted as well, but the fear had been the stronger of the two emotions.

'Are you afraid of what I can do?' Sam asked. The question left her feeling like she'd torn herself open, leaving a ragged and bloody cavity for everyone to see. It was a question she hadn't even known she was afraid to have answered until she'd asked it. She wanted to take it back.

'No,' Hale said, answer quick and without hesitation as he moved closer to her. There was no fear in the connection between them. But that didn't mean he understood the risk.

'You don't know anything about my power,' she said, dropping her eyes to his lips. It felt wrong to feel the attraction with a body sprawled on a tarp just a few feet away, but it was better than being afraid. 'I killed an entire section of the forest healing you.'

'The forest can regrow,' Hale said, tucking a strand of her hair back from her face, fingers delicate as they brushed her skin. 'You haven't killed it.'

'What if you're wrong?' Sam whispered. The Land flitted around her. If she let herself connect, she'd know for sure if the area was dead. But she didn't. She wasn't sure she was ready for that answer. What would have happened if another person had been here, and it had been their energy she'd taken?

Hale leaned down and placed a light kiss on her lips. 'I'm not wrong,' he said, pulling away before it could become more. 'Do you want to go back inside?'

Sam shook her head, trying to chase away the last of her doubts. 'No. Let's finish this.'

Hale ran his hands down her arms before he let her go. The heat of his touch lingered for a heartbeat, then faded. She shuddered at the loss, wanting to hold on to the feeling.

But his words had helped ease some of the knot in her stomach. At least for now.

SAM LED THE WAY back through the woods––in part so she didn't have to see the tarp that Hale was dragging behind him. It was heavy enough that there had been no chance of Sam moving it on her own, though she'd offered to help. They'd had to dig out a large section of soil to remove the blood.

The Land prodded at her, pressing at her to connect to it as she walked. It had been growing more insistent the longer she'd been outside. But she still wasn't sure she wanted to risk the pain just yet, so she pushed it away.

Hale left her as they reached the edge of the woods, moving around to his car where he'd lay the wrapped body down behind it to be removed later. Despite the seriousness of what they were doing, those tendrils of desire flared up again as she watched him walk away.

The Land dulled to a faint buzz as soon as she stepped onto the veranda, and it was an effort not to sigh in relief. The lingering smell of the burgers helped replace the smell of blood and gore.

If anything should have tempered the desire, that thought should have been it. But instead, it slid low in her stomach as she felt Hale head back towards her. Her whole body felt like it was burning up.

If she'd been touching Hale, she might have been able to blame his lust. But she wasn't. This was all her. Her need. Part of her thought she should have worried about that. But she was done holding back, and so very done with waiting.

Hale inhaled sharply behind her as he came into the kitchen. She turned around to face him, his erection obvious even through the jeans. Hell, it had been obvious even before they'd left to go outside.

This time, she didn't wait. She moved towards Hale. He growled low in his throat and met her halfway.

There was no talking this time, no hesitation, as she wrapped her arms around Hale's neck. He walked them backwards, pressing her into the long back wall opposite the window. The curtains were open, but she had no fear that anyone would spy on them here.

She moved her hand lower to get rid of some of the clothes between them, but her elbow caught something sharp. The plant holder that had been on the wall tipped to the ground as the nail gave way, spilling the mix of herbs to the floor and spreading dirt over her bare feet.

She gasped as the energy of the Land buzzed against her mind. It tore at her walls, trying to send her images. She pushed it back; the Land wasn't what she wanted right now.

'Shit,' Hale said, chest heaving and face flushed as he stared at the dirt. He'd felt something too, she was sure.

'Ignore it,' she whispered. Whatever the Land wanted, it could wait. Right now, she needed Hale, so she pulled him back. He tasted like the burgers still. When Hale started to object, she added, 'If you stop, I might kill you.'

Hale chuckled softly, the sound vibrating through her core, but he settled more solidly against her again, moving to run a series of kisses down her neck.

Part of her wanted to draw this out, but after the shower, she wanted more than just a release. Hale clearly had the same idea because his lips didn't linger on her throat long. His hands moved lower until they slid under the dress to find her panties. He groaned against her lips, not finding anything but bare skin.

Sam smiled, glad she'd made that choice as she pushed him back just enough that she could get her hands on his zip.

The Land pushed against her mind again, seeping in through the edges. She tried to ignore it, focusing on Hale--on his lips as he leaned in and ran a trail of kisses over her collarbone and how the sound of the zip lowering seemed so loud in the small space.

Images broke through her walls to the Land. *Grass bending under someone's feet.* She pushed the connection away, focusing on Hale. She didn't care about the forest right now.

Hale shuffled to one foot, kicking off a shoe. But he didn't stop kissing her as his lips moved to her ear, teeth scraping along her lobe, making her body tighten.

Metal brushed against a tree. It was cold and unnatural against the rest of the sensations.

Sam looked past Hale out the window. Light flickered off something in the distance. Something that didn't belong in her yard. Something that wasn't invited.

Sam shoved Hale away from her, hands moving even before her brain understood what she was doing. With his second shoe in the process of coming off, she caught him by surprise and off balance. He stumbled back from her easier than she'd expected, and he fell into the kitchen table with a grunt.

The window cracked. A spider web of broken glass spreading outward from a small hole.

Something hit her, shoving her backwards into the wall hard. She looked down, touching her chest. Her fingers came away wet, stained red.

Stained with blood.

Sound ripped through her ears. A sharp bang. A clatter of glass breaking. A scream.

Then came the pain. A fire in her chest.

CHAPTER TWELVE

Hale grabbed Sam, pulling her to the floor and out of sight of the window a second before another gunshot shattered the remaining glass. She screamed as they landed. The connection between them ripped through him until it seemed like he was the one who'd been shot.

It should have been him. If not for Sam pushing him away, it would have been.

'Sam, look at me,' Hale said, trying to keep his voice calm as he pressed a hand to the bullet wound on her chest. Her blood was a warm, steady flow around his fingers. Not enough that it was an artery, but it was already soaking into the green dress.

Sam blinked rapidly, not looking at him at all. The wound was high, hitting her just under the collarbone. He didn't know if that was good or bad. The wounds he was used to were bites and claws, not bullets.

His wolf screamed at him to help her. To fix it. But he didn't know how. The pack healed when shifting forms. Sam wasn't a wolf. She couldn't shift.

'Sam, listen to me. You have to heal yourself,' he said, but Sam wasn't listening, or maybe she couldn't hear him.

Cursing, he looked around for something that would slow Sam's bleeding. He grabbed a towel that was hanging from the cupboard door by the sink, then searched for something he could tie it on with. On the floor by the wall, the rope from the herb shelf lay in the dirt from the broken pots, more than long enough to wrap around Sam's shoulders and apply pressure. He grabbed it too.

'This is going to hurt,' he said, trying to draw Sam's eyes as he touched her uninjured shoulder gently. She still didn't seem to hear him, but he didn't have the time to wait for an answer.

He pressed the towel down hard on her wound. Sam cried out, jerking under him. He hesitated, but only for a moment as he wrapped the cord behind her back, then tightened it over the wound, keeping the pressure as tight as he could as he knotted it off.

A third gunshot pinged off the wall opposite them, taking a chunk out of the stone already stained with Sam's blood. How long would it be before the shooter gave up wasting bullets and came after them? Going by the damage and the distance of the sound, it was a rifle they were using. They could just stay where they were and keep shooting until Sam bled to death.

'Sam,' Hale said, tucking a strand of hair out of her face. She was shaking, but her eyes focused on him at last. 'Please, you have to heal yourself.'

'Can't,' Sam said, voice harsh as she struggled to breathe.

'You have to try,' Hale said. Fear tightened his chest as the towel started to turn red.

'Can't. Heal. Self,' Sam said. Her skin was pale as she licked her lips. 'Not how it works.'

Hale cursed under his breath. She'd saved him...healed him. He wouldn't fail to do the same for her.

His wolf raged at him, threatening to force him from one form to the other, to tear out the shooter's throat. He pushed him back, reminding his wolf that they couldn't help Sam without hands. Not to mention, claws were all well and good, but against a gun, they were just about useless. They had to be patient.

Slowly, his wolf backed off, but it wouldn't last forever. He needed to get Sam out of here now. But how? The shooter would see them through the large window above if he tried to move her. The back door was half glass and opposite the only door out of the kitchen. Even if he knew a safe place to carry her to, he wasn't getting her out of here without being seen.

He needed help. Needed the pack. Even though he knew they probably wouldn't be close enough to help in time. Calling them through the pack bonds was a bad idea, especially with his wolf raging in fear for Sam.

Hale pulled his phone out of his pocket. He heard the crunch of it even before he saw the screen; it was smashed. Cursing, he looked around for some kind of landline, but there was no sign of one anywhere.

'Where's your phone?' Hale asked, searching for it. There was nowhere to store it in her dress, and he hadn't seen it today at all.

She exhaled slowly, face tight with pain as she shook her head. The meaning was obvious even if she couldn't get the words out. It wasn't here.

Out of options, he risked lowering his mental walls that muted the pack bonds and reached out to them.

There was nothing there.

He gasped, fighting a wave of disorientation as his wolf pushed out further, searching. But it wasn't that they were distant. The pack was simply not there. All he could feel was Sam.

Had something happened to the pack?

No. He'd have felt that, even with his walls high.

Stolen, Fang snarled in his mind, pressing again for them to shift.

But he'd have felt that too. Unless what Sam had done to save him had affected the pack bonds? But if the pack had felt the link be severed, then they'd have been here by now? They'd have thought he was dead.

Hale shook off the thought. Whatever had happened, it mattered little right then. Hale was alone, and he had no way of calling them. He was going to have to deal with the shooter alone. He searched the room for something he could use. There were knives and broken glass. But nothing that would help him at a distance.

Another bullet came, this time hitting a knife block on the worktop, sending sharp blades spinning. Hale covered Sam's body with his. One blade slashed his arm before it skidded to the corner.

'Hale,' Sam said as she struggled to catch her breath. She put her hand on his arm, her energy stuttering around him at the contact. 'You have to go.'

'No. If I––' Hale shook his head, but she tightened her grip on his arm.

'If you stay...they'll shoot us both,' Sam said, swallowing hard. She was shaking with the effort to get the words out. 'You have to...go after them.'

Leaving Sam tore at every instinct Hale had. He'd bought them time by putting pressure on the wound, but he had no idea how long it would hold out.

Another gunshot sent glass sliding over the worktop onto the floor beside them.

'Go,' Sam said again, letting go of his arm to shove him. He let her, though the move was weak.

Hale growled, the sound vibrating through his chest before he could stop it. His wolf wanted to fight and protect. The two needs warred against each other.

But she was right.

'I'll be right back,' he said at last, moving to a crouch, then realised he only had one shoe. He kicked it off rather than searching for the other one, leaving his feet bare.

But still, he hesitated.

'Go!'

The smell of her blood had overpowered everything else. He couldn't smell if she was afraid or not, which was probably just as well. He wasn't sure he'd have been able to turn away from her otherwise. Tears stung his eyes as he tried to shove his pain down into a box.

The window was a gaping hole above the counter, most of the glass missing now. The external door was further along the wall. It was solid at the bottom but had a glass panel on the top. He'd be visible the moment he tried to leave the room, so he'd need to be fast.

He didn't look back, though every instinct he had screamed at him not to leave Sam. He crouched low through the kitchen over to the back door and waited for the gunshot, then he launched himself to his feet and bolted through into the hallway.

Another shot shattered the glass door behind him. But it was too slow. He was already in the living room to his left. It had a massive window on the far wall. He grabbed a short stool to throw ahead of him; it crashed into the glass, shattering loudly, making it easier to dive through.

Glass sliced at his bare skin, but he barely felt it as he cleared the veranda and hit the ground hard.

Without letting himself slow, he rolled to his feet and was up and running before the glass had finished falling behind him and in the woods before a second shot ripped through the clearing.

The land hummed under Hale's feet as he ran. It no longer spoke of safety. Had it changed while they'd been clearing up after the imp? Or was it more recent?

Either way, it didn't matter. He didn't need a reminder it wasn't safe, so he pushed it away, blocking it like he did the pack bonds. It worked, leaving him with only the sense of Sam behind him as he darted through the trees, trying to get behind the shooter.

Sam watched Hale disappear down the hall. She still felt the vibration of his growl. The feral sound should have scared her, but it wasn't even registering on her radar of things to worry about at the moment.

Glass shattered somewhere in her house, but this time before the gunshot. She wanted to scream for him to run faster but pushed down on that instinct. Right now, she was just a distraction.

Was he okay?

Why had she left her damned phone upstairs? If she hadn't, they'd have been able to call for help, though who would have been close enough to do anything she didn't know. At least she could have done something. But now he was out there alone, without anyone to help him.

There were no more gunshots, which might have meant anything. She felt helpless and blind. She couldn't do much about the former, but there was a chance she could do something about the latter. If she could reach the spilt dirt. It was spread out over the floor along with the glass and blood. Her blood.

Ignoring what she was touching, she reached out towards the dirt, dragging a small pile towards her. Her shoulder burned, and her vision dimmed, but she got a handful. She also managed to pick up half a dozen glass shards that cut into her palm, but the pain was nothing against the fire in her shoulder.

Taking a breath to slow her heart, she let the Land into her mind. It wasn't a good connection. The dirt had come from her Land, but it had been in the pot for a while now, and her hands were shaking so badly that the dirt kept slipping between her fingers. Then there was the pain that made it hard to focus.

She caught flashes of feet hitting the ground, artificial soles pressing into the dirt, moving fast. Running. She tried to hold on to the images, to get more details. Was there one person out there? More? The Land tried to show her, but the images fractured.

Sam cursed, trying to sit up, to concentrate, but the pain cut through her, making sweat bead on her skin. The Land slipped out of her grasp as she collapsed back down. She fought for each breath, her chest aching.

Tears stung her eyes as she tried to slow her breathing. It didn't help the pain. Didn't help her connect back to the Land. She tried the connection to Hale instead, but all she sensed was that he was moving away from the house. That tugging told her nothing useful at all.

Stupid Land magic. Why couldn't she just heal the wound like she'd healed Hale? Then he wouldn't be out there alone. Vulnerable. But she couldn't channel the energy into herself when she was the conduit. Even if she could stay conscious through the pain long enough to control the energy.

She tried to focus on the Land again, feeling the dirt against her fingers. The Land flickered at the edge of her mind, the connection coming and going like static TV. It sent her the feel of something heavy and metal hitting the ground, the heat of it burning the leaves. There wasn't enough there to tell her what was happening. Who was hunting Hale?

She needed more. But every breath was like a lead weight was crushing her chest, spreading pain out in a spider web through her whole body.

The room spun around her. She had to stay awake. She tried to push herself upright again, but the pain rippled through her, making her gasp. Her stomach twisted as nausea rose with the spinning.

She fought against it. She had to stay awake. Had to find a way to help Hale.

AFTER THE INITIAL SHOT in Hale's direction, nothing else followed. Hale cursed, keeping low as he turned back around. He caught a flash of colour as someone disappeared into the treeline opposite, towards the yew tree clearing.

His feet itched to run after the shooter, but it was too risky to cross all that open space. He'd be an easy target. He'd have to go around the edge of the woods, which would give the shooter time to get even further ahead of him. But at least if they were in the woods, they weren't anywhere near the house. That brought a small measure of relief. Sam would be safe.

Hale ran around the edge of the treeline, the summer greenery providing decent cover. He strained his ears for any sound. All he heard was the panicked retreat of the forest creatures. If the shooter was still running, he was too far ahead for Hale to hear his footsteps.

Inhaling deeply, Hale tried to pick up a hint of the shooter's scent, but that didn't do much to help, either. All around him he smelled the pack, and Sam's blood, still wet on his fingers. Neither helped his wolf's mood as he pushed again for Hale to change.

Too risky, Hale said. They could shift faster than most, but it wasn't instant. He'd be vulnerable during the change.

But his wolf didn't care. They were in the woods. Their senses would be sharper as a wolf. They could move quieter on four paws, faster. Hunt and trap their target.

No pack, Hale whispered. They were alone here in this fight. There would be no one else to hunt with them.

His wolf reached for the centre of their mind where the pack bonds usually resided, forgetting that it was gone. The hole scraped against their senses like sandpaper. It only made the anger sharper.

Hunt alone, Fang said, but he had hesitated.

We can't fight bullets as a wolf, Hale said as he strained to hear any signs of the shooter ahead, but the forest was quiet around him.

He wasn't sure his wolf would listen. Logic wasn't always something that worked against instinct. Slowly, the need to shift dissipated. He wasn't fooled into thinking the fight was over, but he let out a sigh of relief as the pressure eased.

Cautiously, he moved forward slower than before, using the trees as a shield as he neared where the shooter had entered the woods. The shooter's hearing would probably take longer to recover than Hale's, but he was still careful to make no sound. There was no way to know for sure if the shooter hadn't just settled in to wait for him to catch up.

The gunpowder was a bitter taste in the air, the only hint that someone else was out there. He should have been able to smell the shooter, but there was still just the pack.

As he had done earlier that day, he ignored the path and kept low to the ground, using the ferns to shield him from sight. Years spent in the woods as a child made it easy to move without disturbing much more than a few leaves. He just had to hope his shooter didn't have the same experience, or he could be crawling straight into a trap.

As he moved closer to the clearing, Hale kept expecting another gunshot. But there was nothing. No new sounds at all.

He wasn't close enough to see past the edge yet, but he could already smell the lingering scent of dead Rift imp and his own blood. Thankfully, the fallen leaves would hide the amount of blood he'd lost, but it was so strong that no one in the clearing would be able to smell that he was close.

He was beginning to think the shooter had kept running when he heard a voice ahead of him.

'Don't speak, I don't believe your lies.' Shane's voice was a sharp crack that rose above the normal forest sounds.

'You weren't strong enough to challenge Hale, so you shoot him instead?'

Hale stopped, crouching lower. The scent of the pack he'd been following hadn't been old, he realised. It had been fresh. It had been Shane. But there was another scent there, along with the sharp tang of gunpowder.

Hale risked moving forward the last few feet so he could see past the trees that protected him. Shane stood under the half-dead yew tree, the dead branches doing little to block the late afternoon sun. He held his hands up in the air as he faced Amelia, who was pointing a handgun at him, body stiff and unwavering in her aim.

The lack of other scents hit Hale with a stomach-sickening realisation. There hadn't been something missing. The shooter had been one of the pack. But why would Amelia want to hurt Sam?

Except Sam had pushed him out of the way. That bullet had been meant for Hale. Sam had been hurt because of him.

Hale struggled to control his anger as he stared at Amelia.

Not pack, Fang snarled. *Dangerous.*

His wolf hadn't been a fan of Amelia before. Now, without the pack bonds, he couldn't sense her. She was an invading wolf. They both were, even though Shane was the one with a gun being pointed at him. But why? Why not just shoot Shane and keep running?

No matter what her reasoning was, Hale couldn't afford to let this play out. He needed to get the gun away from Amelia and get back to Sam. Every second he delayed, she was losing more blood.

The Land prodded at Hale, trying to push past the block as if it were responding to Hale's rising anger. He didn't let it in. He didn't understand how that magic worked, and this was definitely not the time to find out.

Amelia had her back to Hale, feet spread wide, with only one hand on the gun. This was the best chance Hale was going to get.

He launched himself forward, bare feet crushing the dead moss and fallen leaves that came up above his ankles as he ran. Shane heard him, mouth opening as if to shout, but he was too slow. Hale was already on Amelia.

Except he'd undershot, expecting her to turn the gun on him where he could grab it. He hit her arm, forcing her hand to open reflexively, sending the gun tumbling to the ground. It disappeared into a pile of dead leaves.

Hale fumbled, trying to recover, grabbing her arm and twisting it behind her back instead. She didn't even try to fight back as he disabled her. Not verbally or physically. It was like he was manoeuvring a stiff doll into place. In the short time he'd known her, she'd never been quiet.

'Hale! You're alive. I thought she'd got you,' Shane said, lowering his hands as he scowled at Amelia. 'I got the rifle away from her, but I didn't see the handgun until it was too late.'

Amelia still didn't move or speak as Shane's words hung in the air. Something about this felt wrong. Neither of their reactions was right.

Hale growled as Shane stepped towards him, unable to stop the sound as his wolf took the motion as a challenge. Shane stopped in his tracks, anger slicing through his scent, his own power rising to fill the space.

The power of an alpha.

Shane had taken the pack from Hale.

Hale's wolf snarled, almost forcing him to let go of Amelia to go after the other man.

'I can explain,' Shane said, but he didn't let go of the power. He couldn't. It was part of him now.

But that didn't do anything to soothe Hale's wolf.

Shane had stolen Hale's pack.

THE CRUNCH OF BROKEN glass made Sam open her eyes. She hadn't realised she'd closed them.

Lacey stepped into the room, stopping in the doorway as she took in the chaos around her. She was wearing her familiar pale combats and a white top, the bright, crisp colour looking out of place in the chaos.

Relief flooded Sam. Lacey was pack; she'd be able to help Hale.

Sam pushed herself up, groaning as her body screamed at her that moving was a bad idea. The dizziness threatened again, but she managed to get her back against the cupboards.

'Sam?' Lacey said, voice tight as she stared at Sam, face pale and eyes wide.

'You have to help him,' Sam said. Every word hurt like there was a razor in her chest. Black spots danced across her vision. Her lungs were too small as she fought to find enough air.

Lacey didn't listen to her as she took a cautious step forward over the glass to move to Sam's side. 'What the hell happened?'

Sam shook her head, carefully touching the towel; it was soaked through with her blood. Too much blood. Swallowing back the bile that burned her throat, she shook the thought away, trying to focus on Lacey.

'Someone attacked us. Hale went after them,' Sam said, struggling to get the words to come out. 'Please, help him.'

Lacey flinched at the word attacked, but still, she didn't leave to go help Hale. She let out a breath and crouched down next to Sam. 'Hale can take care of himself. You, however, are going to bleed out without help.'

'I'm fine. Help Hale,' Sam ground out through gritted teeth. Even to her, the words sounded weak rather than assertive.

'No,' Lacey said as she leaned forward to prod at the blood-soaked towel. Dark spots crawled over Sam's vision. 'You're losing too much blood.'

Frustration pulled at Sam. She had to find a way to convince Lacey to help Hale. As if drawn by her thoughts, the connection to the Land flared up, sending her new images. She'd lost most of the dirt in her hand, but she tightened her grip on what was left, trying to hold on to the connection. Her vision flickered like strobe lights spinning around her.

Lacey pulled at the towel on her shoulder.

Sam felt the nearly dead clearing with the yew tree.

'What happened before you got shot?' Lacey asked, voice low.

Something metal hit the ground.

Lacey frowned at Sam and repeated the question.

Sam tried to catch the image the land was sending her. The piece that was out of place. The metal.

Fire seared her brain, pulsing in time with her heartbeat. But the image solidified, like the Land was as desperate as she was. Whatever it was, it sat in a pile of dead leaves. Cold metal that wasn't part of the Land. Its flat L-shaped design was familiar even before she felt the curve of a trigger. A gun.

Lacey said something Sam missed as she fought to hold on to the image. She had to do something.

She threw all her energy and thoughts towards the gun, begging the Land to dig deep into the metal, pull it away. Bury it.

She didn't know if it would work. She'd never tried anything like this before. The Land rumbled in her mind, doing something. But it moved slowly. There was so little energy left in the area after what she had done to heal Hale.

'Sam, can you hear me?' Lacey said, hand pressing against Sam's face.

Sam ground her teeth, holding onto the image of what she wanted despite the pain. But then the fire in her brain exploded, and the connection slipped away, making her scream.

HALE STRUGGLED TO KEEP himself from lunging at Shane as the power rolled over the clearing. It whispered of the pack. Hale's pack.

Thief, Fang snarled. There was no push to shift. They both knew there wouldn't be time. Not against this.

'Are you okay?' Shane asked, motioning to the clearing around them. 'This whole place stinks of your blood and dead imp. What the hell happened?'

'That's the way you want to start?' Hale asked, barely containing his snarl. 'You take my pack and then ask me if I'm okay?'

'I thought you'd died,' Shane said, voice low. 'Hell, we felt you die, felt the bonds break. I didn't know what else to do but pull the pack together again.'

Hale froze, stomach dropping. He hadn't died. Sam had saved him. Except he'd felt the darkness pull him under. Felt the cold even in the shared dream with Sam.

When Hale didn't answer, Shane continued. 'I was going to tell you in person what happened after I'd dealt with the scorpions.' Shane's lips thinned as he turned to Amelia. 'But I found something worse. A cage close to here; it stank of the Rift imp and Amelia. Then I heard the gunshots.'

Hale looked up at Amelia. She still wasn't reacting to him holding her. Even jammed between two angry alphas, she should still have been struggling against him. But she didn't move at all. Her scent was another matter. He smelled her fear and anger, thick in the air around him.

Had she done this? Laid traps of scorpions to bind him as a wolf? Then a Rift imp to kill him? She'd been angry last night, but this angry?

'Did you do this?' Hale asked Amelia. She didn't react, but Shane made a noise in his throat.

'She's never going to admit the truth, and we can't make her since she didn't re-join the pack like the others did. She went rogue,' Shane said, eyes flashing yellow as he glanced at her, then turned back to Hale. This time, when Shane spoke, his voice held an edge of power. 'We have her now. That's the important thing.'

The familiar mix of alpha and pack energy tingled against Hale's skin. Except rather than being part of him, it was separate, making the hole in his chest seem so much larger. A scent that spoke of a home tickled his senses, promising comfort and warmth.

Except, Shane couldn't offer what wasn't his.

Hale snarled as rage flooded him. His wolf rose, shredding the energy like it was tissue paper.

Shane flinched back. Hale wasn't some lone wolf looking for a home. He was an alpha in his own right.

'You think I'm so weak that you can use the stolen power of my pack to soothe me?' Hale said, wanting nothing more than to push Amelia away and go for Shane. But she was the one who'd had the gun.

'I didn't have a choice,' Shane shouted, his anger rising. 'I had to protect the pack.'

'Protect the pack?' Hale snarled. All Shane had done was gather up all the pack connections after they'd been severed from Hale when he'd been near death. He was little better than an opportunistic scavenger. He didn't have the power to offer a real challenge.

'Hale, you have to calm down,' Shane said like it was Hale who was the one who was the problem. That power reached out again, but Hale shoved it aside easily.

'Do you think you're strong enough to control me?' Hale asked, wolf so close to the surface it was a wonder it didn't just come out as a growl. It took more than the power of being alpha to create and hold a pack together. That Shane thought he could wave the power around like this showed how little he actually knew.

Shane's eyes darted to the pile of dead leaves where the gun had landed. But when Hale growled again, Shane took a step away, raising his arm in a defensive gesture.

Amelia shuddered. Being between two alpha powers couldn't have been a fun experience. But why wasn't she talking or arguing? She didn't even try to look at Hale. Or say Shane was lying. Was she just biding her time, or was Shane controlling her?

'Amelia, did you try to shoot me?' Hale asked, this time trying to pull the answer from her. But she wasn't in his pack now, and the magic did nothing except draw her wolf to the surface.

Hale felt it in the air around her. Without her being in his pack, he couldn't sense her emotions, but he didn't need to. Her scent changed, flowing from a mix of fear and anger to just the latter.

'What do you expect her to say, Hale? She has been lying to us since she first came here. You've seen her anger. She tried to use an imp to kill you. Make it look like an accident. I was trying to stop her from finishing the job,' Shane said, lowering his arms, but he hadn't relaxed. 'Come, I'll show you the trap myself. Then you'll see the truth.'

Hale didn't have time for this. He had to get back to Sam and had to help her.

Make pack, Fang said, nudging him.

At first, Hale thought his wolf was talking about Sam, which was impossible, but then he realised that wasn't what his wolf meant. Fang wanted Hale to bring Amelia into his pack.

But it wasn't that easy. Or at least it wasn't something he'd ever tried to do without another alpha giving up at least a piece of the pack bond. Hale very much doubted Shane was going to give up Amelia. Providing she was even part of his pack, of course. Even if she wasn't, she'd still need to accept him.

Make pack, Fang repeated. His confidence didn't guarantee he actually knew what he was doing, or that it was safe. But they were running out of time. Sam needed him.

Hale exhaled and tightened his grip on Amelia. Then he let his wolf stretch out towards her. To her wolf.

The sensation made bile rise in his throat as his wolf touched on the edge of Shane's pack bond. The alien web of power and energy twisted around her like a net, binding her to the point she could barely move. Hale had never felt anything quite like it before. No wonder Amelia wasn't answering him. She couldn't.

'Hale, what are you doing?' Shane asked, trying to lace his voice with his power again, like he could coax Hale's wolf into submission. 'Amelia is the one who shot at you. She tried to kill you. She put Sam in danger.'

But Shane couldn't touch Hale. He wasn't some weak pup who could be manipulated. He was an alpha, even if he didn't have a pack.

When trying to control Hale didn't work, Shane tried to pull on his bonds to Amelia. He drew them tighter around her wolf until she shuddered in Hale's arms. She couldn't speak. Couldn't even scream.

Amelia wasn't attacking anyone. She was a prisoner in her own body. No real alpha would bind their pack like this. It was wrong.

Hale pushed deeper, reaching towards Amelia. He could almost see both her and her wolf in his mind's eye, fighting against the weight of the magic that held them. They were alone, not even having the links to their family pack anymore. Shane had severed that too.

Her wolf turned to Hale, sensing him. It didn't even hesitate as it reached for him. Their pain and anger hit him like a sharp spike of fire in his skull.

Hale's wolf howled, anger overriding their earlier caution as it slashed at the web around Amelia. It shouldn't have worked, even with her reaching out, but the bindings around her shattered, sending energy lashing back painfully around them all.

Hale fought to keep a hold of Amelia's human half as the power lashed around them. She was afraid and struggling against him. She didn't want to be trapped. He felt it as clearly as it was his own thought. On the other hand, her wolf wanted to hold on to Hale, and the two were fighting each other.

Protect. Safe, Fang whispered. Or at least that was the closest Hale could translate the images that rolled through his mind. Communication shouldn't have been possible through the link, and yet Amelia seemed to hear.

But she hesitated, hovering in the space between being part of the pack and being free. He didn't blame her after what Shane had done. It didn't help that Shane was fighting to pull her back, tearing at the shreds of energy like he could wrap them around her once more.

If you wish to be free, I'll release you when this is all over, Hale said, to the very sharp annoyance of both his and Amelia's wolf.

Home, Amelia's wolf said, images of Sam's land passing around them like a kaleidoscope of colour. It wasn't backing down as it stood in the centre of the storm, angry, and ready to fight. *Protect. Fight.*

Amelia argued with her wolf. There were no words, just emotions and images that moved so fast he couldn't follow them. He felt it when they came to an agreement. The pack bonds rose in the space between them, pushing Shane's energy away with a violent shove.

Shane screamed, lashing out, trying to grab a hold of Amelia with power that he didn't understand, but he was too late. Hale's connection to Amelia slammed into place in his mind, and her knees gave out.

Hale gently lowered her to the ground as she gasped for breath. The new pack bond settled into the empty void in his mind, but the connection was brighter and stronger than their previous one had been.

Safe now, Fang whispered. Amelia wouldn't be able to hear the words, only the emotion behind them. Though, after what had just happened, he wasn't entirely certain.

Now save whole pack, Fang snarled.

But it wasn't that easy. The pack bonds to the rest of the wolves were bound to Shane, not Amelia. To save the pack, he'd have to rip all of them away from Shane. Or kill him.

Kill, Fang snarled.

Soon, Hale said. After what Shane had done to Amelia, Hale had no concern over the latter option.

'Shane...' Amelia whispered, body shaking as she looked up at him, struggling to get the words out, '...brought imp.'

Hale saw Shane move from the corner of his eyes. With a sharp shove, Hale pushed Amelia clear and braced for the attack.

CHAPTER THIRTEEN

THE ROOM SPUN AROUND Sam as she struggled against the pain, twin hot rods pulsed in her head and shoulder.

'Sam, can you hear me?' Lacey said, patting Sam's cheek. She was crouched on her heels next to Sam, just to the side of the growing pool of blood. How much time had passed?

'Sam?' Lacey said again, voice sharp. 'I need you to answer my question.'

'What question?' Sam said, struggling to get the words out. Why wasn't Lacey going to help Hale?

Lacey made an exasperated sound and let go of Sam's face. 'How did Hale get healed?'

Lacey's question felt wrong. Sam tried to push herself further up the wall, but her arms wouldn't hold her weight, and she just ended up in a more painful position.

'Did you call for help?' Sam asked, looking for a phone, or any sign that Lacey had done anything but stare at Sam since coming in here. But there was nothing.

What was going on?

Lacey's lips thinned. 'He should have died. We felt him die. Probably the most any of us have ever felt from him. No one comes back from that.'

'Lacey?' Sam asked, wanting to pull away from the woman as her face twisted. How did she know what had happened to Hale? Except that wasn't what had happened. He hadn't died. He'd been close, right on the edge, but Sam had saved him. 'What's going on?'

'I suppose it doesn't matter now. It's already done,' Lacey said, face closing down as she leaned forward, resting her hands on the makeshift bandage Hale had made.

'What are you talking about?' Sam said as she grabbed Lacey's arm in a panic. But Sam wouldn't have been strong enough even if she'd been healthy. 'What did you do?'

'What we had to. Hale made his choice. Now we've made ours.' Lacey's fist closed round the rope wrapped around the towel. 'You shouldn't have got involved. I didn't want this.'

'What choice?' Sam said, trying to push away, painfully aware of what would happen if Lacey removed the pressure. Then she remembered Lacey's words yesterday. 'The land?'

'He should've fought for more time. Instead, he'd rather keep you happy,' Lacey said, pulling in a deep breath, her fingers trembling.

'No! It isn't Hale,' Sam said, head spinning as she tried to pull away from Lacey's hand, but there was nowhere to go. 'The prime alphas blocked him.'

Lacey hesitated, but then her eyes narrowed. 'Is that the lie he told you? Did he even ask you? Or did he ask, and you said no?'

Sam didn't answer.

'That's what I thought,' Lacey said, lips thinning. 'He'd rather keep you happy than give the pack what they need.'

'You don't understand,' Sam said, struggling to take in enough air. Once again, her secret was costing other people's lives. Hale was going to die because of her. If he'd ignored the prime alphas and rented land from someone else, none of this would be happening.

'What's to understand?' Lacey said, anger breaking through her mask. 'You aren't any better than Hale. Happy to watch us suffer as long as it doesn't impact your perfect fucking life. I told Shane to keep you out of it, but I shouldn't have bothered. Now you can die along with Hale. The both of you can rot in hell.'

'Don't do this,' Sam said, tears burning her eyes. The image of Sam's dad flashed through her head. Her mother slamming the door behind her. Both getting into their old beat-up cars as the snow came down.

She'd killed her parents, and now, because of Sam, Lacey was trying to kill Hale.

It was her fault. All of it.

'Don't hurt him,' Sam said, voice breaking.

'It's already too late,' Lacey said, working at the knot on the rope. 'He's probably already dead.'

'No!' Sam screamed, her pain and panic so strong that she couldn't even connect to the Land to find out if Lacey was right. It hurt too much to reach out to that link to him.

'Everyone is going to be upset about your death, I'm sure. Tragic that one of the pack went rogue, and you got caught in the crossfire,' Lacey said. It was like she was telling herself a story. Like the lie was important.

'Until they come in here and smell you on my corpse,' Sam said, but she already knew they wouldn't. All she'd have to do was be the one who found Sam dead in the kitchen. It wouldn't even look like Lacey had been involved. She'd get away with it. Sam clawed at Lacey's arms, both of them slick with Sam's blood.

'Everyone will agree how awful it was to find you like this, dead on your own kitchen floor. Unable to bind your own wounds in time before you bled out.' Lacey didn't even try to stop Sam from scratching her. Why bother? They'd heal long before anyone arrived.

'Please stop,' Sam said, words coming out in a hiss as she reached for the Land again, tugging at it. But there was too much pain, and even if she could grab the land, nothing in the house could help her.

Sam fought tears. This wouldn't be how she died. She abandoned trying to gouge Lacey's wrist, searching for something else, anything. The ground was littered with shards of glass. But they were all too far away.

There was nothing here to help her. Lacey was going to win.

HALE GROWLED AS HE caught Shane's tackle and used the man's own momentum against him to toss him across the clearing. Shane hit the ground hard, rolling through the dead leaves. Clearly, he'd not expected Hale to recover so quickly because Shane was a better fighter than that.

Amelia's anger at being shoved was a sharp lash inside Hale's head and nose, but he hadn't hurt her more, and that was the main thing. The anger shifted target as she turned to Shane, wanting to hurt him like he'd hurt her.

Hale tried to dull his link to Amelia so he could think. It wasn't easy with just the two of them in his pack, especially after the hole that had been there before. His wolf wanted to keep the link open.

Giving up, Hale motioned for Amelia to stay back from the fight as Shane stood and brushed off the leaves that clung to him. She didn't like it, but she was still hurting from what Shane had done and needed time to recover.

'I should have come out here and made sure the imp had finished you off,' Shane bit out, moving slowly, eyes narrowed as he watched Hale.

Hale's wolf paced inside his mind, frustration eating at him. He wanted to be the one to fight Shane, wanted to end this as wolves. But Shane had challenged him as a human. Probably because even with a pack behind him, Shane's wolf wasn't stronger than Hale's. He'd chosen the fight he thought he could win.

'That's because you're a coward,' Hale said, moving so he was between Amelia and Shane. He felt Shane try to repeat what Hale had done, to rip Amelia from Hale. But Shane wasn't strong enough, and Amelia had made her choice.

'You've some nerve calling me a coward,' Shane said, spitting on the ground. 'How many years have you had the chance to give us a home? How easy would it have been to just ask for more? Instead, you sit here in isolation with no mate, no land, and no hope. We aren't a pack. We're a group of disconnected minions for the IRS&D. The pack will be better with me as alpha.'

This was about the land? There was a scent of truth to Shane's words, but it was hard to be certain through the anger. It would have taken longer than a day to catch and hold an imp and several scorpions. This had to have been weeks of planning.

'And you think you could run the pack better? You risk everyone by bringing in creatures from the Rift into our hunt. What if one of the other wolves had stumbled into one of your traps?' Hale said, looking Shane up and down. 'A true alpha would never have risked any of his pack like that.'

Amelia struggled to her feet, her wolf's anger just as sharp as Hale's. He tugged on the pack bonds, warning her to be cautious. She gave him a sideways look that said he was telling her the obvious.

'I'll give the pack what they need. Time to run and hunt. Even if I have to take it,' Shane said, eyes moving to Amelia. 'Something most of the wolves will be grateful for.'

'And when you can't get that time because it's not yours to take?' Hale said, not liking Shane's tone.

'Sam won't need this land when she's dead,' Shane said, voice showing no sign of emotion except for anger.

Protect mate, Fang snarled, trying to force him to attack, but he wasn't that easy to bait.

'Not extending the land rental has nothing to do with Sam,' Hale said, realising that maybe he'd been wrong about the target. It hadn't been one or the other. It had been aimed at both of them.

'You can make all the bullshit excuses you want, but everyone knows it's because you didn't want to upset Sam.' Shane took a step closer, knuckles white. 'But when she's dead, the prime alphas will let us take it for ourselves.'

Hale took a step towards Shane as the threat landed. But only one.

Taking Shane's bait wasn't smart. Sam was still hurt, and he couldn't help her if he got himself killed making stupid mistakes.

'No one in the pack will even object. I've seen how they suffered under you and your cowardice,' Shane said.

'Suffer?' Amelia said, stepping up beside Hale. Her pain echoed through her words, but Shane didn't seem to notice. 'The pack writhes in pain from the way you hold our ties. You almost killed us when you summoned us to you.'

'You don't know anything; you've been here for five minutes. I've been here six months,' Shane said, curling his lip as he looked Amelia up and down. 'You don't know suffering. But you will once I kill Hale.'

Amelia growled, taking a step towards Shane, but Hale stopped her. Her wolf wanted to fight almost as badly as his own did, but he felt her residual pain, and fear, too. This wasn't a fight she'd win. But there was something she could do. If Hale trusted her.

Amelia gave him a twisted smile, clearly sensing the hesitation and concern, if not the reason. He hadn't trusted Amelia last night. Maybe today might have turned out differently if he'd taken the time to listen to what she wanted to tell him. His wolf was suspiciously quiet on the matter, like he didn't think the question even deserved an answer.

'Go help Sam. She's been shot,' he said, having to trust her. 'I'll deal with Shane.'

Amelia growled, giving Shane a dark look before she nodded and stepped back. She turned and jogged out of the clearing.

'You're pathetic. It's already too late. Sam is already dead, and you know it. Amelia won't be able to do anything but help bury the bitch,' Shane said, shifting his weight. He'd clearly been waiting for Hale to send Amelia away so he'd have better odds. 'If I let Amelia live that long after I kill you.'

Hale shook his head, not bothering to answer this time as the rage rippled through him. But he didn't let it control him as he closed the gap between them and threw the first punch. He was done playing Shane's games. It was time to put him down.

Shane dodged under Hale's fist, twisting to return the blow. Hale danced back before it connected. They'd sparred together enough times over the last six months that both of them knew the other's moves.

Hale was faster, but Shane was physically bigger and stronger. But that had been before Shane had stolen the pack. With that, Shane had gained a power boost. He just didn't have any idea what to do with it.

They clashed again, moving back and forth, testing the other's defences. A punch grazed Hale's jaw as he barely got out of the way. He got a hit into Shane's ribs, hard, but not hard enough to break bones.

Shane was breathing heavily as they separated, wiping sweat from his forehead. He'd spent too much time focusing on strength and not enough on endurance. It didn't matter how much stronger or faster you were if you couldn't keep up the pace.

Not that Hale was doing much better. Each draw of air burned his lungs, and his head pounded in time with his heartbeat. He'd spent too much energy over the last day and not put enough back into his body to regain his strength.

He had to end this soon. Sam needed him.

'Admit it, Hale, you're weak. They should have replaced you as alpha years ago,' Shane said, drawing in a deep breath. 'I chose this pack because we are supposed to be fighters, warriors. You can't even fight to give us our own land.'

Hale barked out a laugh. He shouldn't have been surprised that Shane thought that. He'd always thought highly of himself. 'You were sent north,' Hale said, 'because your pack was tired of your shite.'

Shane growled, shaking his head, body tense as his eyes shifted colour. Funny, his wolf had barely shown himself during the fight, but that had upset him. 'Liar. Even the other alphas are sick of you. They told me the truth. Told me how you're lying to us about the land. How they wanted you gone. Quietly. They're going to give us the land we need.'

Hale hesitated, trying to catch Shane's scent, but he was too angry to know if he was telling the truth. Or at least if he *thought* he was.

'And you think the prime alphas will grant you more land if you get rid of me?' Hale said, layering his voice with scorn. Then he smiled, letting his teeth show as he curled his lip back. 'They're the ones who blocked even trying to negotiate with Sam.'

'Liar,' Shane said, shaking his head like he was disappointed. 'But they said you'd say that. Lies and games to extend your time here. Like you've done again and again over the last seven years.'

Was it possible Shane was telling the truth? If someone wanted Hale out, a Rift imp attack wouldn't be questioned, even on Sam's land. Hell, it would have worked if not for Sam. Hale thought about the pressure from the prime alphas to sign the contract with Sam. They'd been angry about the delay because the mayor had new lawyers who'd wanted to review it.

Was it possible that Shane was telling the truth?

'If they're so happy to get rid of me, how long before you suffer the same fate?' Hale said, but Shane shook his head.

'I'll not make the same mistakes you made,' Shane said, moving to strike at Hale again, clearly done with the conversation.

AMELIA RAN THROUGH THE woods, feeling like she was letting her fear drive her. She wasn't. She was going to help Sam. But dammit, it was a hard distinction to make as the memory of being trapped in her own body kept repeating in her head.

Safe now, Luna said, voice weak as she huddled in the back of her mind, still very much hurting.

She'd been foolish to think Hale's control was bad. He'd been downright restrained. She wondered if all the alphas had the power to do what Shane had done. She hoped not, but if they did, she could see why they wouldn't want to let anyone know about it. No one would want to be put under that kind of control willingly.

Amelia slowed as the path through the woods widened ahead of her and Sam's house came into view. From this angle, she couldn't see any obvious sign of damage, though she'd heard the gunshots from where Shane had forced her to wait in the clearing.

Where was Sam?

Amelia was just about to go round the front, when she heard Sam's scream of pain. Amelia bolted towards the sound, moving fast despite the weariness tugging at her.

The back door was a broken mess, open, with glass all over the floor. Amelia entered cautiously, searching for Sam. The scent of her blood hit Amelia like a blow, thick and heavy in the air, along with her fear. Sam was slumped against the cupboards under the window. Lacey crouched next to Sam, hands on her wound, blood and glass all around them.

Amelia started to say Lacey's name but stopped as Sam screamed again. She was clawing at Lacey's wrist, trying to push the woman away from her. To stop her from pulling at the binding around her shoulder.

Stop Lacey hurting pack, Luna growled. But why she thought Sam was pack, Amelia wasn't sure.

'Get away from her, Lacey.' Amelia's voice made Lacey's hand jerk back as she turned to face Amelia.

'What are you doing here?' Lacey said, moving to her feet. Blood smeared both her hands and patches of her white top, but she didn't seem to notice. 'You should be with Shane.'

Amelia's stomach dropped. There was only one reason why she'd think Amelia was with Shane. Lacey had known what Shane was going to do. Had helped him. Part of Amelia wanted to believe that Shane had controlled Lacey, just like he'd controlled her. But there was too much focus in Lacey's eyes for her to be under Shane's control. At least not through the pack bonds.

'Stop this,' Amelia said, stepping closer, glass crunching under her feet. 'Let me help you.'

'Help me? How can you help me?' Lacey said, curling her lip at Amelia. The anger made Amelia flinch back in surprise. 'Shane is the only one who can fix it.'

With Lacey's eyes on Amelia, Sam tried to push herself away, smearing more blood on the floor. There was too much blood. Sam was too pale. Amelia didn't have a lot of time.

'Whatever happened, Hale will fix it,' Amelia said, putting out a careful hand as she took another step forward. 'Please listen to me. Shane's way isn't the answer.'

'I'm tired of not being able to be free,' Lacey said, running her hand over her jeans, smearing blood. 'You've been here for what, a month? Two? But wait till it turns into six months, then a year. Only being able to shift once a month, or in the Rift Scar, isn't enough. It's never going to be enough.'

'You could go south, to Glasgow,' Amelia said, though she knew it wasn't ideal, but the longer she spoke, the closer she could get.

Lacey snarled and spat on the floor. 'That's not a solution. It's a tease. A fragment of hope that never turns out to be as good as you think. If they agree to let you go at all.'

'Your time here isn't forever,' Amelia said, shivering at the pain in Lacey's voice. How long had this wound festered for her?

Lacey let out a bitter laugh, turning slightly away from Amelia. 'Except they extended my time here. Said I still had more to learn, that it wasn't time for me to come home.'

Amelia was almost close enough. She just needed a little more time. 'Then we take it up with the prime alphas. We push for more time, more space. Killing Sam isn't the solution.'

'You're wrong. There isn't another way,' Lacey said, the light catching something in her hand. 'I'm not spending another year here.'

'Knife.' Sam choked out the warning just fast enough.

Amelia dodged the knife, slamming her hand down on Lacey's wrist hard enough to send the knife tumbling away from them. It bounced off the wall and skittered across the room. Lacey followed up with a kick that knocked Amelia backwards into the wall with a grunt. Pain lit up her ribs like fireworks.

Lacey aimed a punch at Amelia's head. She slid sideways at the last second, but Lacey was too slow to adjust, and she hit the wall hard. She screamed as something cracked in her hand loudly.

This time it was Amelia's turn not to wait for Lacey to recover. With a quick shove, Amelia forced Lacey backwards into the kitchen table. The old wood didn't survive the impact, and it crumpled with a crash, wooden shards scattering through the room. Some of them hit Sam, and she let out a small yelp.

Amelia cursed. She needed to end this before they hurt Sam even more. But Lacey was far from done fighting. She kicked away the debris and grabbed for the knife that had fallen beside the table, then scrambled back to her feet.

Amelia tried to back away, but her foot slipped on blood and glass. Lacey took advantage of the distraction and slashed at Amelia. She threw her arm up defensively, screaming as the knife slashed across her arm.

'Lacey, stop,' Sam screamed as Amelia stumbled back against the cabinets, nearly standing on Sam. 'She hasn't done anything to you.'

Lacey shook her head, glancing at Sam. Amelia stiffened, pushing herself away from the counter. If Lacey changed targets, Sam wouldn't be able to protect herself.

'Shane already gave Amelia a choice, and she chose wrong,' Lacey growled, panting as she pointed the knife at Amelia. 'Shane will make this into a real pack. Give us what we need.'

'You expect me to believe that anyone here would've survived Shane's idea of a pack,' Amelia said, heaving in a lung full of air, wanting to move back across Sam, to put herself between Sam and Lacey, but Lacey was too close. 'He doesn't want a pack; he wants people he can control.'

'You're wrong,' Lacey said, eyes flashing to yellow as her wolf shone through. 'You don't know him.'

Amelia laughed. Even to her, it sounded wrong in the gore-stained room. 'How do you think he's going to create stability when his solution to Hale was to let a Rift imp out? To bind me so tightly I could barely take a breath without permission? How many people would you both have let die to have this paradise?'

Lacey growled, taking a step closer. Amelia braced, ready to lunge forward and push Lacey back away from Sam. It was risky, but fighting over the top of Sam was more of a risk. But Sam moved before Amelia could.

Sam stabbed Lacey's leg with something long and sharp. Lacey screamed, her leg giving out as she collapsed. She turned the blade to Sam, moving to slash at her.

Amelia threw herself forward, grabbing for Lacey's arm, stopping her from driving the knife into Sam's shoulder. But the angle was bad, and the blade sliced through the rope holding the bandage in place. Sam didn't even scream as the bandage fell away. Her head fell to the side.

Amelia cursed, forcing Lacey backwards onto the floor hard before the knife could do more damage.

'Shane will kill Hale,' Lacey said, breath coming in short gasps as she rolled, forcing herself on top of Amelia. 'And with Sam dead. No one will stop us from taking the land.'

Amelia didn't bother to waste air arguing as she fought Lacey for the knife. The blood was making it almost impossible to keep a good grip.

The knife slipped, sliding into flesh, hitting bone.

CHAPTER FOURTEEN

AMELIA'S PAIN HIT HALE like a blow, and he stumbled back from the fight, barely keeping his feet. He expected Shane to take advantage, but he also cried out, falling to his knees.

Hale's wolf snarled at him to go to Amelia. To help her. But he couldn't. It would just give Shane the opening he needed to take Hale out.

Shane growled, eyes flashing to his wolf. For a minute, Hale thought Shane was going to lose control and shift as his energy rippled over the clearing. But he just shuddered and buried his hand in the dead leaves in front of him.

What had happened that it had hit them both equally? Hale's wolf growled louder in his head, only able to think of one scenario. Someone else from the pack was here and had been hurt like Amelia. There were two traitors in the pack.

The anger helped Hale straighten. He had to end this now, and then he could help Amelia. He lunged toward

Shane, trying to take advantage of the distraction. But Shane had been baiting him. Overacting his pain. He jumped up and threw dry leaves crushed to dust into Hale's face, blinding him.

Hale flinched back, eyes watering. He blocked the first blow by instinct, but he was far too slow for the second one that hit him in the chest with enough force to throw him backwards. Pain burst through Hale's back as he hit the ground hard. He rolled to his feet, blinking rapidly, braced for another attack. But it didn't come.

He could just about see a blur of Shane moving away, sliding into the leaves where Hale had disarmed Amelia.

Light flared off the metal of the gun as he raised it.

Hale was never going to be fast enough, but he started moving anyway. Feet digging into the crushed leaves and dead moss to give him more speed as he ran towards Shane.

Four metres.

Shane pointed the gun straight at Hale.

Three metres. He was just too slow.

The flash of the gunshot blinded Hale for a second before a loud bang burst through his ears. He missed a step, blind and deaf, waiting for the pain to register.

But there was none.

Then Shane screamed. A long wail of agony that seemed distant as Hale's ears struggled to recover.

Hale blinked away the light shadows, moving forward carefully as he tried to figure out what had happened. Shane knelt on the ground, hands clutched against his chest, blood pouring through his fingers. The gun lay on the ground, the barrel split and fragments of metal spread out around Shane's feet.

Without waiting to see if this was another game, Hale closed the gap between them, grabbing Shane and twisting him into a restrictive hold. Shane's scream cut off with a choked sound as he bucked against Hale, but it was too late. Shane wasn't going to be able to break out of Hale's grip.

'Don't,' Shane growled out as he clawed at Hale's arm. Two of his fingers were missing on one hand. The stumps left bloody streaks across Hale's arm as Shane tried to break free. 'I can help you. Tell you who wanted you dead.'

Hale hesitated, but even if he had time, there was nothing this man could offer him that'd be worth the risk that came with it. Hale needed to be done with this and go to Sam.

End this, Fang agreed, calm now, but watchful. There was no regret from his wolf about what needed to be done. Shane had lost. He was a traitor to the pack.

Shane seemed to realise his begging wasn't having any effect. 'You'll regret this. They'll hunt you down.'

Hale tightened his grip, looking up at the skeleton of the yew tree. 'The only regret I have is being unable to settle this challenge the way it should have been. As wolves.'

Hale twisted sharply, sending a loud crack through the clearing. Silence fell in its wake.

The pack magic rose immediately as the link between Shane and the rest of the wolves snapped. The loose threads fluttered against Hale's senses. All he had to do was reach out and bring them in. As the victor, it was his right, but he hesitated.

Hale let Shane's body drop to the ground, thinking about Amelia's pain. Of the way Shane had bound her and the pack. Hale didn't want to hurt them like Shane had. They'd already suffered enough today, it seemed.

Protect pack, Fang said, urgency in the images he sent him. *Won't hurt them.*

Which was all well and good, but what if others felt like Shane had? That Hale wasn't doing a good job. That they wanted more. Amelia had wanted to be free. He'd felt it.

Need home, Fang growled, nudging him towards the bonds. *Need us.*

His wolf was right. Whether or not the pack wanted Hale, he couldn't abandon them. And if he did nothing, that's exactly what he'd be doing because Shane had severed the connection to their family packs. Two alphas lost in one day was hard enough, but being lost with no pack to call home? That would be even worse.

Drawing in a breath, he reached out to the threads, pulling them close, accepting them. There was no other alpha to fight him like there had been with Amelia, so there was no resistance. One by one, they settled into place in his mind, a chaotic nest of fear and confusion as they felt the echoes of Shane's death.

Hale sent the pack comfort and a promise of safety. It didn't help much. He'd have to call them all together, but that wasn't something he wanted to do through the pack bonds. Even on a normal day that was dangerous. He'd have to find a phone and gather them that way.

But first, he had to check on Sam and Amelia. He carefully closed the link enough that he could think on his own. It was harder than he wanted to admit rebuilding those walls. It felt good to have the pack back, felt like he was whole again, even if he knew the connections would likely dim as the other alphas tried to reclaim their family connections.

Hale took one last look at Shane's body. His face was turned away from Hale. If Shane had been telling the truth, someone out there wanted Hale to follow Shane to the grave.

And Sam with him.

Hale wasn't going to let that happen.

Turning away from Shane, Hale focused on that new sense of Sam. It was faint, barely there. Stomach dropping, he ran in that direction.

HALE RAN ALL THE way to Sam's kitchen door. The room stank of blood, fear, and death. It layered everything.

He saw Lacey first. She lay motionless against the back wall, fresh blood pooling underneath her. Even without going closer, he saw she was dead.

'Hale,' Amelia said, voice strained as she turned to him. She held an arm close to her body, the scent of her blood touching his nose. Her pain echoed through the pack bonds. She turned to Lacey, then back to him. 'I didn't have a choice. She wouldn't stop.'

His wolf rose in anger at Lacey's betrayal. Lacey had been Sam's friend.

'It's okay,' Hale said, letting the link between them stay open enough that she knew he meant it. Then he turned to Sam, chest so tight he could barely take a breath.

She lay on the tiles like a broken doll, arms and legs askew, so still that his heart stopped. But then he heard a faint, laboured rasp as she struggled to pull air into her lungs. She was still hanging on.

Hale stepped closer, the glass cutting into his feet. He ignored the pain; it was a small price to pay to get to Sam.

Amelia moved to block his path, her fear peppering the air to layer over the blood.

'I'm sorry, Hale,' Amelia whispered. 'I retied the bindings, but she's lost so much blood.'

Hale's chest was too tight. He tried to talk and failed.

Help mate, Fang snarled at Hale. Pushing him forward.

'Move.' It was more a growl than a word as it slipped from Hale's lips. Amelia flinched, pulling back from him, and looking down at her feet.

Another day he might have felt guilty about the fear. But not when Sam lay crumpled on the floor.

'Help her,' Hale said, crouching next to Sam, reaching to wipe away a smear of blood off her face. He stopped himself, hand shaking. She wasn't going to care about that now.

Amelia didn't answer.

'Help her,' he said again.

'I can't,' Amelia said. 'If you move her, she won't last more than a few minutes. She'll never make it to a hospital.'

He knew Amelia was right. Could hear it in how slow Sam's heartbeat was. See it in the paleness of her skin.

Help, Fang said again. He raged in Hale's mind, throwing himself at Hale's walls. Demanded Hale fix her. Hale didn't even try to soothe his wolf; he couldn't.

'I'm sorry,' Amelia said, crouching on Sam's other side again, wiping away the spot of blood on her cheek. Sam didn't react.

There had to be a way to help her. She'd healed him. Used the Land and pushed it inside him. She'd said she couldn't heal herself. But if she could heal him, why couldn't he do the same in return? The healing hadn't felt all that different from how the pack magic worked. A transfer of energy through a link.

He'd felt the Land when he'd been outside, pushing at the block he'd built to keep it out. It was quiet now that he was inside. But if he could feel it, could he use it to help Sam?

Hale picked Sam up gently, cradling her in his arms like a child. Her head flopped to the side, body limp and unresponsive. Blood, still warm, soaked into his T-shirt.

'Hale,' Amelia said, voice hitched as she tried to reach for him. Her wolf was so close to the surface that Hale could smell fur.

Hale growled, unable to find words as he brushed past Amelia and out through the back door.

As soon as he stepped off the veranda, he felt the Land again. Felt it dancing like fireflies against his skin. Despite the recent heatwave, there was a stretch of grass that was green and healthy in her backyard. Hale took Sam there and gently lowered her to the grass, laying her out flat. She never stirred.

He crouched next to her and let down the walls he'd built to keep the Land at bay. It flickered around him, showing him images of Sam's blood soaking into the ground under her.

Growling, he tried to push through the images, to reach for more. But there was nothing there to hold on to. He could feel it, but he couldn't control it, couldn't use it.

He needed something else.

Help mate, Fang whispered.

The renewed pack connection sang in his mind. It was similar to the Land connection. A web of power. Amelia was there, a bright spark in his mind. He could feel her sadness, her anger, and worry as she watched him. Like she was afraid of what he was going to do.

But he couldn't feel the Land through that link. It wasn't part of the pack.

Tears burned his eyes. He didn't know how to help Sam.

Desperate, Hale pulled on his wolf, the core of power that made him alpha. The same power he'd used to bind Amelia to him.

'Hale––'

'I have to try something,' Hale said, cutting Amelia off.

'She's human. You cannot make humans pack. You know it's not possible. Others have tried and failed.' But despite her argument, she moved to kneel opposite him. 'Even if you could, nothing short of shifting will help her heal.'

'She's not human,' he said quietly. Amelia's eyes went back to Sam. He hated he was breaking his promise, but he'd rather Sam be alive and mad at him than dead. 'She's an Earth Elemental.'

'That doesn't make it any better,' Amelia said, touching his arm gently, resignation in her voice. 'Elementals aren't the same as us either, Hale. You know that.'

Hale ignored her words. Sam was dying, and he had to do something. He let the feeling of being alpha layer him until he could barely stand the weight of it. Then he closed his eyes, carefully pushing out with his wolf.

He saw Sam in his mind. He tried to push his magic through her, tried to grab some part of her to bind. But Amelia had been right. Sam wasn't a Shifter, and there was no wolf to hold on to.

His head pounded as the pressure of the magic built. It wasn't designed to be held, and right now, he had nowhere for it to go. He needed to build a connection to Sam first.

How had she healed him?

She'd taken the energy from the yew tree and funnelled it into him. But how?

Through the Land. Through Earth Magic.

Which he didn't have access to.

Except that wasn't what it had felt like. The energy had been the Land, but the connection had been more personal.

Sam's heartbeat stuttered, threatening to stop. He was running out of time.

'Hale.' Amelia's voice was distant.

He ignored it. There had to be a way. He reached out to Sam with the Alpha Magic again. But this time, he followed the tug he felt towards Sam and traced it back to its source.

The connection to Sam opened with a wave of searing heat and dragged him under.

CHAPTER FIFTEEN

HALE BLINKED TO CLEAR his vision. He stood on Sam's veranda. Or at least he thought that's where he was. Snow and ice covered everything in a thick sheet, though he didn't feel the cold. The treeline was a distant blur behind a thick fog, and the grass was invisible under the piles of snow.

A teenage girl appeared in front of him, creeping around the house with one hand on the wall as she struggled with her footing on the ice. She was short, with blond hair that hung in untamed curls. The familiarity froze him in place as he watched her move straight past him, not even registering his existence. Then she disappeared around the corner.

Fragments of his own half-dream rose in his mind. The night his mum had abandoned him. He'd watched himself as a teenager, reliving the moment over and over again. Was this the same thing?

He moved to follow her. The teenager stopped in front of a small greenhouse box slightly taller than she was. She looked around, checking to make sure no one was watching as she opened the doors.

Hale moved closer, searching for signs of the adult Sam, but the teenager was alone. Where was his Sam?

Inside the greenhouse box were a few sad, wilted-looking flowers, their petals scattering the soil of their pots. Without warning, they changed, growing healthier until they bloomed despite the frost.

Beyond teenage Sam, the front door opened, and an older man in his early forties with short curly brown hair stepped out. He opened his mouth to speak but stopped, face twisting with horror and fear.

Just like Hale's mother had reacted the first time Hale had felt his wolf.

The older man made a sound, and the teenage Sam turned, face going pale as she tried to block the view of the flowers. But it was too late. He'd already seen them.

'Sam?' the man said, looking between her and the greenhouse.

'Dad, I can explain,' teenage Sam said, reaching out to him.

Her dad pulled away from her, recoiling like she'd struck him.

'Please. I just wanted to make them healthy again,' teenage Sam said, voice breaking.

Hale's wolf lunged at Sam's dad; his black fur seemed all the darker for the snow around them. Instinct made Hale try to pull up walls in his mind to block his wolf, but it did nothing. Here, his wolf appeared like he was real, and he did not like Sam's dad.

Thankfully, this was a memory, not the real world. His wolf passed straight through the man and slammed into the wall beyond him. He snarled and shook himself, giving Hale a dark look. Hale ignored his blame that the house was solid and the man wasn't.

'Sam, honey, you shouldn't be outside without your coat. It's freezing,' a middle-aged woman said, coming out the same door, a coat in her hand. She froze when she saw the expression on the man's face. She was Sam's height, with the same blond hair and green eyes. It wasn't hard to guess this was Sam's mother.

Adult Sam followed her out. She wasn't covered in blood here, but she was wearing the same dress and looked just as pale.

'Sam?' Hale said quietly. Sam glanced at him, barely seeming to register his presence, then she moved back to staring at her mother's face.

'I can explain––' Sam's mum started.

'Don't,' her dad said, voice tight as he turned. 'You knew?'

When Sam's mum didn't answer, her dad curled his lip. 'Of course you knew. How could you not? You're the reason she's like this.'

The image wavered and then shifted so they were standing inside Sam's front hallway. Her parents were by the door. Hale looked around, quickly finding young Sam at the top of the stairs.

'Think of Sam? Maybe you should have thought of her before you got pregnant without telling me what you were,' her dad said, voice going low. 'If you think for one moment I want anything to do with your Rift Freak bloodline, you're sorely mistaken.'

'I can't make it stop,' Sam said, shuddering as the image rippled, but it didn't change. 'I don't want to see this.'

Hale moved to his Sam, wrapping his arms around her. His wolf growled and pressed himself into the back of Sam's legs, offering protection. But they couldn't protect her from the past.

The connection between them grew sharper with the contact, but it wasn't the same bright stream of shared feelings as it had been after Hale had let her in. She was blocking him.

Time jumped around them. They were still by the front door, but everything was dark. Hours must have passed. There was a knock at the door. Teenage Sam appeared at the top of the stairs, moving slowly like she was in pain, holding a shawl close to her body. She opened the door to a man Hale recognised despite the age difference. He worked for the police.

There weren't many reasons why the police would knock on someone's door in the middle of the night.

The image reset again, and they stood on the veranda, a teenage Sam passing them, feet crunching on the frost.

'It was my fault,' Sam said, voice breaking. 'All of it was my fault.'

'You didn't do anything wrong,' Hale said, but Sam shook her head.

'You don't know that. You weren't there.'

'Then tell me what happened?' Hale said, looking after the teenage Sam as she disappeared around the corner.

'They died because of me. Because I was careless,' Sam said. She was silent for a long minute, and Hale thought that was all she was going to say. But slowly she continued. 'I wanted to help my dad. I thought if I fixed the flower, he'd be happy.'

Sam paused again, shuddering. His wolf pressed tighter in behind her, whining. Fang hated that she was in pain, and he couldn't do anything.

'They fought, and my dad left, driving out into the worst storm anyone had seen in years. Then my mum followed him. Neither of them ever made it home,' Sam said, a tear falling down her cheek. 'They left because of me. I killed them.'

'You were a child, Sam. You didn't mean for him to see you,' Hale said, but Sam was already shaking her head. 'You're not a killer.'

'Except I hated hiding what I was. Mum had said we could never tell him, but she'd never said why. I thought she was being stupid.' Sam tried to pull away, but Hale held onto her. 'I let him see my power. I wanted him to know what I was.'

Hale could feel her pain and anger as the connection between them shuddered. She wasn't letting him in, but she also couldn't block him entirely. 'You didn't tell your dad to come outside and watch you fix the flower, did you?'

'No. But——'

'No buts,' Hale said, cutting her off. 'Him catching you was an accident. Them choosing to leave in icy weather and thick fog was a choice they made.' They'd both been reckless, and Sam had paid the price. 'You're not responsible for their choices, Sam.'

'If I hadn't shown my dad my power, he wouldn't have left. My mum wouldn't have followed.' Sam drew in a shaky breath. 'Everyone who finds out what I am gets hurt.'

'That's not true,' Hale said, pulling back so he could look her in the eye. 'If it was, I'd be dead as well.'

Sam pulled away from him, her anger sharp through the bond. This time, he let her go, though his wolf wasn't happy about it. 'You damned well nearly did die.'

'Not because of your power. Someone put the scorpion and imps out there deliberately, to target me,' Hale said, missing out that he was sure it had been aimed at both of them. 'If you hadn't saved my life, and trusted me with your secret, I'd have died.'

Hale's wolf huffed a breath, the connection between them growing tight as he reached towards Sam too, trying to reinforce what Hale was saying. The block between them wavered.

'You asked me earlier today to let you help me,' Hale said slowly, still remembering her words, even if the rest of the image was hazy. 'Asked me if I was willing to abandon the pack?'

As if summoned by his words, the links to the pack flashed up around them as thin as spider webs, flowing from him to his wolf and out in a dozen different directions. Sam's breath caught as she stared at the links. It was a rainbow of shimmering colours, alive with the pack's pain and fear. His connection to Sam was there too, a more delicate thread that looked like it was stretched too thin.

'Now it's your turn to let me help you,' Hale said, drawing Sam's eyes back to him.

'It's not possible,' Sam said, but she didn't sound sure as she looked at the thickest thread around them. It was green, going from Sam out into the distance.

'Do you trust me?' Hale said, moving his hand so it hovered over the edge of the thread.

'Yes,' Sam said, no hesitation. Later, he'd find time to enjoy the pleasure that trust gave him, but first, he had to heal Sam.

Hale touched the link with his hand. It felt similar to the pack bond in how the connection worked, but it was different as well. Almost more like his connection to his wolf.

No, he thought, *exactly like that connection.*

The Land was alive with a kind of base instinct and awareness that spread out for miles around him. Rather than existing inside Sam, like wolves did for Shifters, this was outside of her. But the link was still the same.

He realised he was trying to pull the wrong part of Sam into his pack. The Land was her wolf.

The landscape around him and Sam's form wavered. She was so close to the edge that he felt the darkness trying to pull her away.

Hale pulled on his power as alpha, then reached out to the Land with everything he had.

The dream shattered.

THE LAND SLID INTO the pack bonds with all the delicacy of a sledgehammer. It was all around him, spreading out for miles.

A flower struggled against the heat and not enough water. A fox stalked a mouse. The mouse sensed something danger-ous was close but was too exhausted to move.

Amelia gasped beside him, but he couldn't get enough air to tell her it was okay. Though he wasn't entirely sure it was.

A fish swam against the current in a small stream. A robin landed on a tree, the branch bending against its slight weight.

Hale's head started to pound. There was too much information. His vision started to splinter as the connection tried to tear him apart.

But Sam needed him.

He struggled to hold on to that thought in the storm of images, trying to focus on what he wanted.

To heal Sam.

The pulse of connection grew stronger and more focused. It wanted the same thing. But now he had access to the Land. What was he supposed to do with it?

Sam's pain and fear came to him in flashes. He felt her through the Land, like he felt the wolves in his pack.

She'd used this magic to heal him. But how?

There had been pain. He remembered that part. A fire in his blood and energy flowing through him. Sam had killed the yew tree, saving him, taking life from the Land to heal him.

He shuddered, focusing on that idea as he looked around the clearing, the trees at the edge of the forest, the grass under his feet. Everything around him. The Land rose like a storm in his mind, and without pausing to think about it, he shoved the energy towards Sam. The power moved through the Land, into him, then into Sam.

She jerked under Hale's hand. He pressed down, trying to keep her still.

He felt Sam's muscles and flesh knit back together. Felt it like it was his shoulder, not hers. It hurt, but it was nothing compared to the pain that speared his head until it was like he was being burned from the inside out.

The grass around him turned brown. The trees seemed to shudder at the edge of the clearing, pine needles falling to the ground. But that wasn't the only place the energy came from. It pulled on his strength. On the pack. The pack bonds shuddered under the weight of the connection.

He tried to curb it, to limit where it was coming from, but it felt like he was trying to build a dam in a flood. There was too much power. Too much pain. He couldn't risk stopping the flow, but he could protect the Shifters in his pack. He shut his link to the wolves.

The energy flowing from him to Sam increased tenfold, along with the pain in his head. He couldn't see as black spots danced across his vision.

Sam's body was on fire. He could feel the heat where he touched her and in his own body. The magic trying to heal the rest of her. To replace what was lost.

The connection between Hale and Sam snapped.

Hale grunted as his back hit the grass hard. A weight settled on top of him, but it was a small thing when the pain in his head was so strong, he could barely breathe.

His throat was raw as he swallowed. What had happened?

Had it been enough to save Sam?

'Hale?' Amelia asked, voice hesitant.

Hale forced his eyes open. Amelia sat on his chest, her hands shaking as they checked the pulse at his neck. When she saw his eyes open, she sagged and backed off him.

'What did you do?' Hale asked, struggling to sit up so he could see Sam. She lay on the grass just out of reach, still pale.

'What did I do?' Amelia said quietly, looking back at Sam. 'What did you do? I felt you getting weaker. Like you were dying.'

He tried to be angry at Amelia, but he felt her fear, even though he could've sworn the pack bonds were shut tight. She was right. He'd pushed further than had been safe.

'Sam?' Hale said as he forced himself to his knees. Standing was beyond him.

Amelia looked like she might try to stop him, but one look made her back off, which was just as well. His head was pounding so badly he wasn't sure he'd have been able to win the fight. He crawled to Sam's side, fighting a wave of nausea as the headache grew worse.

He couldn't see Sam's wound, but she looked less pale than she had. Her chest moved more evenly, too. Those had to be good signs. He risked touching her. The link was patchy, like there was static interference. Her pain was bright, but nothing like it had been.

Amelia joined him, kneeling on Sam's other side, checking her pulse, then her wound, peeling the bloody cloth away so she could see underneath it. The wound was closed.

'Her heart rate is good. She's stable,' Amelia said, sounding like she wasn't sure she believed it. 'I think.'

He sagged in relief, despite the 'I think'. It had worked. It had been enough. Sam was going to be okay.

'What happened?' Amelia said again, watching him.

'I'm not sure,' Hale said, rubbing his face. He lowered his walls to the pack bonds, feeling the confusion from his wolves. But not pain, which was a relief.

'It feels...' Amelia trailed off, looking around her.

Hale frowned, following her gaze. Visibly, nothing had changed except for the brown grass. But it felt different. This was more than just his link through Sam. That link wasn't even open.

Home, Fang said.

But it was more than that. He'd only ever felt this kind of connection once before when he visited the Northumberland pack lands near the border of the Northeast England Rift Scar. It was one of the first pack lands to be created in the UK. It wasn't sentient exactly, but it welcomed like wolves who came there.

Some said it was because it had been created by the first alpha when he had bound the first pack. But as Hale looked at Sam, he wondered if there was another answer. From a time before they'd feared Earth Elementals. Or maybe that was what had caused the fear.

Amelia shook her head and turned back to him. 'It feels like home.'

Hale swallowed but didn't say anything. How was he going to explain this?

Sam groaned, hand twitching against the ground as she opened her eyes. She blinked rapidly, looking at Hale. Her fear and confusion came through the patchy link. 'What happened?'

Hale reached out and took Sam's hand, bringing her eyes to his. 'You're safe,' he breathed.

He'd find a way to explain the changes in the Land to the pack because there was no way he'd be able to hide that. But whatever that explanation ended up being, it wouldn't put Sam at risk. He was going to make sure she was safe, no matter what.

He was going to protect his mate.

Protect mate, Fang echoed, the sound almost more like an 'I-told-you-so' than an agreement. But Hale ignored it.

CHAPTER SIXTEEN

SAM BLINKED AGAINST THE sunlight that was trying to burn a hole in her head so she could see Hale properly. Her shoulder screamed at her when she tried to move, but it was duller than it had been, different somehow.

What the hell had happened?

Hale knelt next to her, blood splattering his arm and shirt. He looked pale and tired as he watched her, never looking away. It was like he was afraid she'd disappear if he did. His promise that she was safe had done nothing to answer her question. Though it had helped ease some of the pain in her chest.

'Hale healed your wound,' Amelia said, giving Hale a sharp look before she looked away. Sam remembered Amelia coming into the kitchen. Telling Lacey to stop. Fighting her. Then everything had gone dark.

Pieces of the dream hit Sam all at once. Hale with his arms around her. Her dad walking away. Hale's wolf at her back.

Sam shuddered as the images overlapped, flowing out of order. Most of all, she remembered the web of light flowing through Hale—the pack—and the single green thread that connected her to the Land.

Then the pain as Hale had used the link to heal her.

She didn't know how it was even possible, but she'd felt the connection. Felt it still, though it was distant, like he'd done something to lock it down. It was different from her connection to the Land, or even the tugging that pulled her towards Hale. This was an awareness that 'something' existed separately to her, a bundle of emotions that was at the corner of her eye.

'What happened?' Sam said again, trying to sit up. This time, Amelia helped her, supporting her arm as she moved. 'Lacey? The shooter?'

Amelia paled, looking away. Which was enough of an answer that Sam didn't push for more.

'Shane and Lacey are no longer part of the pack,' Hale said, voice rough, his wolf shining through as his eyes flashed gold. There was no regret there, and Sam had to admit that knowing they'd both been dealt with gave her a measure of relief. Then guilt, as she thought about how desperate Lacey had sounded. How broken.

'We should get you inside and cleaned up so I can see the wound properly,' Amelia said, glancing at Hale, who nodded.

Sam let Amelia and Hale pull her to her feet. It didn't hurt as badly as she'd expected, but it was bad enough to make her stomach roll. Getting upstairs wasn't simple or easy either. Hale tried to help, offering to carry her, but the idea of anything touching her shoulder made the roll in her stomach turn into a storm.

She felt Hale's worry for her. His fear that she was still hurt. None of which was helping. In the end, Amelia sent Hale away with the firm command that he, surprisingly, listened to, muttering something about cleaning, and quieter still, calling the pack.

Amelia helped Sam wash off the blood. Sam didn't have the energy to be embarrassed, even when memories of Hale and her last using the shower rose in her mind. After she was clean, Amelia helped Sam to the bed, taking the time to look at her shoulder before finding something for Sam to put on.

The wound was now a dark bruise that spread from Sam's chest to her shoulder. She looked like she'd been hit with a hammer, not a bullet. Tiredness like nothing she had felt before bit at her heels.

At Sam's suggestion, Amelia put on a dress from Sam's wardrobe to replace her bloody clothes. It was a lot shorter on Amelia than it had been on Sam.

'Try not to move too much, Sam,' Amelia said gently, helping Sam lay back in the bed. 'You might no longer have an open wound, but you need to rest so your body can finish healing.'

Which was easier said than done when her brain kept circling the same thought.

'You try staying still after everything that just happened,' Sam said, then she sighed and softened her tone. None of this was Amelia's fault. 'I'm sorry. I didn't mean to be rude.'

'It's okay. I get it,' Amelia said, sitting on the edge of the bed. She'd wrapped a thick bandage around her arm where she'd been slashed. Though you wouldn't know she'd been hurt by how she moved. 'It's been a lot.'

'How are you doing?' Sam asked.

'I'm fine,' Amelia said, fingering the bandage on her arm. Apart from their rather strained first meeting, Sam didn't know much about her at all. But the woman had protected her from Lacey when she could have walked away.

'Are you sure?' Sam asked.

Amelia looked away, turning to the open window. 'I've never been to the pack lands that feel alive, but this is how I imagined it would be. It's like I've come home after a long time away.'

Sam shivered, nervous energy rolling through her as she followed Amelia's gaze. The Land felt different to Sam too, happier. Like it was glad the pack was part of it now. But it was hard to enjoy the pleasure it felt when it meant her secret was out. How long before the government found out what she was?

'I know what others finding out that you're an Earth Elemental would cost you,' Amelia said, turning back like she'd sensed the direction of Sam's thoughts. Though this was a guess on Amelia's part because there was no link between them like there was with Hale. 'I've no intention of sharing that secret with anyone.'

Sam wanted to believe Amelia, but that fear was old and had been around for a long time. It wasn't easy to dismiss it. 'I'm not sure it's going to make a difference if you tell anyone or not if the Land feels different.'

Amelia shook her head. 'It doesn't feel like it comes from you. If I hadn't been here, I wouldn't know the truth. I wouldn't know what you are.'

When Sam hesitated, Amelia continued.

'If you want to, we could test it?' Amelia said, tilting her head towards the woods. 'See what happens when you use your magic?'

'An experiment?' Sam said slowly. How many times had she thought how much simpler things would be if she could do tests? Now she had someone offering to do those same things with her. She also didn't see any fear at the idea of being near Earth Magic.

'Though I'd recommend waiting until your shoulder is a bit better. Hale might not appreciate us going for a wander right now,' Amelia said, smiling.

'Thank you,' Sam said, voice tight. First, Amelia saved her life and now this. Sam didn't know what to say. 'I'm glad you were here.'

'As am I,' Hale said from the doorway, making Sam jump. He nodded at Amelia as she turned to him. Hale still looked a little pale, but she doubted she looked any better. He'd changed his clothes, probably a spare from his car. Which was just as well. He wasn't going to fit into one of Sam's dresses.

As he took a step closer, she smelled bleach, so it wasn't hard to guess what he'd been doing. The thought of everything that had happened in her kitchen made her stomach roll.

'Did you call them?' Amelia asked.

Hale nodded slowly. 'I told Oliver and Lance what happened with Shane and Lacey. They're together still at his house. I'll be going there in a minute.'

'The pack?' Sam asked, remembering those links again. How they'd felt—their fear and worry—though the link was closed now. 'Are they okay?'

'They're safe now,' Hale said, but Amelia looked away. 'But?'

'They're confused. They need answers about what happened with Shane,' Amelia said when Hale was silent.

Sam shivered. 'Would bringing them here help?' Sam asked, looking between them, desperate to do something. If Amelia was right, no one would know the change had anything to do with her.

'You don't know wh––'

'I felt their pain, Hale. Their fear,' Sam said, shivering again. She never wanted anyone to go through that. 'Bring them here if it will help.'

'It's not that easy. Something has changed here. It feels different,' Hale said. 'Something I can't explain.'

Something that might give her away, he meant.

That he was trying to protect her secret meant more to her than she wanted to admit. But to accept that gift right now with so many others in pain wasn't the sort of person she wanted to be, not after everything that had happened.

'Amelia has already told me about the changes,' Sam said, looking at Amelia. 'How it feels different? But it doesn't feel like me.'

'That doesn't mean that they couldn't figure out the truth,' Hale said, running a hand through his hair. He wanted to protect her, but she wasn't the only one he needed to protect.

'Amelia, if it was you out there with the rest of the pack, afraid and needing answers. What would you want?' Sam asked, ignoring Hale's huff of annoyance.

Amelia looked at Hale first, like she wasn't sure if he'd like the answer. But that same defiance she'd shown yesterday flared up, and Sam could appreciate it this time.

'I'd want to be here, together, the whole pack,' Amelia said. 'Even without all the answers, being here would help.'

He shook his head. 'There are other places I can gather the pack.'

Sam reached out to Hale; he took her hand, wrapping his around it. 'They'll have to come back here, eventually. Whatever has changed, the pack will figure it out on their own, won't they?' Sam took his silence as agreement. 'Bring them here. Let them feel safe again.'

Hale sighed, tightening his grip on her hand. But he knew she was right.

'Very well, you win,' Hale said, looking at Amelia. 'But first, I want to make sure the place is clear of any signs Sam was hurt.'

Sam let out a breath she'd not realised she'd been holding. Hale would bring the pack. It wouldn't fix everything, but she was sure it would go a long way to helping.

Amelia nodded, placing her hand on Sam's arm and giving it a squeeze. 'Thank you,' Amelia said, then she stood and walked out.

Hale stepped further into the room as Amelia slipped past him.

'They're going to want answers,' Sam said, stomach twisting despite her earlier confidence.

'And I don't have to tell them what really happened,' Hale said. 'Nothing has changed since I made my promise to you.'

Except everything had changed. Not just the Land but what Sam knew about the pack. Lacey's desperation was still vivid in Sam's mind.

'But things can't stay the same,' Sam said. Bringing the pack here now was only part of the solution.

Hale stepped close enough that she could feel the heat of his energy, his eyes flashing gold as his wolf peeked through. He sat down where Amelia had been but didn't touch her. 'This is your home, and I'll not let anyone take it from you.'

'The pack needs more than once a month to shift,' Sam said. Hale started to speak but Sam stopped him, raising her fingers to his lips. It took her a moment to remember what she'd been about to say as the soft warmth registered. 'I know you want to protect me. I appreciate it, really. But they need more. The prime alphas can go screw themselves.'

Hale watched her, but she hadn't quite convinced him yet. 'I'll think about it,' Hale said, kissing her fingers.

Sam shuddered; the desire was so sharp that it was almost painful in its own right. She wanted him, even though she knew he was just trying to distract her from pushing.

She gasped as she tried to move her arm, reaching for him. The pain overrode the pleasure, making sweat bead on her skin. Hale backed off immediately, forehead furrowed with worry.

'I'm okay,' Sam said, but even her words came out shaky.

'You need to rest,' Hale said, standing up. 'I'm going to help Amelia clean.'

'I meant what I said,' Sam said, catching his hand with her good arm. It still hurt, just not anywhere near as much.

Hale hesitated, holding onto her hand for a minute, then he let go and left. She closed her eyes, wishing she could go back to earlier that day when they'd been alone in the shower. As chaotic as everything had been then, the moment had been simple. Just the two of them.

Until her shoulder healed, that wasn't something she was going to be able to recapture for some time. But she was patient.

AMELIA STOPPED IN THE doorway to the kitchen, gut twisting. Hale had removed Lacey's body while she'd been helping Sam, along with most of the glass. But it was too easy for Amelia to see the body in her head, with the smell of death and blood still strong. Though the bleach made it impossible to tell whose blood it was.

It would be easy to let the pack believe it was Lacey's.

Amelia closed her eyes. Some of the blood had been. Warm as it had run over her arm from the wound in Lacey's gut. It shouldn't have come to this. Amelia opened her eyes again. The image was there either way.

Two of the pack had betrayed them and tried to kill the alpha.

Shaking her head, she stepped into the room and picked up the mop that Hale had left in a bucket of bleach and water. It was stained red and wouldn't be any use until it was rinsed out and refilled.

Everything was changing. A shift of more than just the pack lands being created under her. The other alphas weren't going to let the creation of true pack land go. All of them were going to want it.

She doubted Hale was going to let it go. Not when it connected him to Sam, along with her secret. Earth Elemental. Amelia was surprised Hale hadn't asked her to keep that secret yet. Or commanded her. But he'd said nothing.

Trust, Luna said, floating, content. The gore in front of them wasn't bothering her at all. *We protect pack. Protect home.*

Amelia didn't argue as she picked up the bucket and poured out the water, watching it drain away slowly. She heard Hale come downstairs and go out the front, beyond where she could hear him making a call. At least she hoped that was what he was doing.

She continued to clean, stomach tight as she waited for Hale. Despite his agreement with Sam, part of Amelia was still worried.

Hale bring pack home, Luna said, clearly more confident than she was.

After a few minutes, Amelia heard and felt Hale come inside, entering the kitchen behind her. He was silent, and thoughtful, the connection between them more solid than it had been before. A little more open. She especially felt his worry for Sam through it.

'What did Oliver say?' Amelia asked, putting the wet mop back in the bucket as she turned to Hale. The water was already pink again.

'They're on their way here,' Hale said, playing with the phone in his hand. It looked to be Lacey's, but it wasn't like she was going to need it anymore. Bile rose in Amelia's throat, and she had to swallow hard.

'That's good,' Amelia said. 'Bringing them here will help.'

'I'm sorry,' Hale said, hesitating, then he shook his head. 'I shouldn't have pushed you away yesterday.'

Amelia winced, looking away. 'I was angry.'

'You had a concern, and I ignored it,' Hale said, raising a hand as Amelia started to object again. 'I ignored a lot of things. I would have seen it coming if I'd been paying better attention. Then, I could have dealt with Shane sooner.'

'I don't think anyone could've predicted this,' Amelia said, touching the bandage on her arm. It didn't hurt badly, but it was a reminder of what had almost happened because of Lacey's desperation. 'But maybe you could stop it from happening again. The pack needs land to run and hunt more than just once a month. You need to let us stay connected.'

'Sam said the same thing,' Hale said, covering her bandage with his hand gently, drawing her eyes back to his. She couldn't feel anger from him, but there was hesitation still. 'And I don't disagree.'

'Why do I feel there's a "but" in that statement?' Amelia said.

'It's going to take more than the new pack land to build the connection you're talking about. This pack is transient, members coming and going so often that it's like I'm accepting someone in, only to have to let them go again,' Hale said, looking out the broken kitchen window. 'The type of pack you're talking about might not be possible.'

'Just because something has always been that way doesn't mean it always will be.' Her wolf rose in her head, adding weight to her words. 'Not everyone wants to leave.'

Hale inhaled sharply. 'You wouldn't have said that yesterday.'

'Yesterday I didn't understand what it meant to really be part of a pack,' Amelia said, trying to find the words. 'When you broke my bond with Shane, your wolf protected me. I felt safe in a way I haven't felt before. Then you brought in the Land. You made us a home. This is what being in a pack should feel like.'

There were more reasons for her to want to stay. But as much as she liked this new pack with Hale, her past wasn't something she wanted to bring into the mix here. If Hale sensed she was hiding something, he let it lie.

'There are people who wouldn't be happy to hear that anyone wanted to stay,' Hale said, letting the silence hold enough that she risked looking him in the eye. She could see his wolf there, his frustration as he added, 'Sending wolves here has always been seen as a punishment.'

Her pack had certainly intended it to be that way for Amelia. Something designed to bring her back into line.

'And now?' Amelia asked.

'I think some change is good,' he said, nodding.

Hope rose for Amelia as she considered what that meant for her. A permanent place here. She'd still be stuck working in the Rift Scar, but she'd be free of worse problems back home.

Hale turned back to the window, pulling in a deep breath as the breeze picked up. The air was cooler, a sign that maybe the heatwave was finally ending. His eyes flickered gold for a moment, then he turned back to Amelia.

'Let's get this place clean before everyone gets here,' Hale said, the pack bonds dampening a little, but not all the way.

Not like it used to be.

Despite the gory work ahead of them, she felt good and at peace. Maybe she'd finally found the home she'd not even known she was looking for.

HALE STOOD IN THE middle of Sam's front yard with his pack all around him, sending him wave after wave of their residual pain and fear. They'd arrived an hour ago now, listening to him as he'd given them an abbreviated version of what had happened.

Losing any member of the pack was hard. But losing them like this was worse than if Shane and Lacey had died fighting in the Rift Scar. There was suspicion and doubt. Hale felt it through his mental walls, like a dark cloud around the pack.

It didn't help that he hadn't told them the whole story, and most of the wolves were savvy enough to sense something was being held back. But he couldn't risk Sam like that, not even for the pack.

Sam pack too, Fang said.

She's just our pack, Hale said. The rest of the wolves couldn't feel her. Hale had made sure of that with Amelia before the pack had arrived. His wolf didn't understand the difference, so he ignored Hale. He was just happy to have the connection to Sam.

Leaving Sam alone had been harder than it should have been. Hale's wolf had wanted to lie at the end of her bed and never let her out of his sight until she was healed. Maybe not even then. Only the pack's unease had convinced Fang to leave her.

Protect all, Fang said, rising to watch the pack with Hale.

They were gathered in small groups, talking quietly as they let the feel of the Land seep in and soothe them. It was starting to get dark, and they'd have to find another source of light soon or go home. He suspected the latter wasn't likely this side of the morning.

Hale didn't doubt that their family packs had already started calling him, demanding to know why their wolves' bonds had been severed. But since Hale's phone was smashed, it was an excellent excuse to deal with them tomorrow.

It wasn't like the prime alphas were about to get on a train and head north to take their wolves back. Everyone needed time to heal before messing with the pack bonds again, so it was unlikely there would be any change before the next full moon. Hale wasn't looking forward to that fight with his wolf.

Oliver and Lance appeared at the edge of the woods, drawing Hale's eye, nodding at him. It was done. He exhaled sharply, returning the nod. They circled round to the back of the house to clean up before rejoining everyone else. The pair had been part of the group Hale had sent in to remove the scorpion traps.

They'd taken them, the dead imp, plus Shane's and Lacey's bodies, and put them in a van that had been found near the edge of Sam's woods. It had a cage that had stank of the Rift imp, as well as both Lacey's and Shane's scent. If anyone in the pack had doubted Hale's word, that would have been enough to convince them.

Not that anyone had questioned him. Hale had to wonder whether that said more about him than Shane, but he didn't linger on the thought. This wasn't the place for those kinds of doubts. His pack needed his confidence now more than ever.

Those outside the pack would be told that Lacey and Shane had died doing their duty, fighting in the Rift Scar. The lie was bitter on his tongue, but he couldn't afford the questions that the truth would bring. What had happened was pack business, not the Institutes', or the prime alphas'. Though Hale knew that at the very least, the latter would find out the truth soon enough, but after Shane's words, Hale couldn't have cared less.

The pack lands was something else that wouldn't stay secret, though, and that was a lot more worrying. Had the first alpha known how he'd created the link to the Land? Or had it been accidental like today? There was no way of knowing, no way to ask questions without risking Sam. Besides, that alpha and his mate had been dead and buried for years.

Oliver came back out of the house, moving to where Amelia stood to one side of the gathered pack, alone. She'd surprised him today in more ways than he could count. The prime alphas wouldn't appreciate it if the other wolves wanted to stay. It reduced their control over the Shifters. They weren't going to be happy about any agreement to extend the Land usage, either.

Hale looked over to Sam's bedroom window.

Mate, Fang whispered in his mind.

Hale wasn't sure she'd appreciate his claim. But maybe he was wrong. Changing the contract was a big step, one he wasn't convinced she wouldn't change her mind about. If she did, he'd let her. And if she didn't?

He turned back to his pack. Everything was about to change one way or another. He just hoped he was strong enough to protect everyone from the fallout from the prime alphas.

CHAPTER SEVENTEEN

Less than a week after Hale had nearly died, he sat in a small, stuffy office with Sam, the mayor, and his solicitor. They were seated around an old, slightly dusty table that took up most of the space.

The time had done wonders for Hale and the pack, though Sam's healing had been slower. She'd been in so much pain those first days that he feared she might break. Even now, she favoured her good arm as she turned the pages of the contract.

Needless to say, the week had been rather frustrating.

Hale re-stacked his copy on the table in front of him and waited for Sam to finish reading hers. There was very little difference between this contract and the original one they'd signed seven years ago.

Just one paragraph that really mattered.

A few changed words.

It was funny what a difference those few words would make. Being able to shift and run as a wolf all month long instead of just one day.

His wolf paced inside his head as they waited for Sam to finish reading. Though he was impatient rather than afraid she'd change her mind. She'd been insistent, even though he'd tried to make her wait before arranging this meeting.

All that waiting had done was allow Amelia to work with Sam to test how much the pack sensed of Sam's magic. So far, unless she used magic right in front of them, it was easy to assume it was just the pack land energy. The wolves couldn't sense that Sam was anything other than human.

Her secret would be safe.

Of course, after that had been determined, Sam was done waiting to change the rental agreement. She'd booked the meeting herself yesterday, and the solicitor had been ecstatic to make the changes. Oddly so.

Hale hadn't wanted to risk telling the pack just in case this didn't work. Even if Sam didn't change her mind, the prime alphas might have still found a way to stop it.

When Sam finished reading her stack of paper, she turned them back over into a neat pile the same as he'd done, arm brushing his. The contact sent a thrill through him as their connection flared up.

Her excitement and nervousness ran across his senses. Along with her slight fear. If she said no, he'd walk away from this deal. Find another way to find land for the pack.

'Are the changes to your satisfaction?' the solicitor asked, leaning forward, looking between them. He was an elderly man in his fifties with a receding hairline. He hadn't tried to make conversation or distract either of them while they'd been reading, happy to sit patiently, waiting for them to finish.

The mayor wasn't quite as still as he tapped his fingers on the edge of the desk. He was a trim man in his fifties, with a receding hairline that had left him nearly bald. Because of the laws around shifting, he had to sign off the contract as well. He'd already verbally agreed to the changes. Hale hadn't even had to resort to a gentle reminder that the pack's continued presence kept them all safe.

'This is exactly what we were looking for,' Sam said, giving Hale a wide smile, then turned back to the older man. 'Can we sign it?'

The solicitor smiled and offered them both a pen.

'You're sure?' Hale asked one last time. The mayor sighed like he was worried they'd gone through this for nothing.

Sam responded by taking the pen and signing her name. 'I've never been more sure.'

It took Hale a minute to remember he was supposed to be signing the page as well, as his imagination took him somewhere entirely different and far more private.

The solicitor took the completed documents and smiled as he handed the paper over to the mayor to provide the last signature.

'I hope you know what you're doing, Hale,' the mayor said as he signed his name without waiting for an answer. The man wasn't easy to read, but Hale suspected he knew exactly what the document they were signing was going to do. 'I'll make sure they are filed in all the appropriate places.'

Reading between the lines, that meant he'd send the details to the prime alphas. But it was too late for them to do anything about it.

Hale stood, feeling a level of relief that surprised him. Part of him had been sure something would stop them from changing the contract. He offered a hand to Sam, though she didn't need help to stand. She accepted, the connection springing up between them like a live wire. Her relief echoed his.

'Are the pack all coming round tonight still?' Sam asked him as they left the council building.

Hale nodded, touching the pack bonds as they spread out to each of his wolves. Amelia was still brighter than the rest, but they were all there, a sense of everyday calm coming from them. 'They're all coming.' Though he'd not told them why, just in case. The Elementals had been surprisingly willing to cover the extra shift.

'Good,' Sam said, looking at him, eyes bright. 'I think I might have some burgers left in my freezer.'

Hale's body twitched as he caught the look in her eye, but he resisted doing more than smiling at her as he opened the passenger side door of his car. *She was still hurt,* he reminded himself. He needed to be careful.

Unfortunately, his body took no notice as he got in the driver's side and headed in the direction of her house. It was a long drive.

SAM ENTERED THE HOUSE, Hale following behind her like a furnace. She'd felt it the whole drive home. Signing the contract might not have been magic––it was only words on a piece of paper––but somehow it felt like something more. Something new and exciting. Especially now she was sure the pack couldn't sense her.

Her kitchen was halfway to being repaired, and she couldn't help but finger the fresh plaster on her wall as she walked through the room. It was rough, still in need of a sand, but you'd never know there had been a bullet hole there. Unless you'd lived through it.

Which she had.

'It's looking good,' Hale said behind her. He'd stayed in the doorway, fingering the new glass on the door, opaque rather than clear. The window had been replaced now as well, though she'd drawn the line at making it opaque.

'You didn't have to do this. I could've afforded to fix it,' Sam said, moving back towards him since he didn't seem to want to come all the way inside. He'd been keeping his distance for the last week, like he was afraid she'd snap in half, and she was done playing games.

'It was caused by my pack, it's the least I could do,' Hale said, pulling in a deep breath. Her scent, her arousal. His eyes flashed to gold. 'How's your shoulder?'

'Good,' Sam said, rolling it to prove the point. It had only taken a few days to heal to where she could move without pain. Well, almost without pain. Not that Hale seemed to believe her.

'I should go,' Hale said, but he didn't move. Sam took another few steps closer. 'I'll be back before the rest of the pack arrive.'

'Actually, while you're here, maybe you could help me with something,' Sam said, brushing back a loose strand of hair that had escaped her plait.

Hale's forehead furrowed, and he looked her up and down like he was searching for injury. Or at least that's how it started. He got stuck about chest height. She'd picked this dress for exactly this reaction.

'It's been a rather frustrating week,' Sam continued, taking another step towards Hale.

Hale looked away, closing his eyes. His grip tightened on the doorframe. 'You were heal––'

'I healed days ago.'

'Being sho––'

'So, you think you know my body better than I do?' Sam said, raising her eyebrow. Hale sighed and gave up, eyes rising to meet hers. She might not be able to smell his arousal, but she saw the outline of it in his jeans well enough.

'I'm not made of glass, Hale,' Sam said, closing the last few steps. His heat burned into her. How many times had she brushed past him and felt this? How many times had they both said no? That one time in the shower wasn't enough.

Hale's heat spiked, and his energy became sharper. 'I've said no to myself for so long, I don't know how to say yes,' Hale said, reaching up to touch her face.

The words struck a chord in Sam's chest like it hit a nerve. She hadn't even realised she'd been worried he'd not felt the same until that moment. 'It's easy,' she said, breath catching.

Hale blinked at her, opening his mouth to speak, but Sam was done talking. She reached up to wrap her arm around his neck and pulled him down so she could capture his lips, stopping the words.

The kiss was as good as she remembered. Better even without the pressing need of hunger that had driven them before. Hale wrapped his arm around her back, pulling her flush against him.

'You do it just like that,' Sam said as she pulled back to take a gulp of air. She wasn't the only one who was struggling. Hale's breath came in soft pants, and his eyes were flecked with gold.

'Well, if it's that easy,' Hale said, lifting her up with one smooth motion. She squealed, wrapping her legs around his waist. 'Why don't we continue this upstairs?'

Sam didn't get a chance to reply as Hale stole another kiss from her. She let him carry her towards the stairs, not letting go even for a second.

She'd found someone she could share her secret with, something she'd never imagined she'd ever be able to have. After almost losing him once, she wasn't going to let him go.

CHAPTER EIGHTEEN

HALE DIDN'T WANT TO leave Sam's bed, but he already felt the pack getting closer. It was nearly time to tell them the news.

'Did you tell Amelia?' Sam asked as she ran a hand over his hip, sending tendrils of pleasure all the way through his body.

Hale returned the favour, feeling the echo of the sensation bouncing between them. They'd abandoned the sheets, having a far more interesting way to keep warm, and now Sam lay curled against him, sweat drying on them both.

'No. She went through more than most. If things hadn't worked out, it would have been cruel to get her hopes up,' Hale said. Though he felt Amelia's hope through the bond. She was smart, and stronger than she gave herself credit for.

'We should get up,' Sam said, but she didn't move.

He wanted more time. But he had a job to do. With reluctance, he pulled away from Sam and slid out of the bed to look for his clothes. They were in one piece, which was good.

'I really do have burgers, you know,' Sam said as Hale pulled on his jeans. She stretched delicately, then she stood and headed towards the bathroom. She paused in the doorway to look back at him. 'I think they'll make an excellent breakfast.'

Hale smiled, wishing he was taking his jeans off again rather than putting them on as she closed the door. The offer had been very deliberate, and so very welcome.

Our mate, Fang said, pleasure filling them both at the idea of waking Sam tomorrow morning and crawling into bed beside her after the hunt.

The pack was drawing closer, and he forced himself to finish finding his clothes, skin itching as his wolf hovered close to the surface.

It took another half an hour for everyone to arrive. There was caution in the bonds, along with confusion. Outside the full moon, the pack rarely gathered like this, so they all knew something was happening. Sam joined him, standing by his side with his scent marking her skin. That she'd not washed it off made him far happier than it should have.

Amelia stood at the edge of the pack with Oliver beside her. After everything that had happened, Oliver had been even more protective than normal. Hale felt the guilt through the bonds, the need to have done more. He made a note to find time to talk to Oliver about it. None of this had been Oliver's fault. Not dealing with Shane sooner was on Hale's shoulders.

'Thank you all for coming,' Hale said, looking around at his wolves. Those who'd been visiting home had returned this week, and there were two shy of thirty Shifters watching him. 'I wanted you all together for this. After everything we've been through this last week, it's about time. I've good news for you.'

Whispers spread through the pack, and Hale felt Amelia's hope surge.

'Sam and I have signed a new contract today for the land rental. One that will allow us to shift here as often as we like,' Hale said, bringing every eye to him.

Their confusion came first, then excitement and joy, as they realised he was serious. One of the pack split off, stripping, abandoning his clothes in a pile, making Sam blush. When Hale nodded, others followed until almost all the pack was moving into the woods so they could shift out of sight.

'Thank you,' Amelia said, taking the time to hug Sam, eyes flaring the blue of her wolf before she too went into the woods.

'You didn't have to do this because of them,' Oliver said, looking between Hale and Sam. There wasn't any doubt who 'them' were. Shane's and Lacey's motivations had been one piece of information Hale had shared.

'I did it for you, all of you,' Sam said before Hale could reply. 'I just wish I'd been able to do it sooner.'

Oliver looked into the woods.

'I'm sorry it took so long for me to deal with Shane,' Hale said, putting a hand on Oliver's shoulder, so he turned back. The amber of his wolf shone through, not in challenge. Just watching. 'I should have seen his anger and done something about it sooner. That's on me.'

Hale put emphasis on his words, opening the pack bonds so Oliver knew he meant what he said. The guilt was still there, but it loosened.

'Go, hunt, run. Have fun,' Sam said, nodding at the woods. They were the last of the pack not yet beginning their shift. 'I'll see you tomorrow.'

Hale nodded, feeling his own wolf rise close to the surface as he nodded at Sam. He wanted to kiss her, but he didn't trust himself to leave it at just a kiss, so instead he turned towards the woods with Oliver.

The feel of the pack flowed over him. Freedom. Happiness. Excitement.

Whatever the consequences with the prime alphas, tonight was worth it to see his pack totally free for the first time.

A FEW DAYS AFTER the pack had been told they could shift anytime they wanted, Sam stood at the edge of the Rift Scar with her work gear. She'd taken some time off while she'd been healing, and today was her first day back.

Memories of the last time she'd been here with Lacey made her stomach twist, but right now she had bigger worries.

She flicked the switch on the Corruption Detection Scanner, but nothing happened. Sighing, she bashed the side of the device, watching the meter on the screen flicker, then flash to life. She really needed to get them to send her a new one. Though, maybe after this, they would.

'You shouldn't hit it,' Amelia said without looking at Sam. She kicked at the ground with the heel of her combat boots. She was dressed in a dark grey Kevlar vest, almost as ill-fitting as Sam's. 'You'll hurt your shoulder.'

Sam didn't answer. She wasn't going to admit she'd felt a twinge. Amelia was already overprotective enough.

The weight of the CDS was familiar in her hands as she took out the cone scanner to run it over the area she was standing in. The high-pitched whine that should have come out of the device was absent.

'Well?' Oliver asked, head coming around from where he'd been staring out into the Rift Scar. The brown-haired wolf was also kitted out in full combat gear. He was her actual bodyguard for the day, not Amelia. But she'd arrived here just as Sam came to do her readings, along with another two wolves.

Sam rolled her eyes, then wiped her forehead. The temperatures might have dropped, but now it was just humid and sticky. She wanted the dry heat back. 'I have to load the CDS results into the computer, to be sure.'

'Why do they even need the machine? I can see the grass growing just as well as you can,' Oliver said, frustration lacing his voice.

'Seeing it and proving it aren't the same thing,' Sam said, but her eyes went to the vibrant patch of green that had come up after the rain that had followed the heatwave.

The grass itself wasn't the issue. The fact it was growing on the wrong side of the Rift Scar barrier was.

Sam took a deep breath, regretting it as the rot settled into her nose.

'Let her be,' Lance said, turning around to glance at the machine. 'They want proof. We'll give them proof.'

He was larger than Oliver, which was saying something, with close-cropped hair and a dark glove covering one hand. Sam had never seen the scars under them, but the rangers knew how to gossip. Or at least Lacey had. Sam pushed away the thought.

Sam gave Lance a grateful smile. He didn't exactly return it, but he gave her a quick nod that was about the best you got from the quiet wolf.

'Fine, fine. Let's get back and do the "computer" thing then,' Oliver said.

She couldn't blame him for his impatience. The whole pack had been buzzing about the patch of grass for the last day. It was the first and only sign that it might be possible for the Rift Scar to change size since records had begun.

Sam sighed and turned back to the grass. It might not survive, but the change happening within weeks after what she and Hale had done to the pack lands made her nervous.

When she'd been afraid of the consequences of healing Hale, or him healing her, this hadn't been something that had crossed her mind. Amelia caught her eye, like she'd sensed the direction of Sam's thoughts. There was hope there. For the first time in over a hundred years, they might finally have a way to push back the damage from the Rifts.

Except none of them had any real idea what they'd done.

And telling anyone could cost Sam everything.

But first, she needed to get IRS&D to validate her readings, then she could worry about what they meant.

TO BE CONTINUED IN BOOK TWO OF THE HIGHLAND RIFT PACK SERIES

Prequel Short Story

Want to find out more about Sam and Hale? Join my newsletter to read Hope and Lies. https://jemmaweir.co m/newsletter/

In Hale's story, we see the full story of how he shifted for the first time, and in Sam's, we see how she uses magic to heal her father's plants. Then, at the end, there is the moment the two of them meet for the first time.

If that isn't enough to entice you over, you will also find other free short stories, as well as a sneak peek into the next couple from book 2.

https://jemmaweir.com/newsletter/

HIGHLAND RIFT PACK SERIES

Bitten By Frost

Book 2 of the Highland Rift Pack Series

Amelia's Pack sent her north as a punishment for rejecting the Alpha's son as her mate. But for the first time, she feels free. Now, she's never going to let anyone close, not even the frustrating scientist who's testing her patience and self-control.

For years, Mitchel has hidden his Frost magic, protecting his family's reputation. But when he goes north to investigate why the Highland Rift Scar has shrunk, the cold is making his magic slip. Or maybe it's just the stubborn Shifter who is assigned as his escort.

As an investigation turns into a rescue mission, Amelia is left injured, and Mitchel on the edge of losing control of his magic. To give them a chance to heal, the Alpha benches the pair, but it's not long before more trouble arises, and only the two of them are left to help.

When Mitchel has already lost control once, and Amelia can barely stand, will they be able to learn to work together? Or will this new threat tear them apart?

Filled with suspense and romance, Bitten by Frost is a thrilling paranormal romance that will keep you on the edge of your seat. If you enjoyed the first book in the series, Buried by Earth, you'll be sure to love what this book offers.

https://jemmaweir.com/books/highland-rift-pack/bitten-by-frost/

Battered by Storms

Book 3 of the Highland Rift Pack Series

Staci's storm magic has always set her apart from the rest of the town, but she's always had her mum. Until now. With her mother's mind and health in decline, Staci faces the prospect of a life of isolation.

Oliver's family has always told him that he'll never amount to anything, but now he's an Alpha with a pack of his own. But not for long. At the end of his year at the Highland Rift Scar, he must give them both up, even if he has more than one reason to stay.

When a dangerous storm hits the town, Staci's magic fails her, and only Oliver can protect her from the destructive force trying to drain her magic. As the storm finally dissipates, Staci is blamed for the storm's creation, and

Oliver is faced with an impossible choice that could put everyone he loves in danger.

Can Oliver find a way to keep Staci safe and protect his pack, or will forces beyond their control tear them apart?

Join Staci and Oliver in this thrilling paranormal romance novel as they weather the storm and find a way to be together. Will they be able to withstand the storm and find a way to be together, or will they be torn apart forever? Find out in the third book of the Highland Rift Pack Paranormal Romance Series.

https://jemmaweir.com/books/highland-rift-pack/battered-by-storms/

WISHING FOR TRUTHS

Contemporary Fantasy Short Story

Vanessa considers her mother's drinking and crazy schemes her biggest problem. Until she meets the Genie.

When Vanessa finds a bottle on her doorstep, the last thing she expects is a wish-granting Genie. What could go wrong with a wish for her two friends and herself? Everything.

On top of that, her mothers' newest scheme is starting to unravel, and the only help Vanessa can think of is the Genie. But he's refusing to come out of his bottle. Now Vanessa must use nothing but the truth to help her friends before her mother ruins everything.

This is a story about wishes gone wrong and a Genie who isn't telling the whole truth, served with a dash of Romance.

Buy this Short Story now and join Vanessa as she learns what it means to 'be careful what you wish for.'

https://jemmaweir.com/books/standalone/wishing-for-truths/

THE LIFE AND CHAOS OF A RETIRED OLD GOD

Humour, Magic and Old Gods who should know better: A Collection of Ernie Smith Short Stories

Being retired was supposed to be easy. No drama, no family, no problems. Considering Ernie is a god, he should've known better.

In this collection of short stories, Ernie struggles to live a quiet life as Death loses his scythe, a genie wants a holiday, and Ernie's family keeps dropping in.

Then there's Ragnarok. Because who doesn't need an end-of-the-world event to keep things calm and quiet?

But it doesn't stop there. This collection contains a brand new bonus short story where Ernie is asked to mediate a feud between Dragons. With tensions running high, maybe the poker game wasn't the best idea.

Also included in this collection is a series of flash fiction originally published on my blog. Follow Ernie as he deals with Cupid shooting the wrong person, Wererabbits for April Fools, Santa stuck in the chimney, and what happens to snowmen when the weather changes.

The Life and Chaos of a Retired Old God is a collection of humorous short stories where Ernie learns that quiet is the last thing he's going to get.

https://jemmaweir.com/books/the-life-and-chaos-of -a-retired-old-god/

ABOUT AUTHOR

Too many Ideas - Never enough time

How many jobs let you build your own world? Create strange magic? Develop a diverse cast of people who will live on in the minds of others?

As an author, Jemma Weir gets to do all these things and more, as her cats chase unicorns across the breakfast table, and werewolves dig holes in the garden to torment her chihuahua, it is always an interesting day.

Fantasy books have always been her first love, from dragons to werewolves, and vampires to elves. Now, as she writes her own stories, she pulls together myths and legends, and all the crazy worlds that are her own to create stories she loves.

Working from her Scottish home, she writes fantasy, with a dash of humour, and a pinch of sass.

Want to keep up to date on new releases and get some free stories? Check out my social media or join my newsletter by clicking on the link below.

https://www.jemmaweir.com/newsletter

https://www.jemmaweir.com/blog

https://www.facebook.com/JemmaWeirAuthor

https://www.instagram.com/jemmaweir